Return of the Salmon

Somnauth Narine

Best Wishes
Somnauth Narine

Published by Somnauth Narine, 2024.

RETURN OF THE SALMON

First edition. June 27, 2024.

Copyright © 2024 Somnauth Narine.

ISBN: 979-8227780287

Written by Somnauth Narine.

To my wife, Mala.

Chapter 1- Release

It was a dreary morning when the metal door in the massive concrete wall yawned open, and Sarju Beepat emerged from Sing Sing prison like a worm from the bowels of the earth. He flinched as the heavy metal door clanged shut behind him with an audible bang and looked around him in awe and wonder as if seeing the world for the first time. It was a cool, overcast day, but a feeling of warmth spread across his chest as he realized that he was finally free after sixteen years of incarceration. He pulled the duffel bag over his shoulders and headed out to the roadway. The prison guard at the final gate had given him instructions on how to get to the railroad station: "Proceed to the road. Make a right and continue to the intersection, then make a left towards the bus shelter. The bus will take you to the Metro North Station. Good luck and don't return to this place."

As he walked to the intersection in the shadow of the huge concrete wall topped with razor metal and barbed wire, Sarju Beepat contemplated the imposing prison buildings glaring down behind the wall that imprisoned the will, spirits, hopes, and dreams of the inmates. He was lucky to have made it out after spending a relatively short time there, but that luck came with a price. He heard a babel of voices as he came to one side of the building and saw a crowd of people close to the prison gate. Men, women, and children were interspersed with lawyers in suits who came to visit the inmates. He paused as he considered the looks of the people closest to the road. There was no joy, just a sense of duty, shame, and trepidation on their faces.

He crossed the road to the other side at the intersection and noticed the Hudson River flowing lazily under the dim morning light. Every day, from the prison yard and from the small rectangular window in his cell, he had reflected on that river as memories of his childhood near another river on another continent periodically served to lighten the weight of incarceration. He made a left turn at the intersection, and with the Hudson River behind him, Sarju felt a pang of sadness, as if he were saying farewell to a faithful friend.

About a quarter mile ahead, he saw the bus shelter with a waiting bus. Two figures were walking ahead of him, arm in arm—a man and a woman. The man had a duffel bag just like his. Sarju surmised that he was another prisoner on parole. The man removed his spring jacket and wrapped it around his waist. He was a tall, skinny African American with a bald head. Sarju recognized him. He was known as "Gums" and worked in the cafeteria, cleaning the tables and floor. Gums had been in prison for more than thirty years. Some of the most garrulous prisoners joked that Gums was among the first laborers who toiled on the concrete foundation of Sing Sing decades ago. They joked that his job was to fetch concrete in a wheelbarrow, and after he stole the wheelbarrow, he was sentenced to life in the same prison he helped to build. Truth be told, Gums, at thirty-five, had robbed a jewelry store, shot and killed the owner, and was sentenced to forty years in Sing Sing.

Sarju caught up with Gums and his companion. They had stopped to examine a billboard advertisement that showed a man quenching his thirst with a giant bottle of beer. Gums smacked his lips and glanced at Sarju.

"You too get parole, brother? My sister here is taking me to a restaurant near the train station. Want to join us for a beer? We are free now. We can drink until we get drunk, no guards to control us," Gums declared, and his top jaw glided smoothly over his bottom jaw without any teeth to encumber its movement. Apart from losing his freedom in Sing Sing, Gums had also lost all his teeth, hence his name.

Sarju grinned. "No, thanks, Gums. I will skip that beer today."

"You must be a Muslim, then. Many people enter prison as drinkers, then come out as Muslims," the woman reflected, adjusting her very black wig that was out of place with her very tired and wrinkled face.

"No, no," responded Sarju. "I just want to keep the first day free from the evil spirits."

"Your loss," intoned Gums. "I will down a case by myself today." His jaws glided effortlessly in his mouth as he laughed toothlessly at Sarju.

"Just one beer, Cornelius. I can only treat you to a beer and lunch. When you remember where you hide that jewelry, then you can think about that case," ordered the woman and prodded Gums toward the bus.

"Okay, Delilah. When I recover those diamonds, we will live like the rich people on the east side."

Gums entered the bus first, stopped by the driver, and dug into his pockets. Sarju felt the sharp edges of his card in his pocket, pulled it out, and waited behind the woman, who was furiously searching her bag.

Gums found his card and gave it to the driver, who inserted it into a card-reading machine and returned it to him.

"You can go. Your fare is paid."

The driver looked at Delilah, who had found a few quarters in her purse. "I don't have enough quarters. I only have dollars."

"This bus only accepts cards and change," the driver explained. "You with him?"

"Yes, that is my brother. He just got parole."

"Okay, you can go. Compliments of the city. It's not my money. And your brother did his time and paid his fare also."

Sarju handed him the Metro card. The man glanced at Gums, seated behind him, and looked quizzically at Sarju. "The two of you together?"

Sarju nodded, and the driver took the card and inserted it in the machine. "Never used a card like this before, eh?"

"No," Sarju muttered. "This thing is a modern invention for us. First time I experienced this."

"First time I experienced driving two parolees out of Sing Sing at the same time."

Sarju made his way to the back and sat on the last seat. There were no other occupants in the bus. He threw his duffel bag on the seat and felt the warmth and vibrations through his clothes. Gums was peering through the window, still fascinated by the advertising board. Sarju could see his jaws gliding back and forth in anticipation of the beer. A feeling of nausea overcame Sarju. He felt his stomach rebelling. He got up, walked quickly to the front of the bus, and exited the door. He heard Delilah laughing and joking with Gums. "It looks like your friend already got homesick! He is running back to Sing Sing."

Sarju ran to the back of the bus shelter and doubled over on his haunches. He heaved, and a few drops of liquid spewed from his mouth. He heaved several times. The liquid stopped coming, and he squeezed his stomach. After a while, he heard thumping sounds coming from the bus. He saw Gums slapping the window and making signs that the bus was about to go. Sarju stood up and slowly made his way to the bus. As soon as he climbed aboard, the driver pulled away from the curb, and Sarju fell against Delilah, shifting her wig.

"It is the smell of freedom. The excitement can give you an upset stomach," grinned Delilah, adjusting her wig.

"Beer is the best medicine for that. You can change your mind and join us to put your stomach to the test, you know," suggested Gums.

"That would make it worse, but thanks," Sarju declared, tottering his way to his seat at the back of the bus.

Sarju retrieved his duffel bag from the vibrating back seat and placed himself in a single seat by the backdoor. As the bus rolled through the town of Ossining, making periodic stops to pick up passengers, Sarju glanced through the windows, drinking in the passing scenes of traffic and shops through the residential and shopping districts. The seat in front of him was occupied by a blonde woman with a little girl on her lap. The girl was pulling her mother's face, giggling, and gesturing to the front of the bus. Sarju followed her gaze and saw that she was amused by the antics of Gums. Gums's face was pressed close to the window and was moving left to right in quick succession to capture the fleeting street scenes of freedom. In his excited state, his extended jaws alternately glided back and forth like those of a young alligator. Other passengers began to look at Gums with amusement on their faces. Sarju looked around discreetly. He hoped that no one could see that he was as excited as Gums to be on that bus to freedom; he was relieved to find that no one was paying attention to him.

That day was the last day that he and Gums were wards of New York State, but it was the first time that Gums had been out of the prison gates in more than thirty years. Sarju had been out once before. The previous year, he was transferred to the city hospital, where he spent three weeks receiving medical care, but it was as if he were still locked in prison. He did not get to see much of the world outside the prison. The ambulance collected him from the prison yard and transported him in the dark to the emergency department of the hospital, where he was whisked to a room on the fifth floor. There was one sealed window in the room, and a prison guard was constantly on duty outside the room. But that wasn't necessary as Sarju was shackled to the bed; the only thing he could see through the window was the brown brick wall of another hospital building. Even though the food was better and the environment of the hospital was cleaner and more peaceful, it was still a prison system. There was nothing of interest to see from his room; at least in his cell in Sing Sing, his faithful friend, the Hudson River was always in the distance, the water tumbling playfully downriver.

Finally, the bus stopped at the Metro North Station. He was the last passenger off, and he found Gums and Delilah waiting by the entrance to the station.

"You changed your mind about that freedom beer?" Gums inquired hopefully.

"No, man. I will skip that for later."

Gums extended his hand. "Well, I hope to see you around. I will be staying in Queens with my sister. I have to live close to the probation officer. So they told me."

Sarju pumped his hand, and the duffel bags fell from both their shoulders. "I will be in Brooklyn. At a rooming house arranged by my probation officer. All the best, Gums."

Gums smiled, and his eyes twinkled. "That was my prison name. Not in jail anymore. Cornelius is my name. It was my father's name too."

"Very sorry, Cornelius. Yes, you should be proud of your father's name," Sarju remarked, extending his hand to Delilah. "And best of luck to you too, Miss Delilah."

"Best of luck to you, son, but I didn't get your name."

"Oh, I am sorry. I was so used to people reading my name on my uniform. But it is Sarju."

"Yes, I remember your name now. The boys used to call you *Sarge,*" added Gums.

Delilah smiled. "You deserved that rank of sergeant. You were in the prison service and wore the uniform, so you can call yourself Sarge. But don't do anything to go back and become a general."

Sarju adjusted the duffel bag over his shoulder. "Well, it was nice being in your company. It is time for me to catch that train."

"And I have some beers to drink." Gums took Delilah's hand and headed in the direction of a nearby bar to quench his thirst.

―――――⧫―――――

SARJU AMBLED INTO THE subway station. He joined a short line by the ticket booth and purchased a ticket to Grand Central Station in New York City, where his friend Hassan promised to pick him up. The girl in the booth informed him that the train was still at the station and directed him to the boarding platform.

There were not a lot of passengers on the platform, and Sarju entered the first carriage in view. He plunked himself down on a plush seat and deposited his duffel bag beside him. The few people in the carriage were all engaged with their varied electronic devices. As the train eased out of the station, the duffel bag fell to the floor, blocking the aisle. Sarju leaned over to retrieve it when he noticed a tag hanging by a strap. The name of the benevolent organization that donated the bag was printed on the tag. Sarju ripped the tag off and stuffed it into the bag. He clutched the bag close to him on the seat as he recalled how it came into his possession.

―――――⧫―――――

THE DAY BEFORE, THE welfare officer had sent for him. The guard escorted him through the maze of hallways to her office in the personnel section of the building. The officer, Mrs. O'Connor, a tall and serious-looking Irish woman, was sitting at her desk with his file in front of her.

She motioned for him to sit on a chair a few feet away from her desk. She contemplated him over her reading glasses and smiled faintly. "Your stay with the state is finally over, Inmate Beepat. You told me before that you had no relatives who wished to accept you in their homes."

Sarju's voice quavered in embarrassment. "Yes, Mrs. O'Connor. But my friend had recommended a rooming house in Cypress Hills that may be able to accommodate me. I provided the address to you."

O'Connor leafed through the folder and held up a document. "Yes, you did. We sent the information to the Brooklyn office, and a probation officer made contact with the landlord. He agreed to have you stay there for two months."

"Don't worry, it may even be less than that period," assured Sarju.

The welfare officer returned the document to the file and made a few notes. "Good, good! Tomorrow, when you leave, you will be given some documents to take with you. You will have to contact the probation officer when you get there. Do you have any money in your prison account?"

"Yes, I saved the money that I came here with and from what my friend had deposited in my account. I also have some money from doing work in the prison library and the supply shop."

"Well, I hope it is a lot," she smiled and removed her glasses. "You are going to need a lot to live in that wild world outside. Before you leave tomorrow, you can withdraw all the money from your account. Now, what about clothing?"

Sarju looked down at his prison garb, confused.

She closed the file and laughed. "We can't send you out like that. You will be arrested for stealing clothes that belong to the state."

Sarju appreciated the humor and smiled. "I have a few items of my own in the cell, Mrs. O'Connor. I will be fine."

Mrs. O'Connor got up. "You will be better off with what we have. We receive donations of very good clothes and shoes from charitable organizations for parolees and other prisoners. Come with me."

Mrs. O'Connor led the way to a store room adjoining her office. The room was filled with crates of shoes, clothing, and duffel bags. She picked up a duffel bag and threw it at him. "This is yours. You can fill it with whatever you want."

Sarju had worked for many years in the garment industry in Manhattan and knew quality. Every item of clothing was of excellent standard. He filled the duffel with several items and was preparing to leave when she indicated a section with shoes and sneakers.

"You know your size. Take a pair of sneakers and a pair of dress shoes. There may be a welcoming home party for you."

Sarju looked at her with gratitude. "Thank you, but my days of boisterous parties are over. Maybe a farewell is slowly catching up."

She nodded her head. "You did your time. Now is when you move on and leave everything in the hands of your maker. You may take the bag to your cell. See me in the morning before you leave to collect your papers and money. Keep the faith, Inmate Beepat."

The welfare officer headed back to her office, and Sarju hoisted the duffel bag to his shoulders and made his way back to his cell, accompanied by the guard.

HE CLOSED HIS EYES, and the gentle rocking of the train induced a short doze. He awoke to see the walls of Grand Central Station passing slowly by the window. Sarju draped the duffel bag over his shoulders and followed the other passengers, who were hastily making their way to the exit. He dawdled under the great arch of the station and gazed at the murals on the walls. When he exited the building, he found that the clouds had gone. Manhattan was not as dreary as Ossining, and with the bright spring sunshine on his face, he felt a greater sense of elation since emerging from the gate in Sing Sing prison.

It was just after noon, and 42nd Street was throbbing with life as people walked with both purpose and abandon. The traffic stormed along the street noisily, and the screams of the engines and exhaust noises blended with the voices and laughter of the people to create the effect of a symphony of freedom. Sarju knew that part of Manhattan very well. He had worked in the Garment District that stretched between Fifth Avenue and Ninth Avenue for years. Before attaining the title of "inmate", at Sing Sing, Sarju Beepat was the supervisor of a textile business that imported fabrics and materials from all over the world. Sarju loved Manhattan and had always felt that if God wanted to show the world the success of his creation, he would point proudly to Manhattan, the epicenter of the universe.

He stood for a long time observing life on the street, then started walking slowly along 42nd Street. Even though he remembered the way to Brooklyn by subway, Hassan told him to call him as soon as he reached Manhattan. Sarju strolled along but could not see a public phone booth. With the passing of the years in Sing Sing, cell phone technology had taken over, and all public telephones were discarded. He noticed a food cart on Lexington Avenue. There was a short line of people making their purchases, and Sarju noticed the vendor attending to them while talking on a cell phone wedged between his shoulder and his ear.

Sarju joined the line, assessing the vendor and the items on display. "A muffin and a can of soda, please."

"Anything else, sir," muttered the vendor as Sarju extended a ten-dollar bill.

"Yes, one more thing. Can I borrow your phone to make a call?" implored Sarju. "I can't find a public phone around here."

The vendor halted with the change in midair. "You are new to this place? You just came into Manhattan?"

"Yes," responded Sarju, taking a small bite of the muffin. "I have to call my friend to pick me up. He is expecting me."

The vendor, a middle-aged Hispanic, eyed Sarju carefully. "And you want to use my phone!"

"I will pay you for it. Just one call."

The vendor rapped the phone on the small counter of his cart. "A few months ago, a man asked to borrow my phone to call his cousin in Harlem. You know what happened?"

"He stole your phone."

"No! The dog did worse. The puta called some other cousin. After I got my bill, I learned he called his cousin in Ecuador. You know how much I had to pay for that call? You know how much that call set me back?"

The vendor looked sharply at Sarju to elicit a response. Sarju had no rejoinder for that, so he ignored the look. He pleaded, "My friend is right here in the city. Here is his number."

Sarju pushed a piece of paper across the narrow counter with Hassan's name and number boldly printed. The vendor took the paper and inspected it as if he were inspecting counterfeit currency. "Okay." He relented and waved the phone at Sarju. "I will call and put the phone on speaker. We'll know if this call is transferred to India. A lot of phone scams are going on there."

The vendor called, and after about five rings, Hassan answered. "Hello, this is Hassan!"

The vendor held his hand out so that Sarju could speak into the phone.

"Hassan, Hassan? This is Sarju! I am using the phone of a food cart vendor," shouted Sarju, leaning over the vendor's hand.

"Where are you, Sarju? Give me your directions, and I will pick you up in an hour."

Sarju looked around. "Lexington and 42nd," chimed the vendor.

"Yes, Hassan, Lexington and 42nd Street. I will be waiting by the food cart," yelled Sarju.

"Okay! Wait right there. In case of any change, I will call the number of your food cart friend," instructed Hassan.

The vendor put away his phone and handed Sarju the change.

"How much for the call?" asked Sarju.

The vendor waved him off. "Don't worry about that. Today is my day to help an old immigrant."

"Old?" objected Sarju, sipping the soda. "How old do you think I am?"

The vendor eyed him all over. "From that gray roof to your thin body, I would guess around sixty. Am I right?"

Sarju smiled sadly. "You were not close to fifty-five."

"You probably had a hard life in your country."

A group of tourists passed by, laughing loudly. Sarju looked at them, then picked up his duffel bag. "Now, you are finally right. I definitely had a hard life."

"Well, now that you are in America, you can take it easy for a while. There is a chair at the back of the cart. You can sit there while you wait for your friend," the vendor offered, dismissing Sarju to attend to another customer.

Sarju sat nibbling at the muffin and sipping the soda as he watched the people waltz by in the bright sunlight. He flicked the empty can into a trash can nearby and walked up to the front of the cart. The vendor was refilling his styrofoam container with soda cans.

"You know where I can go to take a leak?" Sarju asked.

The vendor shut the box with a loud snap. "You asked to use my phone; now you are asking to use a bathroom? Look around! This is a food cart, not an indoor restaurant."

"I really need to go, man. I haven't used the bathroom in hours. Where do you go when you get the call of nature?"

The vendor grimaced. The hard demeanor slowly receded from his face. "I use the restroom in that restaurant over there. They allow me to use it because I am a small business owner. We business people have to cooperate."

"Customers can use the bathroom there?" asked Sarju, hopefully.

"Yes, but only paying customers who order lunch. And you have to call and make a reservation, so you are out of luck if you have to go now."

"But man, I have to go."

The vendor shuffled a few feet onto the sidewalk and pointed a few buildings down. "You see that dumpster there. I noticed a few homeless bums hide at the side and do their business there. But if you do it and the police catch you, they will ticket you or carry you down to the station."

As a condition of his parole, Sarju was required to obey all the rules of society, so he could not risk going afoul of the law.

"No, no," he mumbled. "I am not breaking the law by peeing in the street."

"Then go back where you came from," suggested the vendor.

"What do you mean?" asked Sarju in a shocked tone.

The vendor realized the confusion and laughed. "No, I don't mean it like Trump to go back to your own country. I mean, walk back to Grand Central Station and do your business. They have facilities where you can do any number you want, one, two, three, whatever."

Sarju looked relieved. "Okay, okay. But if my friend calls, tell him I will be back in a few minutes."

"Go on!" encouraged the vendor. "If he is a good friend, he will wait for you."

Sarju hoisted the duffel bag over his shoulders and hustled back along 42nd Street to Grand Central Station like a man on a lifesaving mission.

———◉———

WHEN SARJU RETURNED to the food cart, he saw his friend Hassan leaning over the hood of a white Dodge SUV. Hassan was the same age as Sarju but looked much younger. He was clean-shaven, stocky, and muscular, and he boasted a shock of jet-black hair. He was everything that Sarju wasn't, but Hassan had never experienced Sing Sing.

The vendor saw Sarju first and called out to Hassan. "That is the man you are looking for."

Hassan turned around to see Sarju approaching, his duffel bag across his shoulder. He left the vehicle, walked a few steps, shook Sarju's hands, and then embraced him warmly.

"Welcome home, Sarge. Welcome home. The sun is rejoicing that you are out!"

"Nice to see you, Hassan. Thanks for coming to get me," retorted Sarju.

"If you had told me that you were being released today, I would have driven to Ossining to get you."

"That would be a waste of time. The train here was faster."

"Well, are you ready to go home?" grinned Hassan, opening the back door and casting Sarju's duffel bag in the back seat.

"All set after using the bathroom at Grand Central," Sarju gushed, waved to the food vendor, and jumped into the vehicle.

Hassan continued on Lexington Avenue, and Sarju's eyes caressed the glittering electronic billboards and the buildings as they passed.

"Manhattan looks different now. Like scenes from a distant fairy tale, Hassan. But still the capital of the universe."

"You always loved Manhattan, Sarge. Now, you are part of it again," Hassan laughed. He leaned forward, opened the glove compartment, and tossed a small box at Sarju.

"What is this?" Sarju echoed, opening the box to reveal a cell phone. "I don't need this, Hassan."

"So, how do you intend to make and receive calls? Are you planning to live with that hot dog vendor? You probably noticed that there are no public phones anymore. Your number is written on the box. Just don't make overseas calls."

"I was warned about that already," grunted Sarju. "Thanks, Hassan. What plan do you have for this phone? I heard phone plans are expensive."

"Nothing to concern you. I took care of it."

Hassan glanced back at the duffel bag in the back seat. "Is that all you have? I thought you would be arriving with a suitcase."

Sarju glanced at the bag and then at Hassan. "I was at Sing Sing, Hassan. Not on a Caribbean vacation."

"But you spent sixteen years there, man," countered Hassan, still smiling at Sarju.

Sarju looked away and contemplated a bus that had stopped in front of them. "Yes, in a six by nine cell with four shirts, three pairs of pants, and two pairs of boots. All my material possessions in sixteen years. All the other items belonged to the state."

Hassan leaned over to pat Sarju on the shoulder. "You are out now. I have enough clothes for you to fill ten suitcases. Do you want to stop at a restaurant now or have lunch at my place?"

Sarju smiled ruefully. "Don't spoil me now, Hassan. The place you were telling me about, is it far from your place?"

"No, it is about ten blocks. I know the landlord. I did some fumigation work at his place a few times. He had roaches there, but it is alright now. Did you get the paperwork for his place? He said he accepts housing vouchers from the state."

"The prison made the arrangements with him. My probation officer called him, and they arranged everything," Sarju shared.

"Did they make arrangements for two months? He said that they normally send people there for two months minimum."

"Yes, they did. But I won't need two months. I would be out long before."

Hassan looked at him approvingly. "That's the old Sarju. You will be out on your own two feet in a jiffy. After being locked up for such a long time, it is better to pick up the pieces quickly and put your life together. Nothing can keep the old Sarge back."

Sarju looked through the window and gruffly responded. "Definitely out in two months, Hassan. There is no doubt about that timeline."

Hassan had crossed the bridge over the river from Manhattan to Queens. Sarju strained in his seat to see the water below.

"How does it feel to be out, Sarge?" asked Hassan with an amused look.

Sarju turned to Hassan with a solemn look on his face. "Have you ever worn a smaller size shirt, Hassan? A shirt so small that you feel that you can't breathe?"

"I can't say that I did. But if ever that happens, I will tear it off instantly."

Sarju nodded his head in agreement. "That is how I felt for sixteen years, trapped in a tight shirt. Now, the shirt has burst, the buttons are off, and I can breathe again. It's still painful, but I can breathe again."

Hassan looked at him soberly. "You will be fine as usual, Sarju. I have never met anyone who could match your resilience. Now, where do you want to have lunch?"

"Later, with lunch. Let's go to the room, Hassan. I have to call the probation office from there, too."

Chapter 2- Rooming House

The SUV stopped outside a house on Fulton Street in Cypress Hills, Brooklyn. Hassan switched off the engine and looked at Sarju. "This is it, Sarge. Here is your new home."

Sarju leaned his head through the window of the vehicle and surveyed the two-family brick house that Hassan had indicated. There was a rose bush by the gate, exhibiting signs that it had survived the harsh winter. Along the front of the house were several pots with dried stalks that looked like pepper or tomato plants from the previous summer. A short flight of stone stairs led to an iron grill door lined with perspex, behind which was a heavy wooden door. Flanking the front door of the house were two pots with a few crocus flowers peeping out.

"You can see it is a very secure house. You are safe here," observed Hassan. He opened his door and then the back door to grab Sarju's bag. "Well, don't stand there admiring your new palace. Ring the bell so you can meet your new landlord."

"I hope he is not like my previous jailor," joked Sarju as he climbed the stairs. He pressed the bell and heard a sound like a church bell pealing inside the house. He sensed Hassan climbing up behind him just as the inner oak door opened inside and the metal security door swung out. A short, bald-headed Indian man with a thick sweater and short pants stood holding the handle of the security door.

"Yes, what you looking for?" The man barked, then noticed Hassan hidden behind Sarju. "Oh, it's you, Hassan. I didn't call for any extermination. The building is free of cockroaches now."

The man's voice betrayed his Trinidadian accent.

"This is not a business call. I have a new tenant for you."

"Oh! Well, come in, come in." He ushered them into a little foyer and closed the doors behind him. His right knee was heavily bandaged around a heating or cooling pad.

"You were released from the department of correction?"

"Yes. The name is Sarju Beepat."

"Yes, yes, Beepat!" he boomed and shook Sarju's hand. "My name is Terry Ramsingh. The probation office called this morning. They faxed me the papers yesterday. Do you have your discharge papers from the prison?"

Sarju grabbed the duffel bag from Hassan and searched the pockets. "I have them here," he declared, and he handed several pages to Terry.

Terry leaned against the wall and read the documents carefully. He pursed his lips and nodded his head several times.

"Didn't you say that they faxed you the paperwork yesterday?" queried Hassan as Terry ran his finger slowly over every printed word.

"This is good!" Terry exclaimed with some satisfaction. He waved the papers at Hassan. "Sometimes the office sends papers missing very important information. I know the mistakes they make. I am a retired prison officer."

Terry considered Sarju, who stood with the duffel bag at his feet. "Sometimes they even make the mistake of sending you a pedophile," he clucked. "I have to be very certain. Accepting rent for the rooms is not all. You must consider the reputation of the neighborhood."

"Well, this man is not a pedophile. He is a respected man with a family," Hassan remonstrated.

"I know, I know, but he just come from prison. I must be certain that he is not dangerous to the community. There is a school nearby, and I don't want my house listed as a sexual den for a perverted former inmate," asserted Terry.

Terry opened a side door, dropped the papers to the floor, and hauled out a large bunch of keys from behind the door. He removed two keys from the bunch and handed them to Sarju. "The key with the red cap is for these two front doors. They must be locked at all times. Do you smoke?"

"No," Sarju assured him.

"Good. Don't start, or you will get cancerous lungs. I had tenants who left their rooms to smoke outside, and then they forgot to lock after them. I can't be running after tenants to lock doors. You see my knee. I have serious arthritis in my joints."

Hassan and Sarju nodded sympathetically.

"This key with the green cap is for your room. Keep it closed at all times. You don't know when good or reformed people could turn malicious and rob you of everything in your room."

Terry handed the second key to Sarju and started up the stairs. He held on to one rail and inched up slowly, with Sarju and Hassan creeping behind. On the landing, at the top of the stairs, he held on to the wall for a while to catch his breath.

"I can't explain this shortness of breath. Like the arthritis rushing to my lungs," he wheezed, squinting at Sarju.

He turned and opened a door to the left. It was a bathroom. The bathroom contained a stand-up shower and a toilet bowl. Above the little sink, there was a cabinet with a broken mirror. A strip of duct tape ran over the cracked glass. Lined up on the floor beside the toilet bowl were a brush and cleaning fluids in plastic containers.

"Well, this is your master bathroom. Every time you use it, you must clean it properly." He tapped the mirror, and his lips curled in disappointment. "A paroled prisoner broke the mirror. After six months I am still waiting for the Department of Corrections to replace it. Now, let me show you the kitchen."

To the right was a small room that served as a kitchen. A small circular table with three plastic chairs was in a corner. There was a little sideboard with a microwave and an electric kettle. Terry pointed to three standing cabinets, about five feet high and three feet wide on one side.

"Each one is for a boarder." He opened one and showed it to Sarju. It was empty. "This one is your food pantry. You can store whatever you want here."

He limped across the floor and opened a fridge. "This is a new fridge," he announced with pride. "Make sure you keep it clean. You can find dishwashing soap and other things under the sink. If you need anything else, let me know."

He gave the kitchen a final glance, then pointed to a passageway. "Now, to your room."

He led them to a room that was near the front wall of the house. On top of the door was marked in white: *No. 1.* "This is your room. Room number 1. You have the key. Open it and let's see if it is better than where you came from."

Sarju inserted the key in the lock and pushed the door open. Opposite the door, mounted on the wall, was a mirror as tall as Sarju. There was a single bed, a chest of drawers, a small nightstand with an antique-looking lamp, and a small stool nearby. The room was tidy, and the bed was made up.

Terry pushed aside a panel on a wall to expose a small linen closet. "Here are extra sheets, blankets, and towels. Now, don't expect me to give you maid service. There is a laundromat down the block. If you keep everything clean and tidy, then I wouldn't have to hire the exterminator, Hassan."

Hassan deposited the duffel bag in a corner and surveyed the room. "How come the prison only allows people to spend two months here, Terry?"

Terry looked at Sarju and the duffel bag. "Two reasons. The first reason is that some of them learn to be independent. They find jobs or sweet women and then leave."

Hassan laughed. "That is my boy, here. Sarju wouldn't be spending two months here, so you better start looking for another boarder."

Sarju smiled. "And the other reason?"

Terry limped to the door and leaned against the doorpost. "That reason shouldn't bother you. The second reason is that some of them get up to their old tricks that led them to jail in the first place and repeat the same mistake. Before the two months, the police catch them and ship them quickly back to prison. Well, enjoy your stay here, Beepat. If you need anything, just knock on my door."

Terry left the room and clumped down the stairs. Hassan sat on the bed and bounced gently while Sarju paced up and down the room.

Hassan crossed his arms and considered Sarju. "Are you measuring or exercising? Don't you like the room?"

"This is bigger than six by nine. It is a palace compared to my cell."

"Forget about that cell. The only thing I don't like is that the bathroom is outside. You would have to share it with two other men."

Sarju stopped pacing. "Better yet. I don't want a toilet in this room. I had a toilet in my cell. Many times there was no water to flush, or it clogged up for days. You had to literally sleep with your poop. This is okay, Hassan."

"I told you that you could stay with me. You don't have to stay here, you know."

"Thanks, Hassan. But you have done enough."

"Well, at least you could have all your meals at my place. You notice the kitchen has no stove for cooking! Just a microwave."

"That is okay by me. I am learning to survive on very simple meals. I am not a great fan of cooked food these days. Fruits and milk are enough for me."

Hassan looked at him thoughtfully. "So, that is why you lost a lot of weight. You should market that monkey diet and make a lot of money. So, when are you going to contact your wife?"

Sarju looked sharply at him.

"Sorry, sorry, I mean ex-wife or former wife, whichever suits you. Does she know that you are out?"

Sarju lowered himself slowly onto the stool. "No. Only you know, Hassan. But I will call her tomorrow." He glanced quickly at Hassan. "I need to see my kids, now."

Hassan nodded slowly. "You will be surprised. They are not little kids anymore. They are grown adults."

"Doesn't matter. There are still my kids."

"Well, you have a phone now. Call her and make the arrangements. So, what are you doing? You are not going to have lunch with me at my house?"

"Some other time, man. I am not hungry right now. Later, I may go out to get a few things from the supermarket. And I have to make a call to the probation office."

Hassan raised himself off the bed. "Alright! Well, you can call me anytime if you want anything. I am going to complete a termite inspection now. Here is some spending money to tide you over."

Hassan proffered some money to Sarju; Sarju pushed his hand away. "No, no, Hassan. You have done enough."

"What enough? Like you have a short memory. You think I can ever do enough to repay you, Sarge? Remember, when I came to New York, you put me up at your house for two years? You never took one penny. Who would do that for another man?"

"We are brothers Hassan, not other men. I have enough money from my prison savings. Remember, you used to put money in that account? I still have them all with me."

Sarju pushed his hand into his pocket and showed Hassan a roll of bills.

"And you think that is enough? Two spins around the supermarket, and you will see how that wad would melt in your pocket."

"I really can't take any more money from you, Hassan," objected Sarju.

Hassan stuffed the money in Sarju's hand. "What kind of brother would I be if I couldn't leave you with a few dollars, Sarge? I will drop by later."

Hassan strode to the bedroom door. "Meera doesn't live far from here. Give me a call, and I will take you there when you are ready."

Sarju followed Hassan to the front entrance, and remembering the admonitions of his new landlord, he locked the doors carefully and mounted the stairs to his room. As he closed the door, his eyes caught his reflection in the full-length mirror. The sixteen years had aged him terribly. In his mind, he felt like the old Sarju, but the mirror told a different tale.

Chapter 3- Reconnection

As Hassan had indicated, Meera's place was not very far from the rooming house. Sarju knew Ozone Park was on a bus route but couldn't remember the bus that plied there. He noticed Terry in the yard attending to some plant pots and sought information about the buses from that part of Brooklyn to Ozone Park, Queens.

Terry dropped a pot and gestured. "You have to go in that direction. The bus, B13, stops at the head of the street. Take it to Euclid Avenue Station and transfer to the Q7. That passes through Ozone Park. You can climb the subway steps and purchase a Metro card from the ticket booth to travel on the bus. You have a Metro card?"

"No," admitted Sarju, "but I will get one from the ticket booth."

Terry placed his hand in his pocket and pulled out his wallet. He extracted a Metro card. "Here, use this. You probably have money on this card for your excursion. If it is not enough, the driver won't kick you off the bus."

Sarju plunged his hands into his pocket. "Thanks! I will repay you for the card."

"Forget it. It is just a few dollars. If the bus is late, you can always walk. 87th Street is not too far from here. Even I can make it on my arthritic legs in less than an hour."

Sarju strolled to the end of the block. Fortunately, the B13 was at the stop, taking on a few passengers, so he crossed the road and hopped on. The bus took about 10 minutes to reach the Euclid Avenue station. He and Meera had lived not far from the station. He exited the bus, and his memory of the neighborhood slowly took shape. He stood for a while, gazing in all directions like a lost tourist, and allowed the recognition to seep in. Without waiting for the Q7 bus, he started walking east along Pitkin Avenue to Ozone Park. He noticed a woman approaching from the opposite sidewalk. She had long, dark hair that bounced around her shoulders. The sunlight on her face highlighted her caramel complexion. Sarju's heart skipped a beat. She looked so much like Meera.

He had met Meera two years after coming to America. Initially, he had started working as a porter at a firm in the Garment District. As the owners got to know him and learned of his academic abilities, he was soon promoted to supervise the procurement and distribution section of the textile firm. One day, he had the occasion to visit a nearby department store and was smitten by her. It was a slow day at the store, and as she cashed him out, he made small talk at the register. He was captivated by her quick smile, dimpled cheeks, and very brown eyes, and for several days he visited and made inconsequential purchases just to converse with her. Soon, he asked her out, and they commenced a courtship that ended in marriage in less than a year.

They rented an apartment in Brooklyn, and both of them enrolled in college on a part-time basis while working full-time. Sarju started courses in business administration, while Meera took courses in accounting. Their academic pursuits soon came to an end when the children arrived. Child care and working hours conflicted, and both opted out of school, pledging to continue later.

Sarju continued his studies later, when childcare and work were no longer on his schedule, but when years of despair and hopelessness threatened his soul. One night at his cell window, while observing the Hudson flowing, he reflected on how the sediments that the river picked up along the way were deposited at the mouth. He thought of his life and how the memories of his past were flowing through him, and the sediments of his life were being reduced to nothingness. To keep his soul whole, he made a determined move to challenge his mind so that the days and nights in captivity could flow seamlessly.

He met with the prison counselor, who advised him of college courses he could take. He commenced classes in psychology, and in a few years, he was able to obtain his degree. At the same time, he worked in the prison library and tutored prisoners for their high school equivalency examinations. Although his pay was only forty cents per hour, this work paid for the little things he needed at the prison store, but more importantly, it afforded him a degree of sanity and usefulness behind the prison walls.

Sarju turned into 87th Street. Meera had given him the house number and a landmark. She told him to look for a white marble statue of Mother Mary that was in the middle of the lawn at the side of the house. Sarju noticed the statue and proceeded up the short walkway to the front steps. The house was of the high-ranch style. The bottom was made of red brick, and the top was shingled white. He climbed the steps and stopped by the door. There was a large Christmas wreath interlaced with red ribbons still adorning the door. A bronze buzzer projected by the door frame, and he pressed gently. After a few minutes, he heard no stirring from within, so he pressed several times. He turned away from the door and was viewing the roadway when he heard the door opening.

A voice from the doorway bellowed. "We have no time for Jehovah's Witnesses today. This is a Catholic home."

The man standing there was in his sixties and was dressed in a gray sweat suit. He was Italian, but with tanned skin, not unlike a light-skinned Indian.

"Sorry to disturb you. I am not a Jehovah's Witness. My name is Sarju Beepat. Meera is expecting me. I called her this morning."

The man paused with his hand on the door. He scrutinized Sarju, then opened the door wider. "Oh! So *you* are the Sarju? Come in, come in."

Sarju tiptoed in as the man closed the door behind him. The man eyeballed Sarju carefully, then reluctantly proffered a hand.

"Yes, yes, the Sarju indeed. I am Giovanni Nucera, the husband of Meera. Come in, come in! She will be down in a minute."

Giovanni led Sarju to a large living room adjoining a dining room. In the living room, there was a cast-iron staircase that led to the second floor. Ensconced in an area under the staircase was a small bar.

"Come, come, have a seat," invited Giovanni, spreading his hands to indicate three large sofas and several armchairs that were all positioned to face a huge flat-screen TV mounted to a wall. "Meera will be down in a minute."

Sarju's eyes flickered furtively around the lavish home. He felt inadequate and out of place in that setting. "Thanks. I will stand. My visit won't be long. I just require a few minutes of her time."

Giovanni nodded his head approvingly. "Okay, suit yourself, but care to have a drink?"

"No, thanks. I am fine."

"But not me. I will take a hard one. Tell me when you change your mind."

Giovanni ambled over to the bar, where he hummed silently as he mixed his drink. Sarju glanced around the room. He noticed several picture frames mounted on a nearby wall. There was a sizeable frame with a girl in a nurse's uniform posing by a medical machine.

Giovanni returned to the center of the room and caught him gazing at the pictures. "Family pictures. Old and new."

There was the sound of footsteps from the floor above. Giovanni shifted his posture to look at the staircase. Sarju followed his gaze and first glimpsed the hem of a yellow spring dress, then the form of Meera slowly descending the staircase. His heart lurched in his chest, and he caught hold of an armchair for support. Meera, still stately and exquisitely beautiful, with long black hair, stopped at the bottom of the stairs. She opened her mouth in astonishment when she saw him.

They stared at each other for what seemed to be an eternity.

"Sarju is here, Meera," grunted Giovanni, sipping his drink noisily. "He says it would be only for a few minutes; that is why he is not sitting."

"Hello, Meera. I just dropped by to see the kids," Sarju stammered. He couldn't believe his eyes. Just over fifty years old, Meera still appeared like a very young woman.

Meera put her hand over her mouth and stifled a cry. "Sarju, Sarju! This is a surprise. I still can't get over it. This is quite a surprise. We didn't expect you out at all."

Giovanni grinned. "I never expected to see you at all, my boy. We had no warning."

Meera stabbed him with a piercing look, and he quickly took another sip.

"The lawyer said you would not be eligible for parole in twenty years. He never contacted me. How did you get out?"

Meera sat across from Sarju and stared at him. Giovanni crept over to Meera and placed a hand protectively over her shoulder. She shrugged his hand away and almost spilled his drink.

Giovanni's eyes flashed at Sarju. "I hope you didn't break out of prison, Sarju. I don't want the SWAT team or the FBI knocking down my door for you."

Meera glowered at Giovanni. He edged his way to the bar to mix another drink.

Sarju addressed his back. "That won't happen, Giovanni. I made parole without the lawyer's help. A lot of things changed after sixteen years. I am just here to see my kids. That's all. How are they?"

Meera glared at Giovanni, who had topped his glass and was inching his way back to the sofa.

"They are okay, considering," Meera replied quietly.

"Considering what? What do you mean?" insisted Sarju.

Meera met his eyes. "When you went to ...that place, you said you wanted no contact with your children anymore. You never wrote or called them, although they sent you several cards and letters."

"You broke off all contact, Sarju," snapped Giovanni.

A tear rolled down Meera's cheek. She dabbed her eyes. "You stopped me from visiting you in prison. Twice I went, and you refused to meet me."

Giovanni touched her hands. He eyed Sarju with distaste. "You broke off all contacts. You severed all communication, and somebody had to be a father to the kids. That is how I stepped into the picture and their lives. I stepped up and became a husband to her and a father to your kids."

Meera wept openly. Giovanni tried to hug her close, but she shrugged him off.

Sarju appealed to him. "Yes, I admit I did that. But how could I be of use to anyone while I was locked away in a prison?"

Meera stretched across the sofa to a side table next to Sarju and grabbed a box of tissues. She dabbed her eyes and shook her head wearily.

"How could I be a good father in prison, Meera, when I was a poor excuse of a father outside?" pleaded Sarju.

Meera stretched out her hand and laid it on Sarju's bony wrist. "Please don't say that, Sarju. You did what any good father would do. But society didn't see it that way. They prefer to coddle rapists and gang bangers and assure them of rights under the constitution, but deprive law-abiding citizens of these same rights."

"But don't let anything concern you now, boy. The children are all grown. I made sure that they were well-educated. And very well adjusted too. Completely law-abiding," Giovanni announced proudly, taking another loud slurp.

Meera shot Giovanni another disapproving look. He squinted at the contents of his glass.

"Aarti doesn't live here, Sarju. She lives in Connecticut."

"I got the impression she lived here with you," Sarju responded with a catch in his voice.

"She has a daughter," Meera continued and touched Sarju's hand.

"Aarti has a daughter! My little Aarti? I am a grandfather, Meera," croaked Sarju, his eyes welling up with tears.

"And your son Mitra graduated college and is a police cadet. He is in the police training academy," added Meera, smiling as tears of joy rolled down Sarju's face.

"They did well, thank God," uttered Sarju, wiping his tears away.

Giovanni rose from the sofa. "Yes, boy. They both did well. Aarti is a trained nurse, and your son will be a policeman soon. He took a vow to uphold the law and keep society safe from criminals and murderers."

Meera bowed her head. Giovanni glanced at his wife and shrugged. "Just saying, just saying. My father took the same vow to keep society safe. I used to tell Mitra that, and I encouraged him to become a cop."

"Didn't you tell them that I was coming here today?" queried Sarju.

Meera glanced at Giovanni. He sipped his drink and looked at the wall of pictures. "We thought we should have this conversation first before we disclosed anything to them."

Sarju looked at the two and shook his head in disappointment. "Do they remember their father? Do they talk about me at all?"

Meera dabbed her eyes. "Aarti prefers to forget all that happened. We are concerned that it would only open old wounds. We had no hope that your sentence would be shortened. And the children forgot."

"With you gone, the children had to start over from scratch," Giovanni added, placing his hand consolingly on Sarju's shoulder. "To do that, they had to forget you first. We are sorry."

Sarju shrugged off his hand.

"And you yourself said you didn't want to see them. If you had to be locked away for more than twenty years, we should all move on," Meera reminded gently.

"That was your decision, my boy," piped Giovanni with a smug look.

"But forget about their father?" mumbled Sarju.

"That was the first step in moving on," Giovanni smirked. "How do you think they came out so successful? By remembering that their father is in prison?"

"And I couldn't take care of them on my own. It was hard to be a single parent," added Meera.

Sarju collapsed heavily in the armchair by the wall of pictures.

"I think you should take that drink now, Sarju," Giovanni offered.

"No, no," mumbled Sarju.

Giovanni contemplated Sarju, who sat immobile, hunched over in the chair. "I don't know how the children would respond now that you want to reestablish a relationship after an absence of sixteen years. Don't you think that would be selfish?"

Meera snorted loudly. Giovanni was silent.

Sarju shook his head slowly and considered the two. "I am sorry. I was not thinking of a relationship. All I wanted was to see my children. You think that is being selfish?"

"No, Sarju," opined Meera, "you are not being selfish. You are just being a father."

"And that was the role I played all these years. They know me, Giovanni, as the father. Think about how a police officer would react to finding out that his father is a convicted criminal. Meera and I discussed this, and we believe that the past should remain in the past," declared Giovanni with finality. "Let sleeping dogs lie, Sarju. It is all for the best."

Sarju darted a look at Giovanni. "Forget that I was a husband and a father?"

"Well, you should definitely forget about the husband part," insisted Giovanni.

"Sorry! You are right. I will certainly remember that now," Sarju agreed bitterly.

"But you are still the biological father," crowed Giovanni. "I am just the stand-in. You were the husband in the past. I am the husband now. I have been married to her for many years. That is the present. My present is with your former wife, now my wife. Do you feel it is fair to dredge up the past and uproot their future? Just bow out, man."

"Stop that, Giovanni," commanded Meera, "You have said enough! Enough."

Giovanni hustled over to the bar with the empty glass in hand. Sarju got to his feet and examined the picture of the nurse standing by the medical machine. Meera noticed his gaze, left the sofa, and stood by his side.

"That is your daughter. She filled your heart at one time. Do you remember?"

"How can I ever forget my Aarti? You think I can ever erase her from my heart?" Sarju's voice quavered, and he shuffled to the door.

"Wait, Sarju, wait." Meera darted to the adjoining room and frantically tumbled through a cabinet.

Giovanni returned to the doorway and stood shoulder-to-shoulder with Sarju.

"Well, this is goodbye, Sarju. You wouldn't be visiting this house again, would you? I wouldn't want to take out a restraining order against anyone that Meera knew," warned Giovanni.

Sarju stepped away from Giovanni. He hissed, "No, Giovanni. This is goodbye. I will not be here again. But I want you to understand that I did what I did to defend the honor of my daughter. Doesn't that count for anything? My children are adults now. They would understand things differently."

"As I explained, you should let sleeping dogs lie, Sarju. Today, you may be free, but you are still a murderer." Giovanni sneered.

"I did not come here to interfere with your life," Sarju protested vehemently.

"You can't, my boy. I am Meera's husband now. I have been manning the fort while you were gone. And that is the new reality. You are looking at the new sheriff in town."

Sarju peered into the living room. Meera was approaching them with a picture and a brown envelope in her hand.

Sarju's eyes narrowed. "Okay, sheriff, but it is not very often that one is privileged to encounter a human rat. If you ever get tired of that kind of life, I can recommend an exterminator who can promise you a peaceful journey."

Meera joined them at the door. Giovanni rested his hand on her shoulder. She handed Sarju a picture and the envelope.

"This is your daughter. On the first day at her job."

It was a copy of the picture on the wall—the picture of the nurse beside the machine. Sarju slowly departed the house, his gaze fixed on the photo. At the gate, he looked back. Meera was leaning against the door, with Giovanni hovering over her with a drink in his hand. Giovanni raised the glass in the air as his eyes locked on Sarju's.

Chapter 4- The Assault

S arju trudged to the bus stop on Pitkin Avenue. He had underestimated the distance when he walked to Giovanni's house. He didn't want to experience that long walk again. He stood at the bus stop and continued to gaze at the picture of his now-adult daughter. The bus arrived, and Sarju boarded. Oblivious to the demanding look of the driver, he walked past without tendering his Metro card. The driver shook his head in annoyance and muttered, "Another old fare beater."

Sarju took his seat and continued looking at the photo. It was not the way he remembered his daughter. The last time he saw her before being arrested, she was fifteen years old and in high school. The photograph that he had kept in his cell for sixteen years portrayed a young girl with two plaits of long hair, smiling, with mirth and laughter in her eyes. He had to come to grips with the picture in his hand. Time had passed, and his daughter was now a young woman and a young mother. He could discern the same elements in the adult. The hair, eyes, and demeanor were still the same. Even the chin. She had her grandmother's chin, tapered and pointed, attached to a heart-like face. It was indeed his Aarti and his heart swelled with pride as the tears clouded his vision.

The bus stopped. He put the photograph in the envelope that Meera had supplied. He stepped off the bus and crossed the avenue to the other side to catch the B13 bus that would take him to Terry's house. He had traversed this area for many years. The apartment building that he, Meera, and the kids had inhabited was just a short walk away. He heard the sound of the music coming from an ice cream truck that had stopped a block away. He slapped the envelope against his thigh as he recalled the last time that he and Aarti had been together. It was just after purchasing an ice cream cone that the dark cloud of misfortune descended on his family and changed their lives forever.

The B13 bus arrived, but Sarju did not board. He trod past the bus and continued in the direction that his feet remembered. After several minutes, he halted outside an apartment building. There were four floors, and he looked up at the windows on the fourth floor. He and his family had lived on that floor for several years. The apartment building was now well-maintained and freshly painted. The iron security front door was replaced by a tall, shiny glass door framed with gleaming steel. Through the very clear and shiny glass, he could see the hallway layered with cream ceramic tiles. When he lived there, it was covered with a dirty green, threadbare carpet that smelled and sheltered hordes of roaches.

The ice cream truck passed, and slowly, the tinkling music unearthed a flood of unsettling memories.

———◉———

HE HAD COME HOME EARLY one afternoon from work. He stepped out of the Euclid Avenue Station and stopped outside, trying to remember what he had to buy for the house. The apartment building where he lived had no elevator, so to avoid unnecessary trips up and down the dirty stairwell, he and Meera made sure that they remembered to purchase what was necessary before entering the building.

Meera had mentioned something to him that morning, but he couldn't remember. He was trying to jog his memory when somebody came up behind him and hugged him tightly. It was Aarti, dressed in her school uniform of blouse and skirt. Her plaits were long and decorated with butterfly clips, and her eyes twinkled at him.

"What are you doing here, Dad? Planning to panhandle by the subway?" Aarti laughed and slipped her hand through his.

He beamed proudly at his daughter and pecked her on the forehead. He removed her backpack and swung it over his shoulder.

"No. I was trying to remember what your mother asked me to buy, but my memory has gone. Help me out, bread or milk?"

Aarti laughed again. "No, and no. Yesterday, me and Mom bought bread and milk—enough for the week."

"Well, at least I tried. You can tell her that you found me outside trying to read her mind," Sarju teased. "And I know it was not eggs because I bought two dozen yesterday." He tapped his forehead and jested. "So what am I forgetting, my little lady?"

An ice cream truck passed them and stopped several yards away. Aarti turned to the truck as the music played. "I know what you can buy for me, Dad," Aarti replied, tugging him in the direction of the truck. A feeling of joy spread through him. He was so elated about his young daughter.

At the truck, he bought her a cone. The ice cream vendor smiled as he caught the mirth in her eyes and added a dollop more of the ice cream. She licked the top, and some of it stuck to her nose. "You look like a clown, now," Sarju chuckled and gave her his handkerchief to wipe her nose. "What about your brother? What should we get for him?"

"The brat is not at home," Aarti said, swirling her tongue around the side of the cup. "He and Mom went to Grandma's house."

"She didn't mention that to me this morning," Sarju complained good-naturedly.

"That is because you left for work very early. Grandma called when I was preparing to leave for school."

They turned around and headed for the apartment building, with Aarti savoring the ice cream and Sarju basking in the company of his daughter.

Aarti gave him a solemn look. "How come you are home so early, Dad?"

"Well, last week a supervisor in the shipping department was out sick, so I had to work late every day to cover for him. They are compensating for the extra hours by making me leave early," Sarju explained.

"Why don't you save the hours so that we can go on a vacation? Summer is just a few months away," Aarti suggested.

"So, where do you want to go? Did you discuss that with your mother?"

"No. But what about that place where you were born? Wakenaam, the island in that river in Guyana."

"The river is called Essequibo. It is the largest river in Guyana."

"I remember that! When I was in middle school, I researched that for a school project. That is a funny name, *Wakenaam*," giggled Aarti.

"It means a place waiting for a name," remarked Sarju, with a wistful look on his face. "It was named by the Dutch hundreds of years ago."

"And up to now, it is still waiting for a name! But I like it. We should visit your special island. Maybe I can give it a name."

By the time they reached the building, Aarti had finished the cone and was dabbing her lips with the handkerchief. The security entrance door was open wide, exposing the entire hallway.

"Who the heck opened the door? This is a security door. It must be kept closed at all times," huffed Sarju, thoroughly annoyed.

"Maybe some kid was playing around and forgot to lock it," Aarti suggested.

"Maybe the parents were playing around and forgot to teach them about being considerate," rejoined Sarju.

They set foot into the building, and Sarju closed the door with a loud bang. A few cockroaches skidded across the carpet as they ascended the flight of stairs. At the top of the stairs, on the fourth floor, Aarti was out of breath and hung on to Sarju's waist. In the middle of the hallway, close to their apartment door, two figures were leaning against the wall, exchanging money. Sarju recognized one of the figures as Jose, a drug dealer who loitered on the block. The other was a young boy whom Sarju had seen around the building.

Sarju scowled. "Now we know how the cockroaches penetrated the building."

The two in the hallway looked at them and backed away from the apartment door. The young boy smiled shyly at Aarti and waved his hand in a friendly manner.

"Hi, Ricardo," Aarti greeted.

Sarju stopped by his apartment door and thundered, "This is an apartment building, not a pharmacy. If you want to deal in drugs, do it away from my door. Take your dirty business where you live."

The older guy advanced to Sarju's door. "So, who told you that I don't live here?"

"Don't give me that," retorted Sarju, "you live in that drug-infested building on the next block. Go, peddle the poison where you live!"

"Who is peddling drugs here? We are just standing in the hallway minding our own business," shouted Jose.

"But why are you standing in this hallway? You are not a tenant here. Stand in the unemployment line and look for a job like any decent, hardworking person."

The man sneered. "This is not my primary residence, but I can stand here anytime I choose. I can make this hallway my place of business if I choose, so be careful, Gandhi! Be very careful, or you will need drugs from the hospital—and not my type of drugs."

Aarti tugged at Sarju's arm. "Open the door, Dad. Let's go."

Sarju shrugged off Aarti's hand. "What does an illiterate parasite like you know about Gandhi? Gandhi was a man who preached love and non-violence. The drugs you are passing on to the young people can only bring death and destruction."

"Please, Dad, let's go. Don't tell him anything," pleaded Aarti.

"Yes, Dad, go before I give your pretty daughter the kind of drug she really wants."

Sarju dropped the backpack and moved up to the irate man. Aarti tried to hold him around the waist. "Don't you dare say anything about my daughter," he screamed.

"So, what are you going to do?" Jose hissed and crept up quickly behind Aarti. "So, what are you going to do? Who is going to stop me from taking what I like?"

He leaned over and tried to yank up Aarti's skirt.

"Stop, stop!" Aarti yelled and backed away from Jose.

"Do not touch my daughter," roared Sarju, pushing the man away from Aarti.

Jose shoved him against the wall. "Well, then stop me, Mr. Gandhi. Stop me from tasting your young daughter's love."

Sarju, enraged, charged into the drug dealer, and the two exchanged blows. Aarti tried to restrain Sarju, but that allowed Jose deliver several vicious punches to the face and body. Sarju collapsed against the closed door of his apartment, and the drug dealer delivered several kicks to his head and body.

Jose grasped Aarti around the waist and attempted to grope and kiss her. He looked at Sarju, who lay crumpled and crushed against the door to his apartment. "What are you going to do now, Gandhi? How can you stop me from taking this sweet thing?"

"Dad, Dad!" Aarti screamed, squirming to get away from Jose.

Sarju reached for the door handle to raise himself off the floor but fell back in pain, incapable of assisting his daughter.

"Leave me, let me go, let me go!" Aarti continued to scream.

An apartment door down the hallway opened, and a woman poked her head through the door.

The young man, Ricardo, stepped forward to separate Jose from Aarti.

"Let her go, Jose. Let her go. Somebody is going to call the cops."

Jose released Aarti, and he and Ricardo sprinted down the hallway to the stairwell. Aarti slid to the floor and sobbed. Sarju raised himself off the floor to a seated position and banged his head against the wall in anguish and desperation.

<hr />

THE ICE CREAM TRUCK had circled the block and now stopped outside the apartment building. The front door was hidden from Sarju. He turned and retraced his steps to catch the bus to the rooming house, clutching the envelope with Aarti's picture firmly against his chest.

Chapter 5-The Final Diagnosis

Sarju ensured that the two doors were locked securely before descending the stairs to the yard. He found Terry, the landlord, standing against a parked car, looking at his building.

"Morning, Terry," greeted Sarju. "How come you are standing upright like that? I thought you had arthritis."

"I have it but don't want it," grunted Terry. "Standing like this is okay. It's when I move, or worse, when I climb the stairs, then I start seeing stars. Why you think I am standing here? I dread climbing those stairs. But, where you off to this morning?"

"Just going by Hillside Avenue in Jamaica to check out my doctor."

"Oh! You too! I just come from that area myself. I had to do a blood test to see if gout is not part of this arthritis." Terry considered Sarju thoughtfully. "I heard you vomiting your guts out last night. I wanted to come up and check on you, but I didn't want to experience that pain."

"Just a little stomach problem," smiled Sarju.

"Let him give you something for that. First, I thought that you were having some drinks, but I didn't see any bottles in the garbage, so it must be something that you eat."

"I suspect that is the case." Sarju made a few steps to the gate. "I am going to catch the train now before I miss that appointment."

"Change your restaurant, and you will see an improvement. Some of these restaurants are known to serve cockroaches over everything," warned Terry as Sarju strode off in the direction of the train station.

Sarju boarded the J-train a few blocks away, made a change to the E-train, and finally to the F-train. He exited the last stop on Hillside Avenue and walked several long blocks to the doctor's office. When he rolled into the receptionist's area, he was half an hour early; he found four patients sitting quietly, waiting.

The receptionist, a young Hispanic girl with the name tag "Clarissa" on her uniform, looked up from her desk with a nervous expression on her face. "Morning, sir. Do you have an appointment? What is your name, sir?"

"Sarju Beepat. I have an appointment for one with Dr. Chadda."

"Thanks for being here so early, Mr. Beepat. Can you please fill out this form?" She slid a clipboard and a pen over to him.

"How long do I have to wait?" Sarju tapped the clipboard, eying the patients in the waiting room.

Clarissa appeared flustered. She glanced furtively at the patients. "I am sorry, Mr. Beeepat, but this morning the doctor came late from the hospital. We are backed up."

"So you have no idea when I will see the doctor?"

"You will definitely see him. He is not breaking for lunch, but it is going to take a while," Clarissa whispered. She jutted her chin in the direction of a woman whose chin rested on folded hands on top of her walking stick. "That woman has an eleven o'clock appointment. The others are after her."

Sarju snorted. "But when I called you for the appointment, you particularly warned me about being late. That's why I am here early," complained Sarju loudly. The waiting patients perked up their ears and glared at Clarissa. An old man with a very bald head nodded his head in support of Sarju and sucked his teeth loudly.

Clarissa flinched. "I am very sorry, sir. But there is nothing we can do. If you have somewhere to go, you can go and come back later. I will make sure your place is kept," she promised.

"I have no place to go, and I have all the time in the world. I will wait."

Sarju grasped the clipboard and headed for an empty chair between the woman resting on her cane and the old man who had issued the loud suck teeth.

Sarju scrutinized the requirements on the form as the bald man rested his head against the wall and commenced to snore loudly. The lady next to Sarju shook her head in irritation and almost fell over her cane. He signed and completed the form, handed it to the sulking Clarissa, and returned to his seat.

The waiting room had a low ceiling with dark oak-paneled walls that made the room slightly claustrophobic. The chairs were made of cast iron from a different era and were upholstered in material that felt and looked like industrial carpet. It looked vaguely familiar and reminded Sarju of the warden's room in Sing Sing prison.

———◉———

SARJU WAS TUTORING some of the more ambitious inmates in the library when a guard entered the room and beckoned him to the door.

The guard belted out brusquely. "The warden wants to see you now. Wrap it up here and let's go."

Sarju followed the guard out of the general prison area and across a large square to a small administrative building housing the warden's office. They took the elevator and came out in a wide office area populated by several clerks working behind computer desks. The guard escorted him to the end of the room and leaned over a short counter to speak to a young woman in a cubicle.

"This is the inmate you wanted."

The young woman had a purple tint in her brown hair. She moved aside a few strands that were straying over her forehead and peered at Sarju. "What is your name?

"Sarju Beepat."

She consulted a diary in front of her and then picked up a phone. She had a short conversation, then turned to the guard. "Take him in. He is waiting."

The guard made a right, walked down a long corridor, and stopped outside a large wooden door. The metal nameplate announced *Warden E. Knoph.* The guard knocked loudly on the door. He tilted his ear against it and listened carefully while keeping an eye on Sarju. Then, he opened the door about halfway and ushered in Sarju.

The room was huge with oak-paneled walls, and the warden's desk was set against the far wall. On the wall behind his desk were a few photographs of the warden receiving awards or meeting with important officials. A long sofa and two iron chairs were placed along a side wall. The warden was hunched over some documents on his desk. Without looking up, he pointed in the direction of the iron chairs. The guard took one of the chairs and placed it about five feet away from the warden's desk. Sarju stood by the chair while the guard backed up and stood at attention by the closed door, looking at both the warden and Sarju.

Warden E. Knoph was a tall, imposing gentleman. He had a massive frame, and Sarju observed the taut muscles of the man trying to force the white shirt apart at the seams. He had a square face with a snarling mouth that belonged to a bulldog. Sarju had never spoken to the warden before but had seen him several times around the prison conducting his official inspections.

The inmates referred to him as Warden "Head Banger." Sarju had seen him live up to his name. Once in the cafeteria, two prisoners started a fight over food portions. The guards on duty tried to break up the fight. Other prisoners joined in until there was a wild melee. Objects were thrown across the room, and the guards were all over the unruly prisoners with their batons when Warden E. Knoph stormed with his retinue of guards. Immediately, he marched through the crowd and grasped the two prisoners who had started the mini-riot by the scruffs of their necks and banged their heads together. Instantly, they fell helpless to the ground in a mass of unresponsive flesh. He turned to face the other prisoners, but they backed down meekly and returned to their spots. Gums was standing nearby with his mop and a bucket of water. Warden Head Banger grabbed the bucket and emptied the dirty water over the heads of the two men. They groaned and sat up groggily. The medics took them away to the sick bay, where they spent a week recovering from a serious concussion.

Warden Head Banger motioned for Sarju to sit. He peered at him through his steely gray eyes. "We received the report from the parole board, Inmate Beepat. You had applied for expedited parole."

"Yes, sir," replied Sarju, "the welfare officer and the prison doctor helped with the application."

"People have been here for decades and are still waiting for their sentences to be reduced," the warden stated, his steely gray eyes fixed on Sarju's face.

Sarju's heart skipped a beat. "Did they consider my application, sir?"

The warden paused for a while, then continued. "You received clemency after serving sixteen years. They took into consideration the extent of your cancer and granted you parole."

The warden noted the pained expression on Sarju's face. "How much time did your doctors give you?"

"They said it could be between six and nine months, sir."

"Well, I am sorry to hear that. But at least you can leave as a free man," observed the warden.

"Yes, sir. Free to die in peace."

The warden nodded his head slowly and leafed through a few documents. "Freedom should never be taken lightly, Prisoner

Beepat. It should always be treasured and guarded carefully, or it can be lost in a moment of passion or indiscretion. I have a family, and to keep my family, I must be free."

"And I lost my freedom because I couldn't protect my family," Sarju muttered sadly.

"You have been a model prisoner here at Sing Sing, Beepat. You graduated with a degree in psychology and helped many prisoners gain their high school equivalency diplomas behind these prison walls, and you read a lot of the law books in our library. You of all people would appreciate that justice is blind, and it applies to all of us. In a civilized society, one cannot take the law into our own hands. Retribution is not for us."

"You are right, sir. I learned that lesson," agreed Sarju.

"And you have earned a few months of freedom, Beepat. Enjoy the time with your family."

Sarju gazed down at his worn-out prison shoes. The warden continued looking through his documents. He waved a sheet of paper at Sarju.

"But there is a condition to your release, Beepat. Because you are not a U.S. citizen, the parole board and the immigration department have decided that you must leave the country within two months."

"My family is here, sir. America is my home. I have been here for over thirty years," pleaded Sarju.

"That is the condition, Beepat. If you don't agree, you can remain with us until the end. What is your decision?"

"I will leave, sir. That is my decision. I accept clemency and parole."

"Are you going to spend the last months with your family?"

"I don't know, sir. Prison has put walls between us."

The warden nodded and made a few notes in his folder. "Okay, then. The counselor and welfare officer will be in contact with you.

They will find a place for you to stay for two months, and then you must self-deport, or you will have to return here."

"I understand. I won't be back," Sarju assured the warden.

"Well, that is all. I am glad you are leaving. I only wish you didn't have to come here in the first place. You are dismissed. Guard, return the prisoner to his duties."

"Thank you, sir," Sarju rose to follow the guard.

"Prisoner," called Warden E. Knoph, "speaking as a father and not as a warden, I might have been tempted to do what you did. I am sorry the legal system disagreed with you, but that is now water under the bridge. Or more exactly, water that flowed with the Hudson."

The guard opened the door for Sarju; that was the last encounter he had with Warden Head Banger.

<hr/>

IT WAS SHORTLY AFTER three when a nurse led Sarju to the examination room. She took his temperature, weight, and blood pressure and peppered him with a host of questions concerning the medications he took. She inputted all the information on a computer and handed him a gown. "Remove all your clothes. The doctor will be here in a few minutes."

Sarju lay on the examination bed and dozed off. He woke up when he felt a chair roll up beside the bed, and someone touched his shoulder. It was Dr. Chadda, a portly, middle-aged Indian man.

"How are you feeling, Mr. Beepat?" he asked as he consulted his computer.

"I am still feeling alive, doctor," Sarju retorted, searching the doctor's face.

"That is the best feeling to have," Chadda responded, resting his laptop computer on a nearby desk. "Okay, let's take a look at you."

Chadda poked and prodded, giving him a complete check-up. After his anal examination, he discarded his gloves and handed Sarju a box of tissue. "Wipe yourself off, dress, and meet me in my office."

Sarju cleaned himself of the gel that had been smeared over his buttocks, dressed, and joined Chadda in his office adjoining the examination room.

Dr. Chadda studied the computer screen in front of him, wiped his glasses, and regarded Sarju. "I examined all the records the prison doctors sent. The tests done were very comprehensive. I obtained similar results from those that I ordered."

Sarju stared at the doctor with a blank expression on his face.

"It seems like the cancer was diagnosed at an advanced stage while you were in prison," Chadda continued, looking at Sarju accusingly. "Didn't you recognize the obvious signs that you were sick? That all was not well, man?"

Sarju's lips curled in a faint smile. "Doctor, the only thing that is obvious when you are in prison is that you are breathing. Life and death can be considered the same. At first, I noticed blood in my stool, but I did not think it was serious. Later came the stomach pains. I thought that was due to indigestion."

Chadda shook his head in disapproval. "Well, it certainly wasn't! That colon cancer could have been arrested had you taken action earlier and sought the necessary treatment."

"Then I would have been free of colon cancer but still imprisoned in Sing Sing," conceded Sarju caustically.

Chadda ignored that. He continued to look at the report on his computer. "The cancer cells in the colon metastasized, and a bad situation became fatally serious."

Chadda leaned back in his chair and scrutinized Sarju. "The cancer spread to your stomach and then to your lungs and liver."

Sarju was silent. He heard the hum as the fan on Chadda's computer activated. His attention was hooked on a diagram of the human body on the wall, and he identified the organs that Chadda had mentioned. He imagined a long snake slowly squeezing his organs.

"That was what the prison doctor said. That is why they paroled me."

Dr. Chadda rocked back in his chair and observed the ceiling. "We can start an aggressive treatment of chemotherapy and radiation therapy to see if we can retard the spread. I am sure the prison doctor recommended that treatment."

"Yes, but would that cure me?" Sarju leaned forward and quietly addressed Chadda, "You can be frank with me. I am not your ordinary patient, you know. I spent sixteen years behind bars. Cancer is no comparison."

Chadda sighed. "I am sorry, Mr. Beepat. The cancer is far gone. Chemotherapy will just buy us some time. Eventually, the cancer will triumph. All we can do is hope for the best."

Sarju rose to his feet. "The best has passed me by. I knew all this before coming, but thanks for your time, Doctor."

"If you knew, why did you come?" Chadda poked his head over the computer screen to have a better view of Sarju.

"I was hoping you would know of a miracle cure or some miracle trial drug," explained Sarju.

"I wish we knew, Mr. Beepat," declared Chadda, shaking his head. "Medicine is not the exact science we think it is. On my certificate, it is marked "Doctor of Medicine" not "Doctor of Miracles." You can continue with your present diet and medication. When the pain becomes too severe, you can see me to increase the dosage of the pain medication. You must continue with your prescribed diet."

"That is another thing. Whatever I eat tends to come out. I am throwing up constantly."

"That is expected. The cancer and medication cause that. But you still have to eat. At least, before you throw up the food, some nutrients will be digested to help you survive."

"So, I can eat anything?"

Chadda looked at Sarju's gaunt frame. He sighed. "I don't see why not! You said you throw up everything, so experiment until you find what stays down."

Sarju grinned. "What is your advice on drinks?"

Chadda smiled. "Everything in moderation, but with your medication, drinks may not stay down for very long."

Dr. Chadda rose from his desk and walked to the door. He shook Sarju's hand. "I am sorry that I couldn't leave you with good news, Mr. Beepat. Take care of your personal business and enjoy..."

"I know. The rest of my life," interjected Sarju, "of which I can count the months on my fingers! Thank you for your time, Doctor."

Chapter 6- A Celebratory Drink

Hassan, with a bag in his hand, ascended the stairs to the rooming house to find the door open. Terry was extracting mail from the box attached to the wall.

"How are you doing, Hassan? I hope you don't kill any roaches on your visit here. I can't afford your extermination bills," he laughed and handed Hassan a letter with an official stamp. "This is for your boy. It looks like a love letter from immigration."

Hassan mounted the stairs. He looked at Sarju's door and called, "Sarju! Sarju!"

Without waiting for a response, he walked to the kitchen, opened the door of the fridge, and peered inside. He opened his bag, removed a six-pack of beers, and inserted the bottles.

When he returned to Sarju's door, it was wide open. Sarju was sitting on the plastic chair by the window.

"How is everything, Sarge? Sorry, I couldn't give you a lift to the doctor this morning. When you called, I was on a job in New Jersey."

"That's okay. I didn't take long with the train. His office is very close to the train station."

"Well, how did it go? Your plumbing system and pistons working fine? Ready to enter the dating scene?" chortled Hassan.

Sarju looked at Hassan and joined in a short laugh. He recounted the conversation he had with Dr. Chadda. Hassan's face was drained of color. He sat on the edge of the little bed and scrutinized Sarju's face.

"This is shocking news, Sarge. Why didn't you tell me before?"

Sarju looked at Hassan apologetically. "I was hoping to hear some good news from Chadda before I told you."

Hassan addressed Sarju's reflection in the mirror. "So, that is why you got parole before you served your full sentence! I wondered how you got out so early. I could remember the lawyer saying that you had to serve at least twenty years before being released on good behavior."

"Ironic, eh? The cancer that is going to kill me caused me to be free! But free to do what?" Sarju snickered with a tinge of bitterness. "To live for a few more months out of prison so the state can save on medical bills?"

"You can't give up all hopes, man. Take the chemotherapy as the doctor suggested. By the time that treatment is over, they may find a cure for cancer," encouraged Hassan. "You can still look forward to a good life."

Sarju laughed without any merriment. "You don't think I know when it is over, Hassan? Even the doctor reminded me that he is not a doctor of miracles."

"I know some people stopped going to doctors and started seeing witch doctors or obeah men to cure them of diseases," disclosed Hassan.

"Did anyone of those people get cured of cancer?" Sarju demanded.

"I don't think so," admitted Hassan. "Obeah men are just con men, not miracle workers." He looked at the letter in his hand and handed it to Sarju. "Oh, this came for you!"

Sarju glanced at the envelope and slapped it against his wrist. "I don't mind dying, Hassan, but I thought at least my children would have wanted to see me."

"So, what are you going to do? What plans do you have?"

Sarju tore open the envelope. He read the contents, crumpled the letter, and tossed it on the floor.

He stared at his friend. "Home, Hassan! I plan to go home."

"To Meera's home?" asked Hassan, aghast. "That is not your home, man. That is Giovanni's house."

Sarju stood up. He walked to the paper and kicked it. It flew by the door.

"Home, home. To Guyana, where I was born. To die in the house where I was born."

"But this country is your home, Sarge. You have everything here. Family, friends, health care..."

"But I am not a citizen," insisted Sarju. "That was a condition of my parole. I have a few more weeks to leave the country. That letter was from U.S. Immigration. They are reminding me that I have to self-deport or report to Sing Sing. If I stay here any longer, I will become a criminal again."

Sarju returned to the chair and gazed out the window. In the distance, the J-train was weaving its way on the overheard track like a long aluminum snake.

Hassan blurted out, "You have no home there. I heard your brother sold the house!"

"That was my house, too!" retorted Sarju and glared at Hassan. "I didn't know that. I haven't had any contact with him in years. I am sure I can find a place there. In my condition, I won't require a long lease."

"I still have my house in Wakenaam, Sarge. My relatives take care of it, and there is a spare room that I occupy when I visit." Hassan pointed at a glass of milk and a banana on the small table. "And you won't have to worry about meals," he laughed. "They have cows and lots of fruit trees."

Sarju stared at Hassan with a wry smile. "I always imagined that whenever they decided to parole me, you and I would have a drink like old times."

Hassan got up from the bed and strode to the door. "When you called me from prison and told me that you were being released, I was thinking the same thing. I put a few beers in the fridge, but only I can drink now."

"I will have that drink with you," smiled Sarju.

"But didn't the doctor say it would interfere with your medication?"

"He is hoping that some things taken in moderation will not be rejected by my stomach. You only die once, Hassan, and I have a few months before that date with my destiny. Go, bring that beer, my friend."

Hassan brought the beer, and he and Sarju stood by the window, draining the cool liquid from the bottles.

Sarju mumbled with the bottle to his lips. "We had some good times, Hassan. We grew up together; we struggled together in this new land."

"Does Meera know about your condition?" inquired Hassan.

He looked at Hassan with steely determination. "No, no, Hassan! Meera and the children must never know. You are the only person in my circle who knows; you must promise never to tell anyone."

"How can you ask me to make such a promise, Sarge?" Hassan protested. "Don't you think your wife and children have a right to know about your condition?"

"If I can't be afforded dignity, then I certainly don't want pity," remarked Sarju, draining the bottle. "Giovanni was right. The past must remain hidden in the past."

"Giovanni is a vindictive man," sneered Hassan. "Don't you see that he is taking credit for the accomplishments of your children? You set the foundation for their success; he wants to deprive you of your fatherhood."

"But he is right, Hassan."

"No, no," bristled Hassan. "He is not just content with possessing your wife; he wants to control the destiny of your children. You have to put a stop to that, man."

"Don't you understand that I caused all this upon myself, Hassan?" remarked Sarju bitterly. "It was I who created the conditions for this calamity. My actions put all of these events into play."

Hassan sighed heavily. "But at least you should see your children before you leave. Just to see what they have become."

Sarju rested the empty bottle on the table. "Don't you think I want to, Hassan? Even though Giovanni thinks it would hurt them to see me, I want to see them. I want to see my children, Hassan. For sixteen years, every night before I went to bed, I saw their little faces in my mind and heard their voices. My heart ached to see them, but I never wanted them to see their father in prison. I never thought that when I became free I would be faced with this dilemma."

Sarju stared through the window but didn't see anything. He heard the shouts of a few kids playing on the street.

Hassan left the room and returned with two bottles of beer. He handed one to Sarju, then grabbed his vibrating phone from his pocket.

"Hello? Yes, this is Hassan. How are you doing? You want him to call you?" Hassan looked at Sarju. "Well, I can do better. He is right here. You can speak to him now."

Hassan handed the phone to Sarju and grinned. "Meera! She said your phone is ringing out when she calls."

Sarju, after some hesitation, took the phone from Hassan.

"Yes, Meera!"

"Why didn't you pick up your phone, Sarju?" Meera complained. "I called several times this afternoon."

"The phone was in my bag," responded Sarju. "I didn't hear it ring."

"Oh! I thought you were upset about what happened yesterday. About the way Giovanni spoke to you."

"Why would I be upset? It was his house, and what he said was right?"

"No, it wasn't Sarju," Meera sniffed. Sarju knew that she was in tears. "He had no right to speak to you like that. You are my children's father, and you were once my husband."

"Once, Meera. I was your husband *once*. But that is all water under the bridge. The children are better off without me. I know that now, Meera."

"No, you don't know anything, Sarju. I need to explain some things to you," Meera retorted.

"Everything was explained yesterday, Meera. I understood everything."

"I didn't tell you everything yesterday, Sarju."

Sarju was silent for a while. "What is there to know, Meera? What more do you wish to tell me that Giovanni didn't say?"

"Come tomorrow, and you will know everything."

"You want me to return to Giovanni's house, Meera? I am not going to violate the man's house with my presence. We came to that understanding yesterday," Sarju declared.

"No, no, not at the house," Meera sniffed. "Meet me at the park at three, tomorrow. Do you remember the park by Pitkin Avenue? The one where we used to take the kids?"

"The park that is near your house?"

"Yes, yes. Tudor Park. Be there at three."

"Okay, I will be there on time," nodded Sarju and looked at Hassan.

"Oh, Sarju? Do you need anything? Yesterday was so confusing that I forgot to ask you."

"No, no, Meera. I have everything that I need here. Thanks for asking. But wait, there is one thing. Do you still have my Guyana passport?"

"Yes, I have the passport. I have all your old documents. I didn't dispose of anything. Why do you want the passport? It is expired. You can't use it to travel!"

"Not for traveling. Just another document to identify me."

"Alright, Sarju. I will see you in the park. Good night."

"Good night, Meera. See you tomorrow."

Sarju handed back the phone with a dazed expression on his face.

"What is this?" asked Hassan, "Are you planning to change the government? You are planning to overthrow King Giovanni?"

Sarju took a long swig from the bottle. "No. I am just going to retrieve my passport. You can't travel on an airplane without one, you know."

Suddenly, Sarju clutched his stomach and placed his bottle on the floor. He pushed Hassan aside and rushed to the bathroom. Hassan sipped on his beer as he listened to Sarju retching in the toilet bowl.

Chapter 7- The Meeting

Meera arrived at the park a little after three. She was late because Giovanni was dawdling about the house and left later than usual for his weekly rendezvous with his friends on Long Island. She did not want to invite Sarju to the house again because she wanted to avoid a verbal altercation with Giovanni. Although Sarju was in her past, Giovanni was extremely possessive. She knew that after any argument that he could not prevail on, he could be sullen for days. With the children out of the house, she could not bear to have a dark cloud of disagreement hanging over the home, over the two of them.

She had met Giovanni at the bank. After Sarju was incarcerated, she moved from the apartment building in Brooklyn to live with her parents in Queens Village. The children had to change schools, and with her mother taking care of Mitra, she was able to re-enter the workforce. Through an employment agency, she was assigned to a bank as a teller. She met Giovanni there. He was a financial advisor, and after several months, he started showing an interest in her.

The children were growing; Aarti was blossoming into a young woman, and Mitra, showing signs of a rebellious spirit, was crying out for a father figure to guide him. After almost two years of his constant attention and entreaties and no hope of Sarju ever seeing daylight in decades, she relented and agreed to marriage.

They got married in City Hall, and their reception was a very small affair with only very close friends and family. Giovanni had previously been married. His wife divorced him and moved to Florida with their two sons. She remarried there, and the relationship with his children ended as well. Meera recognized a strong longing for fatherhood in him, and when she moved with her children to his house in Ozone Park, at first he was shy and awkward, but later he demonstrated great interest and attention to them. When Mitra decided to take his name, Giovanni was overjoyed. The children grew to love him, and their home was complete.

Meera walked slowly around the small park but did not see Sarju. She called his phone several times, but it was ringing out. She thought it was very strange. Sarju had cultivated the habit of being early for any occasion. Meera knew that no prison could break him. That habit was ingrained in his character. School was out, and there were quite a few kids with their parents there. Many of them were in the children's section with the swings and slides. Meera had a fleeting memory of Sarju pushing Mitra on a swing while Aarti flew by on another, cutting the air in a great arc.

She trailed along the fence, her eyes searching all corners of the park. From the periphery of her vision, she noted a flock of crows hopping around a black garbage bag by the road outside the park. A few of the birds flew a few feet around the bag, squawking hoarsely, "Caw, caw." A few park benches lined the road, and Meera discerned someone, perhaps a homeless man, throwing up into a white plastic bag. She observed the bag inflating and deflating as the man breathed into it. She turned her nose up in disgust and was about to turn her back when the man stood up and shuffled to a garbage bin nearby. She recognized that unmistakable shuffle. The man was Sarju. He had elected to wait outside the park.

Meera backtracked and exited the gate to climb the ramp that led to the road. The benches were under the trees that lined the street, and Sarju was seated on one, his profile facing Meera. At that moment, the spring clouds that had covered the sun blew across the sky, and sunlight beamed through the branches. Sarju swiveled his head upon hearing her footsteps, and a few strips of sunlight fell across his face like prison bars. Meera noticed his face lit up with anguish and pain, and she choked up as tears filled her eyes.

"Sarju, Sarju," she whimpered.

Sarju looked at her and smiled weakly. "Meera, Meera."

His eyes roved over her, almost drinking her in. Her eyes, very brown and piercing behind her tears, snatched his gaze. Her dimples were still evident, little valleys in a slightly plumpish face, and her black and luxuriant hair tumbled over her shoulders. Through the top of her sweater, he hesitated on her cleavage, hinting at her fulsome, unblemished breasts. At Giovanni's house, his eyes couldn't explore all of her. And now she was there. Meera, Meera!

His eyes were still on her cleavage when he heard her voice again. "How are you, Sarju? Are you okay?"

Embarrassed, he took his eyes away quickly and stared at her face. "I am fine, Meera. I am just getting used to freedom."

She opened her handbag and took out a bottle of water. She opened it and took two sips. "I saw you throwing up a few minutes ago. You can't be well, Sarju!"

Sarju looked away to avoid her eyes. "It was just indigestion. Something that I ate early on. The food now tastes different. I was on prison food for a long time, you know."

Meera handed him the bottle. "Here, this water will settle your stomach."

"Thanks. I forgot to walk with water." Sarju walked a few feet away, gargled with a few mouthfuls of water, then drank the rest.

He returned to the bench. "What is it that you want to tell me, Meera?"

"I want to apologize for what happened yesterday, Sarju. Giovanni was caught unaware. Some of the things shouldn't have been said."

"There is no need to apologize. He was right, though. But what did you want to talk to me about?"

"Giovanni! I didn't marry him out of love."

Sarju looked into her dark eyes. "You don't have to explain anything, Meera. We can't undo the past with explanations."

Her eyes clouded over with tears. She reached into her bag for a pack of tissues. "But you need to know that it was not about love."

"It's over, Meera. It's over. We have to get over this."

"But didn't you tell me to stop visiting you in prison and to move on with my life?"

"And I am happy for you, Meera. And you moved on. Aren't you happy, Meera? What could I offer you and the kids in prison?"

"We could have still visited you, Sarju," she persisted. "You were not the only person to be locked away. The kids could have visited and remained connected."

"No, Meera, no," Sarju snapped. "Did you consider the state of your lives if you had visited me in prison? What would you tell your colleagues if they asked how you spent your weekend? That you had gone to Sing Sing to visit your husband? And the children? Would you want them to tell their teachers and friends that they spent their vacation visiting with their father in prison?"

Meera wept silently. Her shoulders shuddered. Sarju felt ashamed of his outburst. He gripped the side of the wooden park bench. He wanted so much to embrace her.

"Giovanni was right. He was thinking clearly."

"Yes," agreed Meera, wiping her eyes and composing herself. "I wanted someone to guide the children and support them. Giovanni was there. He treated the children well, Sarju. He treated them like they were his own."

"I am sure he was a good father," Sarju mumbled. "I should thank him for that."

"He always made the right decisions for them. They trust his judgment."

Sarju nodded his head. "I would trust his judgment, too. Did you find that passport?"

Meera dug into her bag again and took out an old passport wrapped in plastic. "Here it is! Is it for identification purposes, as you said?"

Sarju unwrapped the plastic around the passport and examined the pages. "Yes. And also for traveling. I am going to Guyana."

Meera leaned across him and tapped the front page. "But it is expired."

"After sixteen years, what do you expect? But it is enough for me."

"Why are you going, Sarju? You spent most of your life in America."

"And half of that time in prison. I have done all that I set out to do. There is nothing left for me to do. Besides, if I don't leave willingly, they are going to deport me. I am not a U.S. citizen."

"You don't have to go, Sarju," Meera implored and grasped his hand. "You don't have to leave America. You can go to another state. You know how many millions should be deported, but they are living free as a bird here. It is not easy to deport anyone here."

Sarju placed the passport in the pocket of his jacket. "Not in my case, Meera. I am a convicted criminal. It was a condition of my parole. If I don't leave, they will hunt me down and send me back to prison to serve the rest of my time."

Meera looked at a few crows flitting by, moving freely from tree to tree. "So, where do you plan to go, Sarju?"

"To the island. To Wakenaam. As I get older, I yearn for the place of my childhood. The place of my birth."

Meera looked wistfully at him. "I have never seen your island. Many years ago, you had promised to take me and the kids there."

Sarju looked over the fence to the park where the children were playing. "Yes. The same year that I was imprisoned was the year I wanted to take the kids. But they won't like it there. America is their home. And Giovanni will be here for them."

Meera turned and faced him, staring him in the eyes. Sarju looked away.

"Don't go, Sarju," she pleaded. "It is not over. In time, Giovanni may change his mind. And the children will want to meet you."

Sarju held on to the arm of the bench and slowly raised himself up. He patted the passport in his pocket. "I have to go, Meera. Every day makes the island drift farther and farther away. I must go to my island."

"Oh, there is something else!" Meera groped in her bag and removed an ATM card. She handed it to him.

"What is this for?"

"You had an account before you went to prison, before you left us. I did not close it off. The money is still there."

"I don't need this. You should have used it on the kids." Sarju pushed the card towards Meera; she slapped his wrist.

"There was no need to use this account. I used the one that was in both our names. I kept this one for you. Remember, it was your first bank account in this country."

"I can't take it. It is not mine," Sarju remonstrated.

"But this is from before we got married. Read the card. You are the only Sarju Beepat here. Take it, Sarju. The PIN is still the same—your date of birth."

Sarju reached down and placed the card in her hand. "I told you I don't want this," he declared firmly. "It is yours, not mine."

Meera sprang to her feet and stood before him. Her eyes flashed. "Did you have a job while you were in prison, Sarju? Did they give you a pension for working there? How do you intend to go to Guyana? Grow wings?"

Sarju's lips twitched in defiance. "Don't you understand? This is not what I want. I don't want your money. It is time for me to move on."

"I am not telling you to move on, Sarju Beepat," scolded Meera, and she inserted the card into his jacket pocket. "Don't be difficult. And if you need anything, use your phone and call me, even if you are in Guyana. By the way, why didn't you pick up your phone? I called you several times."

"Sorry. I left it in my room. I am still not accustomed to a cell phone."

An ice cream truck drove down the street and stopped by the entrance to the park. Sarju looked at the truck, and the memory of him and his daughter flashed through his mind. He stumbled slightly. Meera caught his hand, and both of them looked at the truck.

Meera smiled. "Do you remember what we did every time we came to this park with the children?"

"You tell me. It was so long ago, Meera."

"We always stopped and got ice cream. Let's do it one last time."

Sarju smiled. "Your favorite is still chocolate?"

"You remember?"

Sarju smiled and thought, *"How can I ever forget anything about you, Meera?"*

Meera took his hand and led him in the direction of the parked truck.

Chapter 8- The Children

The traffic was light as he took Interstate I-95 to Connecticut. It was his only day off in six weeks from the NYC Police Academy. During the past six weeks, Manhattan was a hive of different activities, from the Heads of State meetings at the U.N. headquarters to the many protests and marches around the city that warranted extra hands to man security barricades and to control crowds. Short on manpower, rookie cops and new recruits were pressed into service. Mitra did not mind the additional hours, as the overtime was substantial and would be channeled into paying rent on an apartment that he shared with a buddy in Manhattan. But what he missed was visiting his mother and Giovanni, and of course, missing his sister when she visited the previous weekend.

Now, he was on his way to visit Aarti, who lived in a township in Hartford, Connecticut. After completing nursing school, she received an offer from a hospital in Hartford and immediately left Queens, New York. She was very excited to be on her own and to leave the congestion of New York City behind. A few months later, she announced her engagement to a former high school friend. When she arrived home for a visit with her boyfriend, Mitra noticed that Meera was not pleased with her choice. Meera was very cold toward the guy and did not encourage any kind of warm association. He knew mother and daughter had serious disagreements over the engagement, so he kept out of their affairs and did not pry. Aarti's fiancé, originally from the Dominican Republic, was employed as a security guard at the same hospital. Mitra tried to analyze the situation to understand the source of the conflict. He ruled out class and social status, as Meera held no prejudice towards any kind of gainful employment. He considered ethnic preference but dismissed that, as Meera and all of them had friends of different ethnicities and faiths. And hadn't Meera married the Italian, Giovanni? Both Aarti and Meera were headstrong, and he knew better not to get between them.

A year after the engagement, Aarti got married in Hartford. It was a very small affair and should have been an occasion for a grand celebration; the coldness and recalcitrant attitude of Meera put a strain on the event. But it was Giovanni who held out the olive branch and brokered a reconciliation. The newly married couple was interested in purchasing a modest property; one of Giovanni's friends owned a rental property in the Hartford area, but the tenants had not paid rent in years. Eventually, the court evicted them, and they left after doing considerable damage to the building. The property owner was ready to cut his losses when Giovanni persuaded him to sell it to Aarti and her husband for a price well below the market value. The property required a great deal of work, but fortunately, Aarti's husband had relatives in New York City who were into building construction. The relatives would leave the city on weekends and put in long hours to render the building habitable.

Mitra turned off the major highway and took the local road to the house. He had been there a few times before to lend a hand with the reconstruction project. He turned into a quiet street lined by pin oak trees and parked outside the house. It was a large, one-family colonial and was still a work in progress. A major portion of a wall of the building was unfinished. The exposed pink insulation material on the wall was screaming to be completed with the appropriate siding. The relatives were still not finished.

Mitra opened the back door and removed a package. Aarti's car, a Toyota Rav 4, was parked in the driveway. Mitra strolled down the paved walkway to the front door and rang the bell. He waited patiently for someone to come to the door. The wooden porch was freshly painted slate gray, and there were a few green plastic chairs around a small round table. He was tempted to take a seat, but he heard scratching sounds from behind the door and a sharp clack as a bolt was drawn back.

Aarti, dressed in sweats, appeared at the door, a huge smile planted on her face. The dimples on her face and her shoulder-length hair reminded him immediately of his mother. She didn't look like she was thirty. Aarti could pass for a teenager. He embraced his sister, and she planted a kiss on his cheek.

She looked at him approvingly with fondness in her eyes. "Hello, stranger! Don't you know that New York cops can't arrest anyone in Connecticut?"

She led him inside and closed the door behind him.

He deposited the package in her hands. "Here is a bribe for not visiting for a while. I am just here to see my niece."

She peeked into the bag and smirked at him. "I am trying to lose some baby fat, and you are tempting me with cheesecake!"

She walked toward the adjoining kitchen and gestured with her chin to a door. "Just take a look, but do not pick her up! I deserve some quiet time for myself."

Mitra set foot through the doorway and stood over the crib. The baby was sleeping on her side, one hand against her face, fingers curled. She had her mother's chin. He was about to slip his pinky into the curled fist when she gurgled. He stepped back quickly. He didn't want to wake her up; he didn't want her to start bawling. He lightly and gently placed his palm on her head and silently slipped through the door.

Aart had put the cake away in the fridge and was sitting at the kitchen table when Mitra returned with a smile on his face.

"She is a living doll. She has grown a lot. What are you feeding her?"

Aart chuckled. "She considers me a dairy cow. She looks at me and only sees milk. What about you? Are you hungry? I have some left-over lasagna."

"No, I am fine. I have been eating pasta and pizza for six weeks. Do you know Dad is out?"

Aarti pushed her chair back and attempted to rise. "Giovanni is outside? He came with you, and you left him outside!"

"No, no," remarked Mitra, and he rested his hand on hers. She sat down and looked suspiciously at him.

"Not Giovanni. Our father!"

"Our father?" She looked at him with a blank expression on her face.

"Yes, Sarju Beepat. Our father."

Aarti got up quickly, pushing her chair back violently. "Outside? In my yard?"

Mitra threw her a serious look. "Sit down. Sit down. He is not here. He is just out of prison."

She sat down and glared at him, her hands twirling a vase with a few red roses on the table. "So, why are you telling me? I spoke to Mom this morning, and she didn't say anything. I am not interested in knowing who is outside or inside a prison."

Mitra looked at her thoughtfully. She had stopped twirling the vase and was cracking her fingers. "Aren't you curious to see him? Don't you want to meet him?"

"Why would I want to meet him now?" she snapped. She leaned forward to look Mitra squarely in the face. "And who told you he was out? Did you use your police contacts to sniff him out?"

Mitra noticed the anger flashing in her eyes. She had been like a mother to him while they were growing up. He could read every cue in her body.

"Hassan, his friend, called me. Aren't you even a little interested? You know he is still our father!"

"Our father," she hissed. Mitra was taken aback by her anger. "Did you disclose on your police application that your father was in Sing Sing prison?"

Aarti headed for the fridge. She opened the door, peered in, and turned to him. "I don't want to hear anymore. I am not interested. The only father that I am interested in is the father of my child. Do you want something to drink, or are you going to rehash things you know nothing about?"

"I will take a soda. That should cool you down, too."

She closed the fridge and set down two cans of soda with the cheesecake on the table. She opened a cabinet and returned with a knife, forks, and two plates.

Mitra took a drink and looked as she cut two generous slices of the cheesecake. She slid a plate and a fork over to him.

Mitra poked at the cake. "Look, I understand what happened, but we can't run from the past. We have to confront it someday."

She took a bit of the cheesecake and pointed the fork at him. "Mitra, what do you know? You were too young to understand anything. The past is too painful for me to relive. Just leave me in the present so that I can plan for my daughter's future."

Mitra took a bite of the cheesecake and washed it down with the soda. "So, when do you plan to return to the hospital?"

She smiled at him. He knew that she was calm now. "In a few more weeks. I wanted to take a year off, but if I do, I may have to be retrained in a few areas. Nursing is not like the police force. You use the same handcuffs and guns all the time, but we have to keep up with technology that changes every day."

Mitra laughed. "Oh, we have the same problems as well. Criminals keep up with new technology to evade the law. So what do you do all day? Just feed her and watch TV?"

Aarti sighed. "I wish it was that easy. Don't forget, I cook, clean, do laundry, and stay awake all night, while she tortures me with her bawling."

"I noticed a park nearby. Take her there. The fresh air will knock her out, and you will have some time to reflect."

Aarti laughed. "Why do you think she is sleeping now? I take her there every day between three and five. Her dad meets us there before he starts the night shift at the hospital. Are you going to see Mom when you get back?"

"That would be too late. Traffic will be backed up, and it will take more than three hours to get there. I will probably see her this weekend to get some home-cooked meals."

"I may even come down. Get a chance to eat some Guyanese curry while she takes care of her granddaughter."

"That's a good idea. Then we will see each other this weekend. I will just give her a peek before I go."

Mitra got up. Aarti wagged the fork at him. "And remember, don't pick her up. I need to digest your cheesecake."

<hr>

IT WAS LATE IN THE evening. Sarju had finished devouring some chicken soup that Hassan had bought when the urge to throw up overcame him. He rushed to the bathroom, but it was occupied by the tenant from Room 2, an old Puerto Rican who usually spent a long time in the bathroom. Sarju rushed back to his room and pulled his emergency plastic bucket from under his bed. He sat on the bed and retched for a long time. He pressed his chin against the rim of the bucket, waiting for another avalanche from his stomach, when he heard a soft rapping on his door. He raised his head and listened. The sound came again. It couldn't be Terry, who would normally announce his presence with a huge racket.

He hastily pushed the bucket under the bed and wiped his mouth with tissues from the box on the table. He lit two incense sticks and fanned the smoke around the room to disguise any offensive smells, then he shuffled to the door.

A young man was standing there. He was dressed neatly in a white shirt and dark pants. He was clean-shaven, and his hair was cut very short—almost to the scalp. There was something familiar about the face; Sarju thought he was some official from the prison.

"Yes," muttered Sarju, eying the young man.

The young man scrutinized Sarju carefully, then his glance shifted behind him to the tall mirror mounted on the wall.

A faint smile appeared on his lips. "I am Mitra Nucera."

Sarju almost stumbled. He held on to the door frame for support. He peered over the railing and saw Terry standing, his big, inquisitive round eyes looking up at Mitra.

Sarju grabbed Mitra and hauled him into the room. He shut the door, and with his back against it, he probed Mitra's face.

"Mitra? Mitra, my son?"

"Yes, yes, Mitra."

Sarju grabbed Mitra and hugged him. Mitra stood awkwardly as Sarju's body pressed against his very white shirt.

"Come, son, sit, sit." Sarju walked to the foot of the bed, pulled out the plastic chair, and placed it by the window.

Mitra folded his hands and leaned against the door; his eyes absorbed everything in the room.

"Thanks. It's okay. I prefer to stand."

Sarju collapsed on the bed, his eyes roving all over his son. He felt a warm glow spreading across his chest. "My son, my son! So big and handsome. I never imagined you like this, Mitra."

Mitra nodded gently. "A long time has passed!"

"Yes, son," agreed Sarju. "Sixteen long years! How I wish I could recover those years to see you grow."

Sarju was ecstatic to see his flesh and blood standing before him. "But, how are you? How is your sister? How is my Aarti?"

"She is well. She is busy with her child."

"Yes, yes," gushed Sarju. "There were so many things I missed. So many things happened. My Aarti is a mother. I am a grandfather, Mitra."

Mitra eyed his father and grinned. "So it seems. You left a dad and came back a grandfather."

Sarju's eyes narrowed as he gazed at his son. "You said your name was Mitra Nucera?"

Mitra's smile left his face. He looked at his father with some embarrassment. "I took Giovanni's name when I turned fifteen. With you in prison, the name *Beepat* would have required a lot of explanation."

Sarju turned his gaze to the window. It was dark outside, and the atmosphere of the room with Mitra standing by the door seemed very eerie.

"I understand, son," he muttered sadly. He looked up from his seat on the bed to see his son's reflection in the mirror.

"Do you know the meaning of your name, son?"

Mitra shook his head. "No. No one told me the meaning."

Sarju looked in the mirror. He met Mitra's eyes. "It means "friend" in Sanskrit, the ancient Indian language. Your friendship was destined to bring light to my life."

"And what about Aarti?" pressed Mitra.

A smile spread over Sarju's face. He beamed brightly. "Oh, she was very special. While you were my light, she was my soul. But she couldn't carry my name through the world. She will carry the name of her husband. But with you, son, it was different. Your light will lead the way."

Mitra looked at his father, sitting on the bed with a sad smile on his face. "I am sorry you missed all the light."

Sarju clasped his hands. He turned from the mirror to search Mitra's face. "Mitra Nucera! My hopes were shattered and contained in the walls of a prison for sixteen years."

"That was not entirely our fault or decision."

"No, no," hastened Sarju. "I remember the last time I saw you. The first day in kindergarten."

Mitra smiled as a memory flickered. "I remember that day, too. You and Mom took me to school."

"Yes, yes," added Sarju eagerly. "And I held your hand all the way to school."

Sarju gazed at his open hands. "I still remember the warmth of your little hand in mine that day."

He cupped his hands and spoke into them. "Every night in my prison cell, I would look at my hands and feel your little hand in mine."

"Everything about you after that day is missing from my memory," announced Mitra, viewing Sarju through the mirror.

Sarju covered his face with his hands. He sighed heavily. "That morning, I knew I was losing you to school. I never thought that very soon after, I would be lost to the prison system."

Mitra unfolded his hands and shifted his legs. "That is what vigilante justice does in a civilized society. It creates pain and brings injustice to all concerned. It is the selfish kind of justice that makes the victim a criminal."

"Love and anger blinded me, so I couldn't reason. But I am so proud of you, my son. Uphold the law. You may not carry my name now, but you will atone for my sin."

Mitra looked at his father with pity. "But how come you are still here?"

"*Still* here?" inquired Sarju.

"You are not a U.S. citizen," observed Mitra. "Non-citizens serving sentences for capital offenses are deported immediately."

"You will make a fine policeman," remarked Sarju proudly. "You are accomplished in the art of interrogation. You will go far in the law."

"So, why did they put you up here?" Mitra persisted.

"I pleaded for voluntary deportation in my parole hearing. I requested a few weeks to settle some personal business, and they agreed."

Mitra's eyes roved over the room once more. "Let me take you to dinner now. You can't cook in this room."

"Thank you, son, but I had dinner already."

Mitra took out his wallet. "Well, I will be busy all week, but have dinner on me tomorrow." He peeled a few notes from the wallet and dropped them on the bed.

Sarju got to his feet slowly. "Keep your money, Mitra. I am okay in that department."

"When do you plan to return to Guyana?"

"Half of my business is done just by seeing you today. I leave in a few weeks."

Mitra peeled off several more bills and dropped them on the bed. "Then you will definitely need some more. Call me if you need anything else."

"I told you I don't need anything, Mitra," Sarju remonstrated, walking to the door. "When can I see Aarti? She is the other half of my business."

Mitra observed the pleading face of his father and hugged him. "See you later. I am on special training but will try to be back before you leave."

Mitra walked to the narrow hallway, and then descended the stairs. Sarju leaned over the railing, his voice trailing after his son. "When am I going to see your sister? Did she say if she was coming to see me?"

Sarju waited by the railing until he heard the doors close behind Mitra. He shuffled into the room and shut the door behind him. With his back pressed against the door, he had a clear view of his reflection in the wall mirror.

Sarju snarled at the reflection. "You piece of shit," he groaned. "You piece of rotten human flesh." Tears streamed down his face, and spittle sprayed from his lips. "Even your children have no use for you."

He stumbled his way to the bed and swept his hands across it, spilling the money on the floor.

"Not only has cancer cursed me," Sarju wept, "but so has my name. *Mitra Nucera! Mitra Nucera!* Not Mitra Beepat! Aarti, Aarti, where are you, my child?"

He clutched his stomach, groped for the bucket under the bed, and began to retch loudly.

Chapter 9- The Rape

He had lunch very late at a little Brazilian restaurant close to the textile firm. Before going up to his office, he turned into the warehouse to check on some fabric that had arrived earlier. The heavy doors of the warehouse were wide open. Genieve, the middle-aged African American lady who was in charge, was haranguing a man who stood against the wall with a sulky expression on his face. The man was Jakie, her son. Jakie was a low-level conman and thief who regularly visited the warehouse to wrangle a few dollars from his mother. Sarju smiled and waved at Genieve.

Genieve shouted, "The office called for you. I told them you weren't here."

Sarju nodded and left the warehouse without checking on the shipment. He went to the side of the building and took the elevator to his office. He entered his little cubicle and saw a note taped to the center of his desk. "Your wife called. She said it was important." He recognized the handwriting of Sarah, one of the secretaries.

Sarju called home. Meera picked up after the first ring. "Sarju, Sarju, come home." She was in tears, and her voice was muffled over the phone.

His heart lurched. "What is the matter, Meera? What is the problem?"

She whispered into the phone, "Aarti was attacked in the building. They attacked your daughter. Come home now."

"Where is Aarti? Where is Aarti, Meera?" He shouted over her sobbing.

"She is in her room. She is crying. Come home."

"Okay, I am leaving the office now."

Sarju left the office. Sarah was standing by the door of the copying room. She noticed the dazed expression on his face. "Is everything okay, Sarju?"

He gave her a blank look. "Yes, yes. Everything is okay. I have to leave now. It is an emergency."

He ran to the elevator bank. The elevator was engaged on the floor above. He ran down the stairs and sprinted up the sidewalk to the subway station. The word *attack* kept playing in his head, and he realized that he didn't even ask Meera for details.

When the train stopped at Euclid Avenue station, he sprinted several long blocks to the apartment building. He pushed his hands into his pocket and realized that he had forgotten his briefcase with his keys in the office. The front door was slightly ajar, but no expression of disapproval entered his mind as he struggled up the stairs to his apartment.

He was out of breath by the time he reached his apartment. He leaned against the door and banged several times. Meera opened the door quickly. Sarju almost fell through the doorway.

"What is the matter with Aarti? he gasped. "You said she was attacked, but you didn't give any details. Where is she?"

Meera closed the door and held on to his arm. "She was raped on the roof of the building," she sobbed.

"My God! Raped? My Aarti? Where is she? Which monster harmed my daughter?" he thundered.

"Don't shout, please don't shout," Meera pleaded through her tears. "She is in her room."

Sarju shrugged off Meera's clutch and zipped to the bedroom. Aarti was huddled on the bed. She drew her legs up when she saw him and crept away.

Sarju approached his daughter and sat on the edge of the bed. She crept closer to the wall, her eyes and cheeks wet and swollen. "Aarti, Aarti, who did this to you?"

"She said it was the drug dealer who attacked you in the hallway," sobbed Meera, hanging over Sarju.

"Aarti, Aarti! How did this happen? I am going to kill that bastard who did this to you." Sarju reached over to touch Aarti. "I swear I am going to walk over his dead body."

Aarti yanked herself away from her father. "Don't touch me! Don't touch me," she spat, tears pouring down her swollen cheeks. "You made this happen. I told you not to tell them anything, but you wouldn't listen."

Sarju recoiled, aghast. His jaw dropped, and his eyes opened wide.

"You made him rape me," she sobbed hysterically. "You made him rape me."

Sarju looked at his wife and daughter in consternation. He got up slowly from the bed. "No, Aarti, no. I didn't make it happen to you. I never wanted that to happen. I only wanted to protect you from evil."

Aarti's eyes blazed with fury. "How could you protect me when you couldn't protect yourself from him? You provoked him and made him rape me."

Her words were like poison darts, attacking every fiber of his being. "Are you satisfied now? Did your protection save me from that monster?"

Sarju backed away slowly from the bed, but her venom followed. "How did being Gandhi help protect me from that evil?"

"How can you blame me for the act of a drug-dealing parasite, Aarti? he pleaded. "I can't be everywhere to look after you. Evil is everywhere. I am not God, only your father."

"And evil found me because you led him here," Aarti spat.

"I told you several times that this building is becoming dangerous with the drug dealings, but you wouldn't listen and search for another place. What are we going to do now?" whimpered Meera.

Sarju dismissed his wife. "Aarti, Aarti, what did you tell the police? Did you describe the drug-dealing scum to them?"

"Don't talk to me," screamed Aarti, "don't talk to me. I don't want to hear anything from you. Leave me alone. Leave me alone. You can't protect me anymore."

Aarti whimpered. Her body shuddered. "I am not your innocent little girl anymore."

Sarju looked dejectedly at his wife. "Did you call the police to report this?"

"No, I was waiting for you."

"Why wait for me, woman? Why didn't you call the police?" Sarju snapped and walked out of the bedroom to the living room. Meera closed the bedroom door and followed him.

"I couldn't call the police. You want everyone in the building and in the community to know that your daughter was raped?" Meera hissed. "She is a girl. You know how that can ruin her reputation."

"So, you intend to keep it a secret?" Sarju collapsed on the sofa. "You don't want the police to catch the jackal that defiled our daughter?"

Meera sat beside him and plucked at his sleeve. "That is not what I meant, Sarju. We will take her to the hospital; they will know how to deal with the police. They will do all the tests and recover the evidence. At least we won't have a whole fleet of police cars around the buildings to broadcast to the neighbors."

Sarju sucked his teeth. "So, how will they catch the beast if they don't surround the neighborhood?"

"She knows who did this. The police can hunt him down without the neighbors and her friends knowing anything."

"This is a crime, Meera. You want to keep it a secret?"

Meera sprang to her feet and headed for the bedroom. "We can't undo the crime, but at least we can try to keep her reputation intact. The police can deal with the criminal, but a woman has to deal with rape for the rest of her life. I will get her ready for the hospital."

Sarju sprawled on the sofa. It was light outside, and bright sunlight was streaming through the window in the living room, but Sarju did not detect that. All he experienced was a feeling of gloom and darkness that rolled like a dark cloud to envelop his soul.

Chapter 10-Vigilante Justice

Sarju arose at the crack of dawn. His body had adapted to the changing seasons while he was incarcerated, and it somehow synchronized with the sun. The first rays of sunlight were tearing the darkness outside; it was his cue to get out of bed. Besides, his bladder was full. He made a beeline to the bathroom, where he found the entrance blocked. Juan, the Puerto Rican from Room 2, was half-lying on the floor with his feet firmly planted against the bathroom door. Sarju thought he was drunk and had fallen asleep on the floor, but Juan was not breathing. Yellow spittle had formed a film that hung from his scraggly beard. Sarju shook him, but there was no response. He heard scratching noises downstairs and peered down the stairs to the first-floor landing, where Terry was tying the ends of two large garbage bags.

"Terry, Terry!" Sarju shouted. "Juan is lying on the floor next to the bathroom."

"He is probably drunk on the floor. Push the man aside or pee on him," suggested Terry in a tone of disgust.

"I don't think he is drunk. He is not breathing."

Terry dropped the garbage bag and looked up at Sarju. "What you said? The man is dead in my house!"

Terry edged crab-like up the stairs and inspected Juan. He dropped to his knee and felt his wrist and neck for a pulse. "He is not dead. It looks like he overdosed on street poison. Call the police and let them handle this."

Sarju returned to his room and called 911. He dressed quickly and joined Terry, who was still standing watch over Juan. Sarju leaned over and tried to move Terry's legs from the bathroom door.

"What you trying to do? You can't disturb the man. Wait on the police and the ambulance."

"I want to pee. I can't hold it," Sarju replied, pressing his hands against his crotch.

Terry looked at him with disdain. "A man is dying here, and you want to pee? Look, my door is open. You will find my bathroom to the left of the corridor. It is right under this one."

Sarju skipped down the stairs and found the bathroom. He was almost finished when he heard the loud buzzing sound of the doorbell.

"Beepat, Beepat!" Terry shouted. "Open the door for the police."

Sarju rushed out of the bathroom, zipping up his fly, and opened the door. A police car was parked outside with the lights flashing, and two policemen were at the door.

"You called for assistance?" A young Hispanic cop asked.

His partner, a middle-aged black man, looked over Sarju's shoulder to the top of the stairs. "Someone reported a man fell and is not breathing."

"He is upstairs, lying on the floor."

The two cops brushed Sarju aside and jogged up the stairs. Terry was leaning against the wall, looking at Juan.

"What happened here?" the black cop said.

Terry gestured to Sarju. "He found him on the floor a short while ago."

The black cop, whose name tag was marked *Thomas*, knelt on the floor and placed his hand in front of Juan's nose.

"I checked his pulse," ventured Terry. "It was very faint."

Thomas felt for a pulse and looked at his partner. "It doesn't seem that he fell and hurt himself, Hernandez."

"No. Not the way the body is positioned. The ambulance should be here in a few."

"Looks like an overdose to me," suggested Terry. "Check the liquid around his mouth."

The sound of sirens burst the silence, and two medics, a white and a Chinese, climbed the stairs. The two cops moved aside to let them examine Juan. Sarju reversed and stood in the doorway of his room.

The white medic stared down at Juan. "We have to take him to the ambulance quickly." The other medic, the burly Chinese, climbed down the stairs and returned with a stretcher. Quickly and expertly, the two medics rolled Juan onto the stretcher, climbed down the stairs, and deposited him in the ambulance.

Sarju, Terry, and the two cops stood peeking into the ambulance as the medics quickly connected Juan to a defibrillator and applied several electrical shocks. Sarju had seen this procedure done once in prison when an inmate suffered a heart attack. The Chinese medic stopped the operations and glanced at his watch. He looked at the two cops and shook his head. The white medic jumped out of the ambulance and closed the door. Without saying a word, he climbed behind the wheel and drove off with lights flashing and sirens blaring.

The two cops looked at each other. "I guess, we have to take a report now," grumbled Thomas and led the way back into the house. He took out his notebook. "We better start from the beginning."

"He knows everything. He was about to use the bathroom when he found the tenant lying on the floor."

The cops recorded the information supplied by Sarju and returned to the second floor, where they examined the bathroom and Juan's room. Thomas's phone rang. He moved into the kitchen and took a call.

He returned and looked at Terry and Sarju. "Anybody else lives up here?"

"Just the two of them," answered Terry. "The other roommate has been in the hospital for over a week."

"Well, we have to secure the place. The man is dead. I must ask you two gentlemen to go downstairs."

"But this is my room. What if I want to use the bathroom?" Sarju complained.

"Detectives will be here to examine the scene. If this is an overdose, it is a potential crime scene. They must gather evidence. I would have to put tape around this part of the house until they are done."

The detectives ushered Terry and Sarju down the stairs, and they all stood on the porch waiting for the detectives.

"Do you know if he was taking drugs?" Hernandez asked.

"The prison papers said he was clean, but he was a drug user before," Terry responded.

"How come he is living here?" queried Hernandez.

"I rent rooms to recently released prisoners. This week would be two months since he has been here."

"So, how did you guess he had an overdose?" asked Thomas.

"Oh! I am a retired prison officer. I have witnessed many cases of overdose."

Thomas focused his gaze on Sarju. "You are a released prisoner? Did you notice him using drugs?"

Sarju looked embarrassed. "I am a parolee. I didn't know him at all. I just met him in the hallway a few times. He told me his name was Juan."

"Well, Juan has gone. You should catch the people who sold him the drugs and put an end to them," Terry fumed.

Hernandez laughed. "We can't do that. It is against the law."

"Not in the Philippines," continued Terry. "The president there, Duarte, makes the laws, and he shoots drug dealers like dogs on the streets."

"Vigilante justice won't solve the problem, Mr. Landlord," advised Thomas and looked sternly at Terry. "When you take the law into your own hands, you are no better than a criminal."

Sarju looked down at his feet. He had dressed quickly, but he forgot his socks. He pushed his hands into the pocket of his jacket and felt a roll of plastic bags.

"You don't need me anymore. I gave you my report already."

"If the detectives need you, they know where you live," replied Hernandez. "But you still can't get anything from your room."

"Well, if I can't go up, I better go and get something to eat. Terry, can I use your bathroom again?"

"Like your bladder is as weak as your stomach? Go ahead. I hope they finish their investigations today, or you might be peeing against a tree tonight."

When he was finished using the bathroom, Sarju pulled the hood over his head and headed for the coffee shop. All the seats in the diner were occupied, so he bought a cup and continued walking. He had no idea where he was going, and about half an hour later, he found himself outside his old apartment building where his daughter was raped. He crumpled the coffee cup in rage and flung it against the side of the building. He continued on for several blocks and lingered outside another apartment building that had seen better days. Garbage was piled up in front in large black bags, with kitchen waste slopping over the sides. He remembered a small alleyway at the side of the building. He paused to look and observed a water-soaked mattress curved like an ominous wave against the wall of the building. His anger built up like a vessel under pressure, and he tasted the bitterness of stomach acids in his mouth. He groped in his pocket for a plastic bag and settled on his haunches to retch in front of the cursed building.

THE DETECTIVES INTERVIEWED Aarti in the hospital while he paced the hallway. They kept her there for a few days. Sarju took the days off to be with Mitra, while Meera camped out at the hospital. The detectives had no news for them; they claimed that they had investigated all the known drug haunts in the neighborhood but could not locate Jose. One even suggested that Jose had fled the country and had returned to the Dominican Republic.

When Aarti returned home, Sarju resumed his work. Aarti was still overcome with animosity towards him, and to avoid any discomfort, he would leave very early in the morning and return home very late at night.

After his official duties in the office, Sarju would hang around the warehouse, volunteering his services until it was reasonably late to go home. Genieve normally worked the late shift in the warehouse, and many times her son Jakie would appear, trying to wheedle a few dollars from her to satisfy his drug habit.

One afternoon, Genieve called out sick. Jakie's face assumed a hound-dog expression when he approached Sarju.

"Mr. Beepat, my mother has great respect for you. I see how you help her with her work, and I appreciate that. I check on her regularly, and now that she is sick, I need a few dollars to visit her."

Sarju considered Jakie. An idea formed in his head. "How do you plan to repay, Jakie? Your mother says you have no job."

"I will get a job soon. My mother knows. That is why she always helps me out. You seen her give me money before, Mr. Beepat."

"Your mother said that you were involved in crime before. You should try to keep out of trouble."

Jakie laughed. "That was a long time ago. I did a lot of illegal things to get money, but not anymore. You will get back any money you give me."

"I am not too sure about that. But I can buy you a meal if you are hungry. I am heading for the McDonald."

Jakie's eyes lit up. "That's fine. Let's have a meal together as friends."

"Talking about friends. I have a friend who needs some help. I am sure you can help him find what he wants."

Jakie furrowed his brows. "Tell me about your friend over that meal, Mr. Beepat. I have a lot of experience getting things for people."

At the McDonald's restaurant, Sarju scrutinized Jakie as he wolfed down the meal. "Your mom told me that you were involved in an armed robbery. Did you ever shoot anyone?"

Jakie slurped at his drink. "I have no stomach for killing. I just shot in the air, and they dropped their money."

Sarju placed a hand over Jakie's. "I know you can get the item my friend wants. He just wants to protect himself."

Jakie stopped chewing. "What does your friend want? A bomb? I can't do that."

Sarju grinned. "No. He is more high-tech. A simple gun would do. Can you arrange that?"

Jakie finished off his burger and wiped his mouth. "Anything for a price, Mr. Beepat. You can get anything you want in this city if you know the right people."

A few days later, Jakie slunk into the warehouse and asked to use the toilet. He patted the front of his jacket as he passed. Sarju joined him in the restroom. Jakie put on a pair of gloves, removed a pistol from his jacket, wiped it down carefully with a piece of rag, and handed it to Sarju. Jakie gave a short tutorial on how to use the gun, then left after pocketing a roll of money.

ONE NIGHT, WHILE HE was prowling around the neighborhood killing time, Sarju noticed the youngster, Ricardo, walking on the street. He trailed him, keeping in the shadows of the buildings on the opposite side of the roadway. Sarju crouched against a building and observed Ricardo in conversation with a man lurking in the alleyway next to a dilapidated apartment building. Someone switched on a light in an apartment above, and the light spilled on the man's face. Sarju recognized the rapist, Jose.

He hastily opened his briefcase, removed the gun, and concealed it behind his back. Sarju crossed the road quickly, his face contorted with rage.

The two jumped in alarm as Sarju appeared before them.

"Take a last look, motherfucker," Sarju spat at Jose. "Take a last look at the rat house that spawned you."

Jose stared at Sarju's face and sneered. "Is that you, Gandhi? Your daughter sent a message for me."

"Yes, she did," hissed Sarju. "Are you ready to be raped by the devil?"

Sarju moved his hand quickly and pointed the gun at Jose. Ricardo attempted to run, but Sarju grabbed him and kicked at his legs. Ricardo fell to the ground and covered his head with his hands.

Jose backed up against the wall, with Sarju dancing from foot to foot in front of him. He noticed the gun jumping in Sarju's trembling hand. "What are you doing with that, you crazy fool? Put it away before you go to prison."

"Prison for me, but hell for you. I hope you have enough drugs on you. The devil is going to rape you eternally." Sarju laughed demonically. "I know you will enjoy that. Rape is the action of the worst scum in the animal kingdom."

Jose's voice faltered. "Put that gun away before it goes off by accident and kills an innocent bystander, man."

"Innocent?" sneered Sarju. "If your mother had aborted you, then she would be innocent. But the whore gave you life, so you could become a drug-dealing rapist. But no more, no more. It is time for you to return to Satan, your true father."

Jose suddenly lunged for the gun. Sarju backed away quickly, out of his reach, and fired at his head. Jose dropped to the ground, landing on his knees with his head thudding against the wall. His body rested there as if bowing in prayer. Ricardo began to scream; he rolled over like a giant worm into the wall of the house, away from Jose.

"That bullet was from me," Sarju yelled, "and these are from my daughter." He pumped two more bullets into Jose's lifeless body.

Sarju swiveled and kicked Ricardo in the head.

Ricardo whimpered, "Please don't kill me. Please! I told him not to harm Aarti, but he wouldn't listen."

"I kill serpents, not rats," Sarju spat. "I just make sure they won't run again. But thank me. Now, you will hobble through life and won't run after evil again."

Sarju turned the gun on Ricardo and shot him in both kneecaps.

"Oh, God, Oh, God!" screamed Ricardo, and his eyes rolled back in his head like bright marbles.

Sarju spat on Jose and calmly left the alleyway with the gun hanging limply in his hand.

———◉———

SARJU RAISED HIMSELF off his haunches and dropped his soiled plastic bag by the garbage bags. His bladder was bursting. He knew he couldn't make it back to Terry's house in time. He looked at the alleyway. The mattress was lying just where Jose's body lay that fateful night. Sarju unzipped his pants and peed on the side of the building where Jose last rested his head.

Chapter 11- Daughter

Hassan turned into the tree-lined street in Hartford, Connecticut, his eyes inspecting the houses and simultaneously searching for a parking spot on the street. He stopped, turned off the engine, and tapped the windshield.

"There is the house!"

Sarju wound down his window to get a better view. From the car, he had a clear view of the front and one side of the building. His eyes caught the patch of pinkish insulating material on the side of the building that looked like a fresh wound seeking the bandage of vinyl siding. He could see the front porch that embraced the front of the house. A baby carriage parked by the front door looked like it was ready to go on a journey. Just a few feet from the side door of the building was a Toyota vehicle.

Sarju pursed his lips and focused on the front door. "My daughter's house," he murmured.

"Why don't you knock on the door?" suggested Hassan.

Sarju snapped at Hassan. "Why? To find out that it is all over?"

Hassan sighed. "Wouldn't it be better than sitting out here and admitting that it is over?"

"Everything unfolds with time, Hassan. Be patient and wait."

Hassan fumbled in his seat and retrieved a small leather binder. He tossed it to Sarju.

"There is your passport. I was able to get it renewed without any fuss."

Sarju opened the binder and explored the passport. He ran his finger over the new expiration date.

"Your ticket to Guyana is there, too."

Sarju replaced the passport in the binder and examined the plane ticket. He replaced the ticket in the binder and groped in his pocket. "How much do I owe you, man?"

"Forget that, man. It was just a one-way ticket." He turned away from Sarju to look through the passenger window at the trees along the street. "I wish I could do more," he murmured.

"I wish you could. But God has decided otherwise. I have no more time. Thank you anyway. A one-way ticket to heaven is all that is needed."

Sarju returned his gaze to the house.

Hassan observed his gaunt profile. "Are you going to tell your family when you are leaving?"

Sarju smiled ruefully. "No need to. They left me already."

Hassan reclined in his seat and shut his eyes.

Sarju focused on the building, willing his daughter to come out. Since the day of the rape, everything had changed for him. Overnight, Aarti became a new person—a person he didn't know. In prison, rapists were considered a filthy breed. They had to be kept apart from the other prisoners, or they could be attacked and brutally injured, often in full view, or with the tacit approval of the prison guards. Prisoners who had murdered, maimed, and robbed were considered morally superior to rapists and child molesters. In society, rape victims experience trauma in accepting or trying to forget what happened to them and in coping with the judgment of the people around them. Sarju reasoned: *Perhaps in trying to forget her pain, his daughter had to forget him.*

The front door of the house slowly opened. A young woman in a long sweater emerged with a baby wrapped in a blanket and a bag over her arm. As she leaned over the carriage to buckle in the child, her face was exposed to the sun. Sarju saw the dimples on her cheek and the pointed chin that belonged to his mother. Her hair dangled over her shoulder in two plaits, the same way it did on the day that started the descent into hell.

Sarju unbuckled his seat belt and yanked it from his shoulder. Hassan stirred, opened his eyes, and looked at the house. Aarti struggled to lift the carriage down the short flight of stairs and then began pushing it slowly out to the sidewalk.

Hassan glanced at his friend. Sarju's face was contorted with a mixture of joy and sorrow.

"There goes your beautiful daughter, Sarge!"

Sarju glanced over to the back seat. He reached over and grabbed one of Hassan's work caps. He pulled it all the way down and turned up the collar of his jacket.

He opened the door, his eyes trailing the figure ahead. "It may be a while, Hassan."

"Take your time. I am not going anyway."

Sarju crossed to the other side of the street and kept a safe distance behind his daughter. She pushed the carriage for several blocks, then turned into a little park. The track that ran around the park was higher than the street level, and Aarti had to lift the carriage again. Sarju had a great urge to assist his daughter with the heavy carriage but painfully kept his distance.

In the center of the park was a pond that housed a few ducks. Their blue and black feathers sparkled under the sun, and their red bills stabbed the water constantly. Sarju pretended to be interested in the antics of the ducks as his eyes followed the baby carriage. There were some benches in the shade of the trees. He chose one that was covered by a large shadow and positioned himself to observe Aarti.

She stopped the carriage in an open area, away from the shade of trees and in the full glare of the sun. She spread a blanket on the grass, removed her long sweater, and walked to the pond in front of her to show her daughter the playful ducks. Sarju leaned over the railing of the bench, and a glow of joy spread across his chest.

Standing there with her plaits reminded him of her teenage years when she was very close to him. Now in her thirties, he had a hard time reconciling his memories with the adult Aarti. Prison had done that to him. Memories of her kept him sane in prison, but now the reality had set in, and their estrangement was like a punctured wound in his soul.

She returned to the blanket and lay there, playing with the child. He listened keenly and could hear the gurgles of the baby. What was the child's name? He should have asked Meera or Mitra. The baby crawled and cooed on the blanket for a while, and then went to sleep. Aarti took a book from her bag and began to read.

It was cool under the trees. He pulled his jacket tightly around him and almost fell asleep with his head hanging over the rail of the bench. He heard a loud whistle and saw Aarti with a broad smile on her face, waving in his direction. Sarju thought that she had recognized him, and he almost got to his feet when he heard another whistle. A young man crept by him with a cane in his hand. He walked with a jerk as if his legs were attached to springs. The man waved to Aarti, and Sarju slunk back into the shadow.

The man directed his steps to Aarti; he dropped his cane, plopped down on the blanket, and they kissed passionately. He tickled the child and woke her. The child chuckled loudly as the man threw it playfully up into the air. He turned his face, and Sarju's jaw dropped as he recognized Ricardo, the youth that he had shot in his knees.

Sarju's mind was in turmoil. He felt the bile in his mouth and searched for the plastic bag in his pocket. He leaned over the bench with the bag to his mouth, retched, and hoped that Aarti wouldn't notice him. The pain in his stomach intensified; he had left his pain tablets at home. In addition, his bladder kicked in, and he felt the pressure of urine bursting in him. Beyond where Aarti and Ricardo sat was a public restroom, but he couldn't take the chance to walk past them. He groaned, gritted his teeth, and bore the pain.

He glanced furtively at them. They were preparing to go. Aarti folded the blanket while Ricardo rocked his daughter in his arms. He gently arranged the baby in the carriage, and as Aarti held him around the waist, they proceeded slowly in his direction. Sarju draped his upper body over the bench to hide his face from view. He heard their voices and the tapping of the cane as they passed.

Her voice hadn't changed. It reminded him of her youthful vivacity and mirth.

"Since you are working again this weekend, I will visit my mother. Mitra will be there as well."

"Her grandparents will be delighted to see her," Ricardo replied.

Sarju would never forget that voice. Ricardo's voice, screaming in pain, had kept him awake many nights in Sing Sing.

"You don't know how overjoyed Giovanni is with her," she gushed.

Sarju groaned inwardly. He was forgotten. Not even a footnote in their memory. Realization hit him like a ton of bricks. By accepting Ricardo, Aarti had to forget Sarju. He who had tried to protect had only succeeded in creating more victims.

He got up quickly to head to the restroom, but he had to change his plan as the dam burst. Sarju peed himself.

Chapter 12-Final Days in New York

It was just before noon when Sarju arrived at the medical office. Three patients were sitting in the waiting area. Sarju approached the receptionist's desk. Clarissa, the young lady he had met before, was rifling through some papers and inputting data into her computer.

She looked up as Sarju tapped on the desk.

"Good morning. I have a twelve-thirty appointment with Chadda."

He looked behind her at the waiting patients. Clarissa followed his gaze.

"I called earlier, and you said that I wouldn't have to wait," he announced tersely.

Clarissa smiled to defuse the tension. She slid over the clipboard with the pen. "Don't worry. You are next. Just complete the form for the nurse."

The nurse arrived shortly and accompanied him to the examination room. She took his pressure and temperature and recorded the information.

"Just sit there. Dr. Chadda will be here in a little while to see you."

"You are not going to ask me to take off my clothes?"

She smiled at his joke. "Not this time. It is not on your chart."

"Good. I don't want him to stick his finger in my butt again."

The nurse chuckled and left the room.

Sarju was half asleep on the examination bed when Chadda eased into the room and closed the door behind him.

Sarju sat up slowly, holding his stomach. "How are you, Doc."

"As well as can be, Mr. Beepat," responded Chadda as he put on a pair of gloves and flexed his fingers.

Sarju eyed the gloved hands. "The nurse told me there was no rectal examination today."

"And she is right. This is just an external."

Dr. Chadda pressed his fingers all over Sarju's stomach, abdomen, and back. He placed his stethoscope on his chest and back and listened carefully as Sarju inhaled and exhaled deeply several times. By the time he was finished with the breathing exercises, Sarju felt tired and light-headed.

Chadda deposited the gloves in a garbage bin, washed his hands, and nodded to Sarju. "Okay, let's go to my office."

Chadda sat behind his desk and looked at his computer screen. Sarju could see the chart on the screen reflected in his glasses.

"I am glad you had the CT scans that I recommended last week."

"I don't know why you had me do those tests when you know that the results won't change."

Chadda smiled and clasped his hands on his desk. "Because I am not religious, but I don't know about you."

Sarju smirked. "So you were hoping for a miracle."

"Perhaps, but how is the pain?"

"A lot more. The last time you said that I may have to use a stronger medication."

"I will increase the dosage. I will write a prescription for a month's supply."

"A month is too short. I need medication for two months."

"I can't do that. This medication is restricted. Drug dealers can get their hands on them and sell them on the streets. We can't prescribe these drugs willy-nilly."

"But I won't be here. I will be gone tomorrow."

"Gone? How do you know?" Chadda leaned forward to peer at Sarju. "If you know you will be gone tomorrow, why do you want me to write you a prescription?"

Sarju grinned. "Not gone from the world. I am leaving for Guyana tomorrow."

"Oh!" Chadda appeared relieved. "I hear Guyana has good doctors. They can prescribe, too."

"Where I am going may not have doctors."

"You said Guyana! You are not going to the moon."

"I am going to a forested area, far from the city, Doc. I would need medication to last me to the end."

Chadda rubbed his hands over his forehead. "Alright. I will prescribe for six weeks. If the pain escalates, you may have to use opioids. But that is for a doctor in Guyana to prescribe."

"And what can you prescribe for my bladder? I have to use the bathroom frequently to urinate."

"That is called "urinary incontinence." Cancer around the bladder and the hormone changes in your body can cause that."

Sarju leaned forward in his chair. "Sometimes, I can't reach the bathroom in time, and I pee myself."

"I can suggest using a catheter to drain the urine into a bag strapped to your leg," advised Chadda.

"How does that catheter thing work?" queried Sarju with some interest.

"Simple," explained Chadda. "We insert a long tube up your penis and lead one end to a bag."

Sarju clamped his legs together. "So, you don't use the bathroom?"

"You pee unimpeded," chuckled Chadda. "The bag is the toilet bowl."

Sarju shook his head slowly. "I don't think I like the idea of sticking a long tube up there. Is there anything else you can recommend?"

"Well, you can always use absorbent underwear."

Sarju opened his eyes wide. "You mean diapers? Like a baby?"

"Yes, Mr. Beepat. Sometimes that is the simplest and best measure we can recommend."

Sarju looked at Chadda and sighed. "You ever heard the saying, *Once a man, twice a child,* Doctor?"

"An unavoidable part of living, Mr. Beepat. As we age, we lose the ability to take care of ourselves. But your case is different." Chadda tapped on his computer. "I have emailed the prescription to your pharmacy. Anything else bothering you?"

Sarju stood and extended his hands. "No, Doc. Thank you for your patience. We definitely won't meet again in this world."

"Go with God, Sarju."

"I thought you weren't religious?"

"I am not. But I sense you are."

SARJU LEFT THE OFFICE and headed up Hillside Avenue. The avenue was teeming with people—shoppers, students, and itinerant vendors. He felt like an ant caught up in a stream of movement, and for a while, he felt very much alive and part of the world. The sun was bright in the early afternoon sky. His mind ruminated on the picture of a man sinking into a black ocean. The last thing before the fatal drop was a bright yellow sun dotting the blue sky.

A young girl was pushing a baby carriage in front of him. At the bottom of the carriage, he noticed a bag that held baby diapers. Sarju walked beside the girl and had a look at the baby. The child glanced at him with very bright eyes while she held onto a stuffed toy. Sarju smiled and glanced at the mother.

"What is the baby's name?"

"Lucinda," answered the mother proudly.

"The name is as beautiful as the mother."

"Thank you." The girl beamed with pleasure, her eyes sparkling under the glare of the sun.

He stopped at the traffic light and glanced over to the other side of the avenue. Around the corner was a medical supply shop. In the display window, Sarju noticed crutches, adapted toilet seats, medical equipment, and different kinds of adult diapers.

Sarju crossed over and peered through the glass door. An old black man sitting on a low stool was assembling a wheelchair. Sarju stepped through the entrance, and a bell on top of the door chimed loudly. The sound startled the old man. He dropped a tool that clanged loudly on the tiled floor.

"You are here to pick up the wheelchair?" rasped the old man.

"No, no. I am looking for adult diapers."

The old man struggled to get up. He held on to a shelf in front of him for support and flexed his legs. "Come with me."

Sarju followed him to the back of the store. On a shelf were different brands of diapers.

"Which one do you want?" the old man wheezed.

"I don't know. I never bought before."

The old man sighed. "I knew you would tell me that it was not for you. You don't have to be ashamed. Not all of us can control our pee at our age."

He hauled down a box and showed it to Sarju. "This one is for all sizes. It fits snugly and doesn't leak, so you can drink as much as you want."

Sarju snickered. "That is the one you use?"

The man grinned, exposing huge gaps in his teeth. "Same one, but I don't drink anymore."

The man placed the box of adult diapers in a shopping bag for Sarju and resumed his task of assembling the wheelchair.

———————◉———————

SARJU STROLLED PAST a McDonald's restaurant. Through the open doorway wafted the smell of French fries. He thought of the last time he was at McDonald's. He smiled as he recalled sitting there while Jakie wolfed down a burger and slurped a soda.

Sarju patted his pockets and was reassured to find his stash of plastic bags. He retraced his steps and made his way into the restaurant. There was a large photo by the cashier of a sumptuous burger with fries and soda—the deal of the day. He made his purchase and was wending his way to a table when he heard someone call out.

"General! General!"

Sarju glanced at his side and saw a lady sitting alone at a table with the "deal of the day" in front of her. She looked familiar, and then he noticed her twitching at her wig.

"General? Oh, sorry, sergeant."

He remembered her. She was Gums's sister. They had met the day he was released.

Sarju plodded over to her table. "Hello, Miss Delilah! Can I join you?"

"Sure, sure. Did I get your name right? Sergeant?"

Sarju laughed. "Sarje. But not yet a member of the military. How is Brother Cornelius?"

"Gums," she responded sadly. "No more Cornelius. He is Gums now, and he went back home."

"Home? Isn't he living with you?"

"His home is Sing Sing. He went back there." Delilah picked up her burger and chewed slowly.

Sarju took a few small bites from the burger. He looked at a sign in the back that indicated the restrooms and confidently took a few sips of the soda.

"What happened to him? How come he returned? His parole was final."

Delilah took a long sip and frowned. "Do you know what causes a criminal to return to the scene of the crime, Sarge?"

Sarju immediately took a considerable bite of the burger and chewed slowly as Delilah waited for a response. Sarju cast his mind back to when he revisited the alleyway where he had shot Jose and Ricardo. What prompted him to return to the scene of his crime? He had no idea why his feet led him there. Was it a criminal instinct born out of survival or just plain morbid curiosity?

"No, Miss Delilah," he admitted.

"You know why Gums was sent to prison?"

"I heard he robbed and shot someone."

Delilah finished her burger and started on her fries.

"Yes! He robbed a jewelry store and ran off with a bag of diamonds. The fool hid the diamonds, then ran home, where the cops were waiting. He went to Sing Sing without telling anyone where he hid them."

"So, no one found them?"

"No. He didn't trust anyone. Not even me. And I visited him several times a year for thirty years. I got old visiting my brother in prison, Sarge. All he shared with me was *three by three; the diamonds were under a tree.*" She grunted bitterly.

"Was that a riddle?"

"I thought it was," she remarked. "He didn't disclose the place where he hid the diamonds. He was in numerous prison fights and sustained several head injuries. He started to have memory lapses. His memory would come and go."

"Did he finally remember where he hid the diamonds?"

Delilah took another bite and sipped the soda. "A few days after he came home, he went for a walk in the neighborhood. He returned, took a sledgehammer from my garage, and sprinted up the road like a madman."

Sarju joked, "Maybe Gums found a construction job."

Delilah gave him a stern look. "He ran several blocks, stormed into a stranger's garage, and started demolishing the concrete floor. When the owner tried to stop him, Cornelius attacked him with the sledgehammer and broke his hand."

"Oh!" Sarju understood. "The police arrested him and sent him back."

"Yes. He violated the conditions of his parole. He has to finish off his sentence there." Delilah tidied up her tray and prepared to leave.

"Why do you think he was breaking the concrete floor?"

Delilah smiled. "The diamonds, Sarje. *Three by three* made sense after I went to the scene. The police called me over to the garage, and I saw where he was trying to break the concrete."

"Under a tree?"

Delilah smiled. "No. But there was a tree stump at the side of the fence. The tree was cut down many years ago before they built the garage."

Sarju grinned knowingly. "*Three by three*. Three feet from the fence and three feet from the tree."

Delilah was surprised. "How did you guess that?

"Those are coordinates. You use them to locate positions. But you have to know where to start. The main point is the tree."

"You are very smart, Sarge." Delilah chuckled. "You should be a general."

"So, what are you going to do about the diamonds?"

"Nothing," said Delilah sadly. "Diamonds are found in the earth, and they will remain there forever."

"You are just going to leave them there?"

"They are not mine, Sarge. They belong to the owner of the property now. Or, if the police investigate using your smarts, they may recover them for the family of the jeweler who Gums killed."

"The diamonds will be forever in the ground!" mused Sarju.

Delilah got up. "That's where they belong. Blood diamonds, Sarge. He killed to get them and is back to Sing Sing because he returned to the scene of his crime."

"Well, when you see him, give him my regards."

"I won't be seeing him. I am seventy-two. I don't have the strength to visit a prison anymore. My brother Cornelius has gone. I may never see him again. He will be buried in Sing Sing as Gums."

Tears trickled down Delilah's cheeks.

Sarju patted her hand. "I am truly sorry, Delilah."

"No need to be sorry. Now, take care of yourself and don't return there. Finish up your meal."

Delilah disposed of the remains of her meal in the garbage bin and vanished through the door.

Sarju continued munching on his fries. He picked up a long fry and examined it. Part was very straight and extended into a half circle at the bottom. Sarju thought of the Puerto Rican, Juan, from the rooming house, and Gums. He recalled what Terry had observed about released prisoners. If they did not become independent in two months, they would revert to their previous life of crime and return to prison. Sarju pondered that theory and decided that Terry had omitted something. He looked at the half circle at the end of the strip of fried potato. Gums had returned to Sing Sing, but Juan had returned to his maker. Sarju put the fry down. In a few weeks, his two months would be over. His circle was closing.

HASSAN ARRIVED AT THE rooming house around eight that night. He climbed the stairs and stood by the open doorway with a backpack in hand. Sarju was sitting on the plastic chair, looking through the window, the duffel bag at his feet.

"You are very early, Hassan. You forgot the time of the flight?"

Hassan looked around the room. "I know the time, but you forgot that you have to check in about three hours before departure." He sniffed the air. "What did you do here? Did you flood the place with aromatic oils?"

"No. I just did some cleaning. Gave the kitchen and bathroom a thorough mopping with some pine cleaner." Sarju got up and placed the chair in a corner. He grabbed the duffel bag by the strap. "Ready when you are."

Hassan swung the backpack like a pendulum. "I know you are traveling light. Can you deliver this backpack to my niece? When people visit Guyana, they are expected to take a few items for friends and relatives."

"I never thought about that. I didn't buy anything for anyone."

"That is because you have no one on the island. Let's go now."

Hassan climbed down the stairs with Sarju creeping behind with the duffel bag slung over his shoulder.

Terry's door was open. Sarju knocked on the wall. Terry limped out and glanced at the duffel bag by Sarju's feet.

"Here are your keys, Terry. I am leaving now. You can check the place to see if everything is okay."

Terry grasped the keys and glanced up the stairs.

"I didn't break anything," joked Sarju. "The mirror in the bathroom is still cracked in one place."

Terry grinned. "I don't have to check. I heard you cleaning all day. I wanted to invite you to clean my apartment, but I was scared of all that pine oil that you used."

"I am sorry I had to leave you so early, man," Sarju declared.

"Don't be sorry. This is just business between me and the prison system. Customers come and go all the time. What do you want me to tell the probation department when they call?"

"They won't call," assured Sarju. "They know that I will be leaving."

Terry looked at Sarju with suspicion.

"Tell them he got tired of this place and went home to sample the new Guyanese rum," Hassan added. "See you later, Terry. We got a plane to catch."

Sarju shook his landlord's hand. "Thanks for everything, Terry. Ask Hassan to recommend an obeah man to help you with your arthritis."

They loaded the bags into the back seat of Hassan's car. Under the street light, it appeared clean and shiny. Inside, it smelled fresh, like the pine oil Sarju had used on the house.

"It looks like you just washed the car, Hassan!" Sarju observed as Hassan drove off.

"I cleaned and detailed it just for you, Sarge. I am sending you home in style. Like a bridegroom going to Wakenaam for a bride," Hassan hooted jovially.

Sarju considered Hassan. "Or a hearse proceeding to the cemetery."

Hassan bit his lips and stared straight ahead. He pointed to some houses beside the highway. "Meera's house is not far. Just over there."

"So? You want me to be an uninvited guest?"

"It was something worth trying. But I guess you don't agree."

Sarju was absorbed in the scenes on his side of the highway.

"You have everything? Passport, ticket, and money?"

Sarju unzipped the jacket. He was wearing a denim shirt with two large pockets. He patted the pockets. "Passport and ticket up here." He patted his pants pockets. "Money is securely locked down."

Hassan smiled at his friend. "I have arranged for a minibus to pick you up at the airport. The driver's name is Mangru. He will take you to Parika."

Sarju looked sharply at Hassan. "I hope that taxi driver isn't another Guyanese shark waiting to feast on me like a blood-sucking mosquito."

Hassan laughed. "You don't have to worry about Mangru. I took care of him. Whenever I go to Guyana, he picks me up at the airport. You don't even have to tip him."

"Why do you do so much for me, Hassan?"

Hassan met his gaze. He paused for a while. "Because we are brothers, Sarju."

Sarju looked away. Hassan continued, "And this is what brothers do."

Sarju pointed to a sign on the highway, "Leaving New York" and whispered, "I totally missed the sign that my children had left me, Hassan."

A tear rolled down Sarju's cheek. "Their little faces and voices are stamped on my soul, Hassan. Why couldn't they show me some love?"

"They still love you, Sarju. They never stopped. They just forgot how to show it," consoled Hassan.

Sarju looked sharply at Hassan. "Your son, Ishmael? Did he ever forget to love you, Hassan?"

Hassan threw a quick look at Sarju while keeping his eyes on the traffic ahead. "When he was very young, he could never bear to be away from me. We were inseparable. Then he became older, and it was different."

"How different? Sarju asked as Hassan fell silent.

"When he became an adult, he gravitated toward his friends. We live in the same house. Sometimes, we barely speak."

"So, is that how he forgot to show his love?" Sarju persisted.

"I remember the old days too, when he was very young," Hassan reminisced, with a smile on his face. "But what I do know is that our love is still there. It has only evolved into a more resilient form."

Sarju searched Hassan's face as if looking for an answer to save his soul.

"No, Sarju. Your children still love you; they show it in different ways, but you can't understand it because there was a huge absence in your lives."

"So, you are saying I can't recognize their love?"

"I am saying that when you come to terms and accept that they are now adults, you will recognize the signs of their love. And that their love never wavered."

Sarju sighed and shook his head. "Now, you are a fucking psychologist! How come I missed that with my degree in psychology?"

Hassan snickered. "Can't an exterminator be a psychologist? How do you think I outsmart cockroaches?"

Hassan pulled up in the lane leading to the departing terminal.

"We will definitely meet again, Hassan," Sarju murmured.

Hassan nodded his head, a sound lost in his throat. "Yes. Tell me when you want me to visit," he grunted.

Hassan stopped the vehicle in the passenger departure area. He hauled the duffel bag from the back seat and thrust it toward Sarju.

Sarju dropped the bag on the tarmac and embraced his friend. "I don't mean our island, my brother," he croaked. "We will meet in another world. Yes, yes! In another but better world."

Hassan climbed into his vehicle, and through misty eyes, captured the last sight of his childhood friend as he melted into the cavernous hold of the departure terminal.

Chapter 13- Return

The departure lounge was crowded. The line to board the aircraft to Guyana was like a long snake; to ensure order and optimize space, the authorities had installed ropes that appeared like the undulations of a reptile, placing the travellers inches apart from each other. The bumping of bags into bodies and the sloth-like movement of the checking-out process presented an ordeal for Sarju. He had not eaten since early in the morning and had only taken a few sips of water. He did not aspire to a bout of vomiting, so he ensured his stomach was completely empty. To address his urinary incontinence, he took the advice of the old man in the medical supply store and, for the first time, wore an adult diaper.

Sarju tried to ignore the pain that throbbed like a pounding wave in his stomach by observing the passengers around him. In a curl of the snake line beside him, a burly Indian man with a stomach that protruded over his waist like an oil barrel was trying to prevent a young child from climbing onto a suitcase. The child, about five years old, suddenly bit the man on his leg. The man tried to shake off the child and fell over the suitcase, taking down the two Guyanese old ladies behind him.

One of the old ladies glared at the man. "When you travel with young children, you must learn how to control them."

A young woman, obviously the boy's mother, held on to him. "He is a young child with A.D.H.D. How do you want him to behave?"

The old woman retorted angrily. "He want a good cut ass. That would cure he of the American D.H.D."

"You want to touch him and see if you don't get locked up at this airport?" The young woman challenged.

"I am too old to go to jail, girl. But if I were you, as soon as we touch down in Guyana, you should use a broad Guyanese leather belt on his spoiled American backside to teach him discipline."

The boredom and impatience were over for a few moments. Sarju looked at the boy, and his mind went back to Mitra when he was that age. Mitra was always respectful, and although he threw a few tantrums, he never made a spectacle of himself in public. The child, now out of the reach of his mother, walked back and forth along the line.

His mother called out to him. "Abel! Abel! Come over here, now."

The child ignored the call. Sarju tried to help. "Your mother is calling you, boy. Go!"

The child turned to Sarju, delivered a sudden blow to his groin, then ran to his father. Sarju held on to the cordon rope for support as a different kind of pain flared through his lower abdomen.

The man with the barrel stomach held the child tightly by the hand. "I am sorry, man. Very sorry for what he did."

Sarju smiled at the man in understanding. He couldn't speak. The pain was too much for him.

A middle-aged African Guyanese man behind Sarju muttered, "Spoiled brat. He wants two fucking slaps to fix his head right."

———————⬤———————

AFTER AN ETERNITY, Sarju completed the check-in process and boarded the plane. With his ticket in his hand, he searched for his assigned seat. His heart lurched as he stopped beside Barrel Stomach and his child. The man was seated in the aisle seat, and the child was in the window seat—Sarju's seat.

Sarju hoisted his duffel bag into the overhead bin. He removed the backpack from his shoulder and indicated the seat. "I believe that is my seat, friend."

The man reached over to his son. "Abel, Abel, that is not your seat. Sit in the middle. That is your seat."

The child held on firmly to the armrest and shook his head. The line of passengers halted in the narrow aisle behind Sarju, unable to move.

Somebody shouted. "Is that fucking little boy again."

Sarju recognized the voice.

A stewardess approached. "Did you find your seat, sir?"

Sarju smiled. "It seems we have a little problem."

Barrel Stomach writhed himself painfully to a standing position. "Do you mind sitting here? I will use the middle seat."

The child scooted over to the aisle seat. "I want to sit here, Daddy."

"Okay, problem solved," beamed the attendant. "You can take your seat now, sir."

Relieved, Sarju entered the space, guarding his groin as he passed the boy.

Sarju closed his eyes as he tried to erase the pain. The plane lifted off, and Sarju took a fleeting glance at the fading lights of Queens, New York. He hoped that Guyana would not be so unforgiving.

He fell into a slight doze and resurfaced when the plane hit some turbulence and fell several feet. He felt a slight movement in his stomach. He heard a retching sound and turned to his right to see his seatmate, Barrel Stomach, with his hands to his mouth. Sarju understood the emergency, dove into his pocket, and hastily tendered the plastic bag. The man gratefully accepted and soon filled the bag. Sarju put a bag to his mouth and, fortunately, only filled it with stomach air.

An attendant came by to collect garbage. Barrel Stomach deposited his refuse, extricated himself, and stumbled down the narrow aisle to the bathroom.

He returned and plunged himself down beside Sarju. The child was fast asleep.

"Thank you, man. If you didn't hand me that bag in time, I would have sprayed the whole plane with stomach juice." He extended a hand to Sarju. "My name is Esau. I am going to Berbice."

"Sarju. I am going to Wakenaam."

"My wife is from the Essequibo, too. How long are you staying in Guyana?"

"Not too long," smiled Sarju.

"I am going to a wedding and to arrange some land business as well. Trap two birds with one stone, as they say. A man is squatting on my land. If things don't work out, I might be tempted to kill that disgusting bird."

"Oh!" replied Sarju, staring at the man. "That serious, eh?"

"Yes. But I met a lawyer at a party two days ago. He promised to settle the matter for me. He said he has a lot of connections. I paid him a lot. He is on the plane, too."

Esau looked behind him furtively. "These lawyers are all crooks, you know. But only they know the laws and how to break them for you."

Esau called the stewardess. "I need a drink to settle this stomach. What you drinking, Sarju?"

"Thanks, but nothing until I land."

Esau swallowed several drinks; soon a group of men gathered in the aisle by him. One of the drinkers, an elderly Indian man in a long black coat, was held in awe by the other drinkers.

Esau turned to Sarju. "That is the lawyer I was telling you about. He is a top lawyer in Guyana—an expert in settling boundary issues, crimes, and other matters."

The lawyer heard, nodded his head, and sipped his drink. "Do you have any legal matters? Let me know now so I can expedite the process."

He took out his cell phone to take notes.

"There are no legal matters in Guyana. Everything is okay," Sarju assured him.

The lawyer returned his phone to his pocket with a look of disappointment on his face. "Then you are a lucky man. The only man without legal issues is a dead man."

Esau retorted, "But before they die, they create issues."

The men around him laughed at his witty comment. The lawyer beckoned the attendant for more drinks.

———◉———

WITH HIS MEAGRE BELONGINGS, Sarju had no problems clearing customs and immigration. The officials dismissed him quickly. They were eager to examine the other passengers, who had several overladen suitcases and had decorated their bodies with an assortment of gold jewelry.

He strolled outside to the pick-up area which was crowded with relatives and taxi drivers.

One man rushed toward him and grabbed his duffel bag. "Where you going, Americano? Town or country?"

Sarju yanked his bag away. "I am looking for Mangru."

The man sucked his teeth and shouted. "Mangru, Mangru! Your passenger waiting on you."

A tall, slender Indian man approached from the back of the throng. "You are Hassan's friend?"

"Yes," admitted Sarju.

Mangru looked skeptically at Sarju. "You have anything else?"

"No, no, this is all I have."

"Well, follow me. If I knew you were traveling light, I would have come with the car."

Mangru led the way to a minibus that was caked with dust. He pulled the side door open so Sarju could deposit the bags.

On the road that stretched in the direction of Georgetown, the capital city, memories of life as a youth came flooding back to Sarju. He recognized the various fruit trees as they zipped by: cherry, mango, guava, star apple, cashew, orange, and papaya. He drank in the scent from the flowering trees and bushes and smiled as he remembered drab New York in the midst of spring. The water in the canals alongside the road glinted and gleamed under the early morning light. As the road curled through a thick bamboo patch, he glimpsed the brown, humus-tainted water of the Demerara River.

Although it was still early in the morning, various food and fruit stalls lined the road.

Mangru glanced at him. "You had breakfast on the plane, or you want to stop somewhere?"

"Just something light for me this morning."

"Restaurant or street food?"

Sarju observed some fruit stalls displaying baskets of bananas, pineapples, and other fruits.

"I can use a banana and some coconut water."

"Monkey food. But that is okay. I can use something light, myself."

Sarju had a banana and tilted the coconut to his mouth. He swallowed the water slowly to refresh his taste buds, but he knew that in Wakenaam, the coconut water would be sweeter.

"Want some more?" invited Mangru, drinking another coconut.

"No, no, that is enough for me. How much do I owe you?" Sarju asked the vendor.

"Breakfast was already paid for by your friend, Hassan," Mangru stated, dropping some Guyanese dollars into the stall owner's hands.

"Now, we drive to Parika. You can cross the Essequibo River to the island by the slow ferry or by fast boat. It is up to you how quick you want to get to Wakenaam."

The sound of the tires humming along the road, combined with the sweltering breeze through the open window, knocked Sarju out. The pain that had kept him awake during the flight had changed to a slightly bearable inconvenience.

He woke up suddenly to a new sound. The humming of the tires and the rhythmic motion of the car had ceased. The mighty Essequibo River of his childhood spread before his eyes, and its lapping water replaced the unnatural sounds of wheels on the road.

Mangru had exited the minibus and was stretching his limbs. Sarju joined him. The hours of sitting in the plane and in the vehicle had cramped his legs.

"The ferry is not here yet, but the speedboats travel every hour. How do you want to travel?"

Sarju looked across the huge swath of roiling brown water. He spotted an island in the distance. The trees on the edge of the island towered over the water and gave it the appearance of a green mountain. Hidden behind that island was his island. A feeling of joy and deep regret filled his heart—joyful to be reunited after more than thirty years and regret at being here alone without his family.

Wakenaam! He thought of the last pleasant conversation he had with his daughter. She had been amused by the name, or lack thereof. What name for the island would she have chosen?

Mangru stopped exercising his limbs and considered Sarju. "So, how do you want to go to the island?"

Sarju looked down the slope to the water's edge. He saw a few multicolored motor boats with tattered canopies bobbing in the water.

"Just five U.S. dollars with the speed boat. It takes less than half an hour. The ferry is cheaper but takes longer," advised Mangru.

"The speedboat is fine. The water is not very rough today," decided Sarju. He dug into his pants and handed over thirty dollars. "This is for the boat."

"I said five," replied Mangru.

"Buy yourself a drink. You earned it."

Mangru took the duffel bag and walked down a sloping path to the boats. He approached a young Indian boy. The boy took the duffel bag and placed it on a seat in the boat.

"The boat will take you across. The captain will put you on a bus to Zeelandia, to Hassan's house. The bus has been paid for."

Sarju shook Mangru's hand. "Thank you, Mangru. You did a great job."

"When you are returning, give me a call. I will take you to the airport." Mangru pressed a card into Sarju's hand and climbed the sloping path to his car.

Sarju smiled at the irony of the card. He placed it in his pocket and entered the rocking boat where about ten other passengers were sitting patiently.

The young boy, who appeared to be the captain, grinned at Sarju and handed him a life vest and a bag. "If you get seasick, don't try to vomit over the side. Use this bag."

Sarju saw a few of the passengers with plastic bags in their laps and felt relieved.

The boy settled down beside the powerful outboard engine; two porters at the water's edge pushed the boat into the deeper part, and with a heavy roar, the motorboat furiously catapulted across the river. The boat cleaved the water into two sliding banks of brown liquid, and Sarju's stomach heaved with the tide. Expertly, he raised the plastic bag to his mouth and delivered all that remained of the banana and coconut water. The bag was still at his mouth when the motor was cut off, and the boat drifted into the stelling or dock at Wakenaam.

Chapter 14- Wakenaam

The minibus pulled out of the stelling and made its way along the road that ran like a belt around the 17.5 square-mile island. As it lumbered its way slowly through the potholed road, Sarju was able to identify many structures and sights. The police station and magistrate's court looked the same as when he left the island more than thirty years ago. He noticed some improvements, though. There were now street lights and many multi-colored modern buildings that were made of brick and stone. When he left, most of the houses were constructed from local wood. Those wooden houses, many old and abandoned, stood silently and sullenly against the new buildings.

Sarju recalled the history of his island. Dutch settlers had first settled on a nearby island, Fort Island, and around 1690, French colonizers arrived and evicted them. The Dutch planters fled to another island, closer to the mouth of the Essequibo River, but they couldn't decide on a name, so they called it *Wakenaam*, waiting for a name. Finally, the British arrived and seized control of the island. The Dutch rule came to an end, but the name was retained.

The island was colonized primarily for sugar cultivation. To supply the labor for the sugar plantations, African slaves were bought and traded at a village called "Free and Easy." After slavery was abolished in 1834, most of the freed Africans left the sugar plantations and began ground provision cultivation. To fill the void in labor, the British brought indentured servants from India; when the indenture ship was over, the majority of the Indians settled on newly acquired lands and turned to rice cultivation.

Sarju noticed the many tractors and agricultural equipment on the roads and in the fields of rice and coconuts; the island still maintained its agricultural flavor.

The bus passed by a village that was marked "Belle Plaine" on a faded sign mounted on a wooden pole. Sarju leaned forward in his seat to stare intently at a new building on a large plot of land.

The minibus driver noticed his stare. "Do you know where in Zeelandia you are going, Big Man?

"Yes," responded Sarju, recalling that *Zeelandia* and *stelling*, were also Dutch names. The Dutch had gone, but their influence was still found in many familiar words and places.

"I am going to Lot 52."

"Who you going to?" persisted the driver, an old Indian man with a long, unkempt beard.

"The third house from the end of the road. Hassan is the owner, but his niece lives there."

The driver nodded. "Nizam lives there."

Sarju nodded. "Yes, his wife is Fazeela."

"Don't worry. You won't get lost. I know the house."

The bus turned down a side track that was perpendicular to the belt road. The potholes were big, like ponds, and filled with water. The driver knew the way through the watery obstacles and meandered his way to a stop outside a spacious modern building surrounded by a white wrought iron fence.

It was the third house from the end of the road.

"This is your house," remarked the driver.

Sarju exited the vehicle with his two bags and stood admiring the house. Hassan had obviously dismantled the old house and invested in this magnificent structure. The huge house was above ground and sitting on concrete pillars. Part of the bottom portion was enclosed to form a small apartment with an open garage port. Fruit and flowering trees dotted the yard, and there was a small standpipe by the side of the house. Another improvement, Sarju noted. *Potable water had reached Wakenaam.*

A young woman, disturbed by the sound of the minibus outside, peered through the window and then climbed down the stairs to meet Sarju by the gate.

She stared at Sarju's duffel bag. "Mr. Beepat?"

"Yes, Yes! You must be Fazeela, Hassan's niece."

She shook his hand. "Yes. Uncle Hassan called last night and told us to expect you. Come in, come in."

Fazeela entered the yard and stopped by the stairs leading to the upper floor. She looked at his bag again. "You didn't get all your luggage?"

"My luggage?" Sarju was momentarily baffled.

"Your suitcases! Is that all you have?"

"This is all I need."

A shocked expression loitered on Fazeela's face. "When people visit Guyana, they usually come with two, three big suitcases. You only have hand luggage."

Sarju chuckled softly. "This is all I need. I won't be here for a long time. Oh, here is something from Hassan."

Sarju proffered the backpack. Fazeela took it, unzipped the main compartment, and peered inside.

"Oh, sweets and things for my daughter. Thanks for bringing it."

Sarju looked around the yard.

"Come, come, you must be tired. Let me show you to your room."

"Isn't your husband home?"

"He will be home in a little while. He and Arifa, my daughter, went to the store."

She attempted to climb the stairs, then stopped. "We have a spare room upstairs, or you can use the apartment downstairs. Uncle Hassan uses it whenever he visits. But it is up to you."

Sarju looked at the enclosed room. It promised all the privacy he needed.

"Is there a bathroom inside?" he asked, hopefully.

A broad smile lit up Fazeela's face. "It even has an A.C. Let me show you."

She led the way to the door to the small apartment; she opened the door with a flourish and ushered him in.

Sarju surveyed the furnished studio apartment. There was a bed, a sofa, a TV, a table and chairs, and a door that led to a bathroom. Hassan had constructed a comfortable den.

"This is mine. This is more than I need," he decided.

"Okay. After you freshen up, come upstairs. I have prepared food for you. And here is the key."

As soon as Fazeela left, Sarju rushed to the bathroom. The diaper was soggy and had made him uncomfortable for a long time. The water from the shower was deliciously cold; it cleansed him of the urine and helped ease the stomach pain.

After a short rest, he climbed the stairs to a spacious and very well-furnished house. A stocky man in his thirties was sitting at the table, monitoring a little girl who was reading a book.

Fazeela beamed with contentment. "This is my family, Mr. Beepat."

The man rose from his seat and pulled a chair for him. He shook Sarju's hand.

"I am Nizam. Do you like the apartment, Mr. Beepat?"

"Yes. It is quite cozy."

Fazeela indicated the child with pride. "And this is our daughter, Arifa."

Sarju smiled at Arifa and patted her head.

Arifa grinned impishly. "Thank you for the book and the other things, Mr. Beepat."

"Oh, that was sent by your Uncle Hassan. That was not from me."

"But you brought it for me. So, thanks for bringing it."

"Okay, you are right. I did bring it. Enjoy the book."

"Arifa, go help your mother with the food," instructed Nizam.

Fazeela and Arifa set the table. There was a bowl of sizzling fish curry and a platter of boiled and fried cassava, plantains, and eddoes. The smell of the curry was quite delicious and overpowering with all the herbs and spices. Sarju took a spoonful and a piece of the cassava. He had not had a home-cooked meal in sixteen years. The spices tingled and exploded in all his taste buds. A feeling of nostalgia hit him, and he put his fork down.

"I hope you like the food. The ground provisions came from the backyard, and the fish was caught from the river this morning," filled in Nizam.

"I recognized the fish! Wasn't it *basha*?"

"Yes, the Essequibo River is filled with it."

"I love basha. That was my favorite fish when I lived here. The food is wonderful, Fazeela."

"Then why aren't you eating?" Arifa interjected, staring at Sarju's plate.

"Oh! I am eating," added Sarju, and he placed a small piece of the fish in his mouth. "I am eating, but very slowly. You start to do things very slowly as you get older, my dear Arifa."

Fazeela looked at his plate. "Is there anything special you would like me to prepare, Mr. Beepat?"

"No, no, you don't have to go out of your way," protested Sarju. "I am not a big eater. I will eat anything you cook."

"Uncle Hassan said you were his special guest. He said we should provide you with everything you need. So don't be shy," Fazeela insisted.

'Yes, she is right. Just say the word, and we will provide it. And later, if you feel like sampling the local rum, I can introduce you to the bar. Uncle Hassan would want that."

Sarju smiled appreciatively. "Thank you, Nizam. But I keep away from bars now."

Sarju felt a familiar uprising in his stomach. He placed his hands over his mouth and darted from the room, down the steps, and into the yard. He made his way to the fence and began to retch. He rested his hands on his knees and glanced over his shoulder. Nizam, his wife, and daughter were standing by the door, watching him with concern and alarm on their faces.

Sarju washed his face at the standpipe and mounted the stairs to rejoin the family at the table. They were all quiet.

"Forgive me," apologized Sarju. "It was easier for me to run to the yard than to go to the bathroom. I didn't want to ruin your furniture."

There was a sad look on Fazeela's face. "Was there anything wrong with the food? I spent a long time and was careful with the preparation."

"It could be the spices, Fazeela," consoled Nizam. "Americans are not accustomed to spicy food. There was a lot of pepper in the curry. Wakenaam people like their fish curry hot with a lot of fresh pepper, Mr. Beepat."

"No, no, the food was delicious. There was nothing wrong with it," declared Sarju.

Arifa giggled. "Then if it was so delicious, why did you throw up?"

"Arifa, mind your manners," Nizam reprimanded. "Mr. Beepat is our guest. Don't speak to him like that."

"No, Nizam. It is okay."

Sarju turned to Arifa. "Arifa, I suffer from something called indigestion. Sometimes I throw up whatever I eat."

He looked at Fazeela, who had a miserable look on her face. "So, you see, Fazeela, it was not your cooking. Your food was delicious, but the problem was my stomach."

A broad smile of relief spread across Fazeela's face.

Nizam chuckled. "I knew it was definitely not her cooking. I only throw up when she doesn't cook. And if that was food poisoning, there would be a line for the toilet."

Arifa considered Sarju thoughtfully. "I know what is wrong with you. You are allergic to food."

Nizam beamed at his daughter. "You see how smart she is, Mr. Beepat. She is going to be a doctor. What medicine would you prescribe for him, Dr. Arifa?"

"A bucket tied around his waist," advised Arifa gleefully. "Then he wouldn't have to dash out the house like an Olympic sprinter."

"Is there anything that wouldn't make you throw up? I could boil or steam fish and vegetables for you," offered Fazeela.

"I am afraid not," Sarju admitted. "But I find bananas and milk tend to stay down longer."

"Then you are in the right place. We have lots of fresh fruits on the island," remarked Nizam.

"You must like monkeys. They eat a lot of bananas," laughed Arifa.

"But monkeys don't drink milk," rejoined Sarju playfully. "Where do you go to school, Arifa?"

"I go to Zeelandia primary school. Not far from here, just down the road."

Sarju picked up a small piece of cassava and chewed very slowly. "I know that school. Many years ago, I was a teacher there."

Fazeela left the table and returned with some bananas. Sarju peeled one.

"I was a student there. I don't remember you as a teacher," Fazeela commented.

Sarju nibbled on the banana. "That was more than thirty years ago. Before your time. When I left, the headmaster was Mr. Rogers."

"There was a headmaster named Rogers. He retired and came back as a volunteer. He had no family."

"Yes. He lived alone while I was there."

"He is dead. But he is still there."

"Dead and still there?" Sarju interjected.

Fazeela shook her head sadly. "He had no relatives. When he died, they buried him in the school compound. That was what he desired for all his years of service."

Chapter 15- Salmon

The sun was dipping into the horizon when Sarju decided to explore the area. He ambled slowly along the side of the potholed main road. He passed a ramshackle building, leaning precariously on one side. A man dressed in shorts, stirring a pot over an open fire, waved at him. Sarju returned the neighborly greeting and turned to enter a smaller side street. He remembered that area well. The street ended at the entrance of the elementary school.

Sarju stopped at the end of the street and gazed at the school building. It appeared so small now, with the passage of time. He felt an eerie tingling in him as if the energy of the many students who had passed through the school was still vibrating in the air, not unlike the echoes of the last string plucked on a guitar.

His gaze halted at the top of the building and focused on the windows there. The small windows belonged to a small attic-like enclosure that had served as a kind of storage room. The middle window was broken while he was a teacher there, and the caretaker had used a piece of plywood to seal it. After so many years, the window was still not repaired. It looked like a little rectangular recess between the two other grimy windows. A little smile appeared on Sarju's face as he remembered the incident that led to the shattered window pane.

He felt a presence near him. About six feet away, a black man was squatting on his haunches with a birdcage resting on his knee. He was dressed in khaki shorts and a dingy white T-shirt.

The man squinted at Sarju, his eyes glinting under the last rays of the fading sun.

"If you are waiting for a teacher or a school child to come out, you have a long wait. You don't know today is Sunday. Or you come from another planet?"

"I know what day it is. I am just checking out the school." Sarju was amused by the introduction.

"Well, if you want to enroll a child here, come tomorrow and speak to the secretary." The man examined Sarju. "But you look too old to have a child."

"I am not here to enroll anyone. This school has a lot of memories for me."

The man nodded his head in agreement. "For me, too. This was the only school I ever attended."

Sarju's eyes returned to the sealed window. "I recall there was a caretaker here called Cyril. He had a daughter who lived with him."

The man's eyes narrowed as he looked at Sarju suspiciously. "Yes, Lalita!"

"She still lives here with him?"

The man blew on the feed trough of the cage. Specks of seeds escaped through the wires. "Nah! Dead! Both father and daughter dead and gone."

"Oh!" Sarju declared with his eyes fixated on the bird cage. When he was a youth in the village, he followed the same custom of keeping songbirds in cages. The warbling and the trilling of the birds had always enthralled him.

"People say that she had two children for two different men," the man continued, "but none of the men lived with her. They said when she left the island, she abandoned the children on the streets of Georgetown."

"Really!" Sarju was shocked by this piece of information. "I used to teach here a long time ago. It's been more than thirty years since I left. I knew her then."

The man nodded his head knowingly. A tiny smile hovered around his lips. "Know her? As in the Bible? Know her inside out to get children?"

Sarju objected quickly. "No, man. I wouldn't go so far."

The man got up. He was a few inches shorter than Sarju. He flexed his bare feet which were flaked with mud. "You said thirty years ago?"

His fingers drummed on the cage as if he were calculating. He stopped suddenly and looked at Sarju. "I should know you! I am forty now! I was ten years old, around thirty years ago. What is your name?"

Sarju stared at the man. "Beepat. Sarju Beepat."

The man placed the cage carefully on the ground and hopped about. "Beepat? Sir Beepat? I recognize your face now. You taught me in the common entrance class. My name is Neblet—Prescod Neblet."

Neblet shoved his hand forward and furiously pumped Sarju's hand.

"I don't remember you," murmured Sarju apologetically. "It was such a long time ago."

Neblet held on to Sarju's hand. "You have to remember me," he pleaded. "Me, Morris, Seerattan, and Pertab used to sit on the back bench. You used to whip us regularly with a cane because we used to cut school and never do our homework."

Neblet let go of Sarju's hand. "Think! You must remember we," he whined.

Sarju thought for a while. "The name Seerattan rings a bell!" he conceded.

Neblet exploded with laughter. "How could anyone forget Seerattan, man? His three front teeth protruded from his mouth like a carpenter chisel."

A memory stirred in Sarju.

Neblet continued. "One day, while you were trying to cane him, he put a bite on you. You don't remember you had to get a tetanus shot at the hospital?"

The memory of the incident arrived like a thunderbolt. "And then his drunk father met me outside the school with a cutlass!"

Neblet and Sarju laughed uproariously.

Neblet recounted, "And the two of you started to fight. When you had his father pinned to the ground, Seerattan sneaked up and bit you again. This time in the ass."

"Everything is coming back now," admitted Sarju. "That was the last year I spent here. But you remember me very well."

"How could I forget?" protested Neblet. "You were the last teacher I had. I never had the chance to go beyond primary school. I always remember you as the *Salmon Man*."

"Why *salmon*?"

"You taught us a lesson on fish one day. It was one of the few times I was paying attention in class."

Sarju was intrigued. "That must have been a remarkable lesson!"

"You taught us that the baby salmon would travel down the river and live for years in the sea and ocean. Then, when it matures, the adult salmon will always return to its place of birth to spawn and to die."

Sarju was quiet for a while. He looked at the school building and at Neblet. "And you still remember that?"

"Yes! Every time I fish in the river, I remember that story. We have no salmon in the river, but I always remembered you, Sir Beepat."

Sarju placed his hand on Neblet's shoulder. "Thank you, Neblet. Your story has made my life worthwhile. So what do you do?"

"Oh! I do odd jobs on the island. I work in the rice fields, clear canals, and make coconut oil. Anything you can think of, I do in this place."

Sarju considered Neblet with pity. "I am sorry you didn't go beyond elementary school, Neblet."

Neblet glanced at the school. A smile of contentment appeared on his face. "Oh, I make out okay. I am free to roam and enjoy the fruit seasons. But Morris went beyond this school. He studied in England. He is a doctor now!"

"A doctor? That is very good. I am glad he did so well."

"He lives on the island as well," Neblet declared, "and he works at the hospital here, but I don't think he would remember you."

Sarju looked sharply at Neblet. "Why? Because he is a doctor?"

"No, no," Neblet added hastily. "I remember you because you were the last teacher in my life, but Morris is a doctor and had hundreds of teachers after you. It would be hard for him to remember you. But I will ask him when I see him."

"You are still friends?"

"Oh, yes," grinned Neblet. "I do all his yard work, and he invites me to all his parties."

Sarju beamed at Neblet. "I am so glad my former pupils are doing well."

The merriment left Neblet's face. "Well, we can't say *all*. Pertab turned out to be a pirate. He is serving a life sentence for robbing and killing two fishermen. And I hear Seerattan finally straighten his teeth and is a pandit in New York. Island people refer to him as the bandit pandit because he didn't pay the American dentist for straightening his piranha teeth."

Neblet picked up his birdcage. It was getting dark. Shadows were creeping up on the school building.

"I heard Mr. Rogers is buried somewhere here, Neblet."

Neblet looked tenderly at the bird imprisoned in the cage. "Yes. Even in death, he didn't leave this school. They said that he put it in his will that he must be buried under that mango tree at the back of the school."

Sarju and Neblet looked beyond the school at a lone mango tree that was almost shrouded in shadows.

Neblet chuckled. "People are scared to go by that tree to pick mangoes. They are afraid of Roger's ghost. But not me. I not afraid of old Rogers. That is my money tree. I pick all the mangoes and sell them."

Sarju shook Neblet's hand. "It was nice meeting you, Neblet. I hope we meet again."

"If you are staying on this island, you can't miss me, Sir Beepat. I am all around. Right now, I am going fishing. I might catch some fish, but certainly not a salmon. So long, Sir Beepat."

"So long, Neblet."

Neblet strode off, holding his birdcage in front of him. Sarju walked alongside the fence and stopped by the mango tree. Under the tree, he caught sight of a slab of concrete, evidence of a tomb that was slowly sinking into the earth.

After he completed high school on the island, Sarju went to the Teachers' Training College in Georgetown for two years. He returned to the island and was assigned to the school as a junior teacher. Mr. Rogers, the headmaster, welcomed the nervous young teacher and mentored and supported him. Sarju had often thought of him when he was in America, but although he had never communicated with the headmaster, he had never forgotten his kindness and friendship.

Sarju leaned on the fence and whispered. "I am back, Mr. Rogers. The salmon has returned. He has spawned in America and has returned to be with you on your island."

The night enveloped Sarju like a shroud as he headed back to Hassan's house.

Chapter 16- Loss of Property

Sarju sat at the table with Nizam. Fazeela had prepared toast and avocado for him. He took small bites while sipping the island coffee. Nizam heartily tucked away at roti and fried potatoes, heavily fortified with tomatoes and onions.

"You should try this," encouraged Nizam. "Your stomach might accept it."

"It looks and smells appetizing. But the stomach is the boss. I must thank your wife for preparing special meals for me," remarked Sarju.

"It is no problem," grinned Nizam. "Toast and avocado is not a meal for me. So what do you plan to do today, Mr. Beepat?"

"I was planning to go to the village of Belle Plaine. I used to live there, you know."

"Yes, Hassan mentioned that. I can give you a lift on my motorcycle on my way to work."

"Where do you work, Nizam?"

"I work with the Ministry of Agriculture as an extension officer."

"What is that? Some kind of manager?

"Not really," remarked Nizam, cleaning the plate with the last bit of roti. "I visit the islands to see what the farmers need and try to ensure they get all the support for their crops."

"When I lived here, the farmers complained about drainage, irrigation, fertilizers, squatters..."

"Nothing has changed. They have the same problems. Some we can address; the others we try to hide under the carpet."

"How do you get around the islands? By ferry?"

"Ferry? That would take forever. No. I have a speedboat. I am responsible for three islands. They are not far away. I try to visit each island at least once a week, and I am home every day for dinner."

Sarju downed the cup of coffee. The toast and avocado were finished.

Nizam looked at the empty plate. "You want to come with me to Belle Plaine? It is on my way."

"No, thank you, Nizam. I will rest a little more and venture out later."

"Transportation is easy here. If you don't see a minibus, tractors with trailers always traverse the road. They stop and pick up anyone."

"It was so when I was here. Someone passing on a bicycle would stop and offer you a lift. The island life that I knew was slow and easy."

"It is still the same in many ways, although many people have left. Many of your friends also."

Arifa, dressed for school, came and sat at the table. She looked at the remains on Sarju's plate. "Morning, Mr. Beepat? Didn't you eat your banana?"

"Stop that, Arifa." Nizam ordered.

Sarju smiled and patted her hand. "Your mother made me something better. Toast and avocado."

A pained look came over Sarju's face. "It seems I spoke too early; my stomach heard me."

Sarju placed his hands over his mouth and left the table. He headed to the yard and heaved into a paper bag. He looked at the landing of the house and saw Arifa looking at him with concern spread over her face. He waved at her and headed for the apartment under the house.

SARJU TROD ALONG THE potholed street to the main road. He did not have to wait long. A tractor coupled to a trailer stopped beside him. Sarju joined the few people standing and holding on to the sides of the trailer.

Sarju took in the fields of rice and coconut trees as the tractor huffed past the small villages. It stopped by a government office in Belle Plaine. Sarju hopped off, thanked the driver, and trekked along the main street. The tractor had stopped in the commercial section. Most of the stores that he knew were torn down and replaced with new buildings. There was even a commercial bank and a funeral home.

He turned down a side street and entered a residential area. He walked slowly, observing the buildings, then stopped beside a large modern house. The house was fenced in and occupied two lots. The empty lot at the side of the house hosted two jet skis and a large motorboat. He stared at two mango trees that lined one boundary of the empty lot. The trees were laden with golden-yellow fruits. Bubbles of water from an earlier rain shower glistened on the leaves and on the bottom of the fruits. He remembered those trees; he remembered the land. It was his father's land, willed to him by his father, Sarju's grandfather. Sarju was born there and lived there until he left for America, but the house that he remembered was torn down to accommodate this present monstrosity.

Sarju's great-grandfather had been an indentured servant. He joined a ship in India and traveled with a little bundle of clothes and a few mangoes. After eating the mangoes on the trip across the ocean, he guarded the seeds and planted them on his arrival in Guyana. The trees flourished in the new land, and when his grandfather bought the two lots in Belle Plaine, he planted the seeds of the fruits from the parent tree; four trees sprouted, marking the boundary of his land to acclaim his ownership and independence. Now, only two trees remained.

Sarju stared at the house. An Amerindian woman with long black hair was at a window, eyeing him. Sarju raised the latch of the gate and inched his way into the yard. He walked on the earth, not on the long concrete path that led to the front steps. Through his shoes, he sensed the familiar land of his childhood. The woman left the window and stood by the landing on top of the stairs.

"Good morning," hailed Sarju. "I am looking for a man called Samlall. He used to own this house."

The woman glared at him. "He don't live here. This house belongs to my husband. We bought this place years ago."

Sarju noted her serious face and belligerent demeanor. "I know. But, do you know where I can find him?"

The woman turned up her nose. "He is a real nuisance in the neighborhood. Continue walking and turn right at the second street. He lives in a rundown flat house near the end. If you don't find him, he is probably lying drunk by some road corner or the riverside."

———◉———

SARJU FOLLOWED THE directions of the woman. He stopped on the road in front of a dilapidated hut that was almost hidden from view by thick overgrown bush. He navigated down a long mud path that led to the hut. Sleeping on a bench in front of the hut was a man with long gray hair. Sarju recognized his brother, Samlall. He took a long look at his brother, whom he hadn't seen or spoken to in over thirty years. There was a rum bottle on the bench. Sarju picked up the bottle, inspected it, and put it down. He winced and held his stomach. He reached into his pocket, and from a pill bottle, he extracted two pills. He reached into another pocket and removed a bottle of water. Sarju took a swig of water and sprinkled some on the sleeping Samlall.

Samlall shook himself awake like a dog. He raised himself slowly from the bench. "What the hell? Raining again?" He rubbed his eyes and noticed Sarju. "What the hell is wrong with you? You think I am a plant?"

He reached into his pocket and fumbled around. He took out a pair of spectacles and settled them on his nose. One lens was missing, and the other had several scratches.

He squinted at Sarju. "Who are you? What you want? You have a job for me?"

Sarju observed his brother for a while. "Your eyes are not working, Samlall? What about your ears?"

Samlall's mouth opened and closed like a fish gasping for air. He stood up slowly. "Sarju? Sarju? You are here? You came back to this place?"

He shuffled towards Sarju, and they hugged for a long time. Tears came down and smeared both their cheeks. Samlall and Sarju sat on the bench in silence for a long while.

Samlall held on to his brother's hand and stared into his face. "You left here as a young man and returned as an old man. But we are all old now. I received little scraps of information that you were jailed for life in America. I kept it a secret here. How did you get out?"

"I was paroled for good behavior."

Samlall looked past Sarju. The tears fell and watered his unshaven cheeks. "I never thought I would see you again. They said you killed a man. I never believed that." He shook his head. "Not my little brother, Sarju."

Sarju looked Samlall squarely in the eye. "It is true. But he raped my daughter."

Samlall tugged at Sarju's shoulder. "Then he deserved to die. You did what you had to do."

"And they did what they had to do," replied Sarju.

Sarju observed the squalid surroundings. "But Samlall, what happened to our house? There is a new house on the land, and you are living in this, this, shed? How come, man?"

Samlall reached across Sarju for the rum bottle. He took a swig and offered it to Sarju, who pushed it away.

"I had some debts, and things went downhill from there." He took another swig from the bottle. "My son took out a loan to go to university. I tried to pay off the loan but lost the house. I lost my job as a clerk at the rice mill too."

———————⟢◉⟣———————

A BLACK TOYOTA CAR drove up to the residence of the attorney, Naitram, and parked in the driveway. The house was a sturdy wood house constructed in the colonial style. The first floor housed the law office, while the upper floor served as the living quarters.

Motielall, a lean Indian man in his forties, turned off the engine and examined Samlall. Samlall was very nervous; his hands, holding a plastic bag, were trembling.

Motielall leaned over and drew a bag from the backseat. He lobbed it to Samlall. "Here, take this. I planned to give it to you after we signed the papers, but it looks like you need it now."

Samlall peered into the bag. A smile appeared on his face as he saw the bottle of rum.

Motielall noted the reaction with satisfaction. "You are trembling as if you are going to the gallows! We are only going to the lawyer's office."

He opened the car door and walked to the front door. Samlall followed with the two bags clutched to his chest.

In the waiting room of the law office, a young black girl sat at a desk, typing on a computer.

Motielall approached the desk. "Where is Naitram? I have an appointment," he barked.

The girl quickly got up and walked to a doorway behind her desk. She opened the door and inserted her head.

She returned and stood timidly at her desk. "Mr. Naitram is on the phone. He would be with you in a minute."

Motielall glared at the girl and looked at his watch. "I hope his minute doesn't stretch into an hour."

A long sofa was against one wall of the room. He guided Samlall over, and the two sat.

Motielall called the girl, who had resumed her work. "Bring a Pepsi and a glass for this client while we wait for your boss."

The girl leaped to her feet and went quickly to a fridge that was almost hidden in a corner of the room. She returned with a can of Pepsi and a glass.

Motielall took the can and glass and handed them to Samlall. The girl returned to her desk and glanced furtively at the two men.

"Here is the chaser for that rum. I know you are nervous about signing papers in a law office, so take a drink and brace yourself."

Samlall removed the bottle from the bag and poured a shot into the glass. He opened the can of Pepsi and filled the glass, then leaned back and emptied it in one long gulp.

He poured another shot and filled the glass with Pepsi. "I am only doing this for my son. Thank you for arranging the loan."

Motielall looked approvingly as Samlall downed another drink. "Don't worry, you will pay it off in a jiffy. It is better to borrow from me than to owe a bank. Mr. Naitram has prepared all the paperwork. You don't have to pay him a cent. I am paying for all the legal work."

"Thank you, Motielall," mumbled Samlall, his unsteady hands clutching the glass. "My son doesn't know about this, but he will be grateful too. He is working at a bank in Georgetown. Now, at least he can pay off his school loan and apply for a mortgage to build a house there."

Samlall glanced at the young girl and lamented. "There is no future on this island for educated young people."

A buzzer sounded. The girl called out. "Mr. Naitram is ready for you, Mr. Motielall."

Motielall got to his feet. Samlall tried to gather the bottle, can, and plastic bag.

"Leave the rum here. You can't drink in front of the lawyer. His office is not a damn rum shop."

In the lawyer's den, Naitram, a dark-skinned Indian in his sixties, was seated at his desk, tapping a pen against his upper lip. There were four armchairs in front of his desk. Motielall took a seat and beckoned Samlall to do the same.

Naitram twitched his nose. "Isn't it too early in the morning for a drink, Motielall?"

"That is not me. I don't drink rum. But this client is slightly nervous, Mr. Naitram. He has never been to a law office before. He needed something to stiffen his back."

"My back is okay," objected Samlall. "I just wanted to calm the nerves. I never wanted to be involved with the law, court, or police."

Naitram held up a sheaf of papers and shook it in Samlall's face.

"Mr. Samlall, you are here to sign the papers for a loan from Mr. Motielall. Do you want to read through all of this?"

Samlall drew back at the sight of the papers. "No, no! I broke my glasses, and reading gives me a headache. Show me where I have to sign, and Mr. Motielall will give me the money. Right, Mr. Motielall? Two thousand U.S. dollars!"

"And that is what we agreed on. Do you have the deed for the property? I have to keep it until you pay off the loan."

Samlall opened the plastic bag and pulled out a document which he gave to Motielall. Motielall examined the document and handed it over to the lawyer.

Naitram read the document quietly. "This states that your brother has a share in the property!"

Samlall blurted out, "In name only. I am in charge. It is my house. He doesn't want any part of the house and won't be returning to this country."

"That is okay. We can accept that," Motielall added quickly. "Here is your money."

Motielall handed over a wad of money. Samlall pocketed the money hastily.

Naitram looked amused. "Aren't you going to count it, man?"

Samlall grinned. "You think Motielall would rob me in front of a lawyer? Show me where to sign. I want to surprise my son with this money."

SARJU SAT ON THE BENCH and looked at Samlall with a shocked expression. "How come you lost that property for two thousand U.S. dollars? That house and land was probably worth around forty thousand U.S. dollars."

"Fifty," insisted Samlall. "Somebody offered me fifty before I took that loan from Motielall."

Sarju sighed heavily. "You took the loan, and now you are on the streets with no house? How? Tell me."

Samlall took another swig of rum. He tapped the bottle. "Rum! That is how. They said that it wasn't a loan. They claimed I sold the property for the sum of two thousand dollars. They have everything in black and white. I signed all the papers in the lawyer's office."

"Don't blame alcohol for your downfall, Samlall."

"You are right," agreed Samlall and took another swig. "After that, my wife left me to be with my son. They are renting a small apartment in the city. I don't hear from them anymore."

"Totally your fault," muttered Sarju angrily.

"My fault for helping my son?" sneered Samlall. "Your father did the same for you. I never told him it was his fault."

"What did my father do that was my fault, Samlall? Tell me." Sarju shouted.

"You forgot that Pa sold the rice field so you could go to America. I lost my rights too, but I remained here on this island, surrounded by trickery and misery."

"I know, I know," sighed Sarju. "And I couldn't even leave America when my parents died."

"It is okay, Sarju," consoled Samlall. "We did what we could do."

"You couldn't report to the police. Tell them what they did?"

Samlall grunted in disgust. "This is not America, Sarju. You killed a man and went to jail. In Guyana, bribery and corruption is the name of the game. This is 2017, and only the rich and powerful know how to play that game."

The sound of a bicycle clanking and screeching made them look to the road. Neblet peered down the passageway and rode up to the bench.

"Sir Beepat! Sir Beepat! What are you doing here?"

Sarju chuckled. "Hi, Neblet! This is my brother."

Neblet leaned over his bicycle saddle and grinned. "I know him. We work together, sometimes. Last month, while we were cleaning a drainage canal, he mistook an alligator for a piece of wood, and it bit him on the foot. He couldn't see with his broken glasses."

Sarju scrutinized Samlall's face. "How come you broke your glasses?"

Samlall sucked his teeth. "Ask him. He was there."

Sarju looked at Neblet.

"He went to Motielall's house, asking for the deed to his house; Motielall slapped him across the face, breaking it."

Samlall waved the glasses in Sarju's face. "No use repairing them. That was the third time he broke them."

"Yes, Sir Beepat. That man, Motielall, is dangerous. He is involved in the drug trade."

Neblett wagged his finger in Samlall's face. "No house is worth losing your life over. I even saved your brother from Crankshaft Willie."

"Who is Crankshaft Willie?"

"You don't want to know him, Sarju?" muttered Samlall.

"He is a murderer. He would kill you, strap a heavy crankshaft to your body, and drown you in the ocean," volunteered Neblet.

"And the police allow this man to go walk free?" Sarju exploded.

"Well, one time they locked him up for murder, and he hired the lawyer, Naitram. Naitram asked the police to produce the body. Who could find a body at the bottom of an ocean? So, they let him go."

"How do you know he wanted to kill Samlall, Neblet?"

"Because I see him talking to Motielall one morning. That same afternoon, he asked me to tell Samlall that he had a job for him on his boat. I get suspicious and hang around his boat, then I see him taking a crankshaft aboard."

"Yes, and I had to hide from him for two days," admitted Samlall.

"So, where is Crankshaft Willie now? queried Sarju.

"We hear that he was in Venezuelan waters transporting a bale of cocaine. The Spanish police collared his ass, and he is in prison waiting for the hangman or the rifleman," Neblet laughed.

"What the Guyana police couldn't do, the Spanish police do," chortled Samlall. "They don't tolerate smart-ass lawyers and murderers over there."

Chapter 17- Paying Forward

Sarju sat at the breakfast table, taking little sips from a glass of coconut water. He observed Arifa as she completed her math homework. She bit the end of her pencil and scowled as she waded through a series of multiplication activities. The scene reminded him of his daughter, Aarti. When Aarti was little, she used to chew on her pencil the same way when doing her homework.

He was very pleased with Arifa. He had shown her a different way to tackle multiplication, and she readily took to it. At first, every time she finished a problem, she would push her book over for him to check. On these trials, she arrived at the correct answers, and now both she and Sarju accepted her mastery. She no longer pushed her book over but still chewed on her pencil as she confidently attacked her tasks.

A motorcycle puttered into the yard. Nizam walked through the front door with two bags of grocery items. He nodded to Sarju and walked over to Arifa, where he planted a kiss on her forehead.

Arifa grabbed him by the arm and blurted out gleefully. "Daddy, Mr. Beepat showed me an easier way to do multiplication. I am getting all the maths correct."

Sarju smiled. He was so used to referring to mathematics as "math" in the American way that it was strange and amusing to hear Arifa use the Guyanese terminology, "maths."

Nizam kissed his daughter again. "That is good to hear. Mr. Beepat used to be a teacher. Maths is a piece of cake for him."

Sarju straightened up in the chair. He placed a hand over his mouth and pushed back his chair, ready to run.

Arifa got up suddenly and pointed a finger at Sarju. "Stay right there," she ordered. "Hold it in. Don't run; just place your hands over your mouth."

Sarju and Nizam watched as she ran to the kitchen and returned with a shiny plastic bucket.

She ran to Sarju's side and placed the bucket on the floor in front of him. "Here! Use this bucket. You don't have to run to the yard every time you need to throw up."

Sarju leaned over and retched into the bucket. Arifa patted him on the back as he made several dry heaves. Sarju leaned back in the chair with flecks of spittle dotting his unshaven cheeks. Arifa handed him a towel to clean his face.

"Thank you, Arifa. Thank you, my child."

Nizam leaned over to have a better view of the bucket. "You are heaving and vomiting your guts out, but only air is coming out of your system. How is that possible?"

Arifa looked at her dad impatiently. "Because he is not eating, Daddy."

Sarju took another sip of coconut water.

Arifa patted him motherly on the shoulder. "You have to eat, Mr. Beepat. Air has nothing. Only food has calories.

Nizam nodded his head in approval. "Listen to the doctor, Mr. Beepat. She knows what she is saying."

"I eat, but I am not hungry now, Arifa. Thank you."

"I bought that bucket today. I bought it for you with my own money."

Sarju reached out and patted the girl on the head. "Thank you. That was very thoughtful of you. Of course, I will repay you for this bucket."

Arifa regarded him with innocent eyes. "You don't have to. That was called *paying forward*. My teacher taught us that. If I do a kind act for someone, a complete stranger will repay me."

Nizam chuckled in appreciation and headed for the kitchen. "That is very deep, Arifa. You too chat while I unpack these bags."

Arifa returned to her seat and closed her book. "My homework is done. I am an expert in multiplication thanks to you, Mr. Beepat."

She examined Sarju's worn-looking face. "Do you have children, Mr. Beepat?"

Sarju choked on the coconut water. He coughed a few times while Arifa waited for a response.

"Well, recently, no one has claimed me as a father."

"You need someone to help you with your stomach."

Sarju nudged the bucket. "You have done a fine job with your bucket."

"But it is empty," Arifa pointed out. "If you had a daughter, she would make sure you filled your stomach."

Sarju closed his eyes and remembered his daughter Aarti in the park in Connecticut with her little daughter. Tears came to his eyes.

"But then the bucket would be full," he mumbled.

"And she would empty it for you," she retorted. "But don't you worry. Eat anything you want, and I will empty your bucket. We will pretend I am your daughter."

Sarju choked on the coconut water again. Arifa leaned over and patted him on the back. "You need some more calories. Let me get you a banana and a glass of milk."

She ran to the back of the house, leaving Sarju staring into the plastic bucket.

Sarju heard Fazeela speaking to someone in the yard. Her voice echoed from the back.

"Mr. Beepat, a man is outside on the road. He wants to speak with you. He says it is urgent."

Sarju got up quickly and moved to the window with a clear view of the street. Neblet was on the road holding onto a bicycle and looking anxiously at the window.

Chapter 18- The Invitation

Sarju balanced himself on the top tube or bar of the bicycle while Neblet, on the saddle, pedaled furiously. He held on tightly as the bicycle sailed through the pools and around the potholes on the road. He had not traveled in this manner since he left the village for America. When he was young, that mode of transport was normal on the island, with few motor vehicles. The rasping breathing of Neblet tickled his ear as they cycled to Samlall's hut to deal with what Neblet had described as an emergency.

They took the road to Belle Plaine, and Neblet navigated the bicycle expertly away from parked vehicles, animals, and other road traffic until they arrived at Samlall's hut. He did not stop on the road outside the hut, as the bicycle had no brakes. Neblet just stopped pedaling and allowed the bicycle to bump and trundle its way down the long mud path to Samlall's hut.

They found Samlall on the bench, pensively looking at a bag in his hands. He glanced up in alarm as he saw the bicycle bearing down. It came to a stop with the front wheel hitting the bench. Sarju tumbled off, landing on his rump on the ground, while Neblet held on to the saddle for support.

Samlall glared malevolently at Neblet as Sarju struggled to get off the ground.

"Who asked you to bring this fucking man here, Neblet? Didn't I tell you not to tell anybody? You don't know what is a secret? Why don't you mind your own fucking business?"

"I bring your brother here to stop you from doing something stupid." Neblet retorted.

"So, you don't think I know about guns, eh, Neblet? I plan to shoot him in the ass today."

Neblet dropped the bicycle. It fell with a clang against the bench. "You are blind as a bat. You can't even see." He held out his hand and waved it like a Chinese paper fan. "How many fingers I have here?"

Samlall pushed his hand into the bag and brandished a gun at Neblet. "I would shoot off your fucking hand just to show you what I can see."

Neblet quickly dropped to the ground and covered his head with his hands.

Sarju took a few steps forward and snatched the gun from his brother. "You think a gun is like a slingshot? Let me see that rusty gun. How many bullets you have in it?"

Neblet got up and stood nervously behind Sarju.

Samlall glared furiously at Neblet. "One bullet! I just need one bullet for that house thief, Motielall."

Sarju poked his brother on the shoulder with the gun muzzle. "What is the matter with you? You drank a gallon of cheap rum today."

Samlall shook his head vehemently. "Not a drop. Not a single drop. I want to be in my right senses when I kill his ass today."

Sarju glared at his brother. "Have you lost your senses, man? Neblet is right. And suppose you miss?"

Neblet looked at Samlall with disgust. He complained to Sarju. "Your brother is crazy, Sir Beepat. I told him that this morning, but the big man won't listen. Instead of taking money for painting a boat, he asked the smuggler to borrow a gun. He believes he is some kind of gangster walking around with dangerous weapons."

Sarju looked at Samlall, who sat on the bench, breathing heavily.

"You work for a smuggler?"

"Yes," volunteered Neblet, "the man smuggles whisky, beer, and cigarettes from Venezuela. But he so cheap he only gave gun slinger Samlall one measly bullet."

Samlall lumbered off the bench and screamed in Neblet's face. "And if you don't shut your fucking mouth, you will get half of that bullet in your ass today."

"And if you had taken my advice, you wouldn't be living in somebody's old shack," Neblet retorted. "You would be living in Motielall's big house."

Sarju observed Neblet with interest. "What did you suggest, Neblet?"

Samlall sat down heavily on the bench and uttered disdainfully. "Obeah! Obeah! He thinks I could get back the property by following the advice of an Obeah man. This madman thinks that witch doctors and black magic have more power than Motielall!"

"The obeah man said you must do the procedure three times for the power to work," Neblet protested.

Sarju viewed the two men with exasperation. "What are you talking about, Neblet? How does a witch doctor feature in getting back the property?"

Samlall huffed and gestured to Neblet.

Neblet sighed. "There is an obeah man in my village. He uses old African powers that can heal and bring good luck to people."

Samlall interrupted. "Why couldn't that obeah man make you rich? He made me poor by taking my money."

Neblet sneered. "The man can restore you to your original condition. He can't make me rich because I was always poor. But he can make you get back your property because it was yours in the first place."

"And he nearly got me killed too. Tell him how I broke my glasses that time," Samlall countered.

Sarju was intrigued. "What happened with the obeah man, Neblet?"

"Well, I took Samlall to the Obeah man. The man asked for money to buy a few items. He bought candles, incense, flowers, and different oils like *Go away evil* and *Commanding oil.*"

"He bought a goat with my money, too!" Samlall interjected.

"That was for the sacrifice to the Dutch spirit who controls the land!" snapped Neblet. "It's the Dutch master of the land who has to guide you to strike down Motielall."

Neblett addressed Sarju. "The Obeah man did all the rituals and gave Samlall three packets. He instructed him to enter Motielall yard on three dark nights and to bury a packet on each visit."

Samlall spat over the bench. "And I entered the man's yard. I was about to bury the first packet by his front steps when he came out and gave me a sound thrashing. He beat me like a drum and smashed my glasses against my face."

"You can't blame the Obeah man for that. It was your fault that you got caught," Neblet chided.

Sarju took the bag from the bench and inserted the gun.

"So the Obeah didn't work. You think the gun would be a better alternative?"

Samlall did not reply. He left the two men and entered his shack. Saju handed the bag to Neblet.

"Take this gun back to the smuggler. Tell him that Samlall changed his mind and would prefer money for working on the boat."

"That is the right thing to do, Sir Beepat. I will tell him that the priest advised him to give back the gun and say the Lord's prayer instead."

Neblet gingerly grasped the bag against his side and wheeled his bicycle out of the yard.

Sarju took a seat on the bench and closed his eyes while he clutched his aching stomach.

Samlall emerged from the hut with a package in his hand. He threw the package at Sarju. It slammed into Sarju's chest. Sarju opened his eyes and clutched the package.

Samlall sat beside his brother and diverted his gaze as Sarju unwrapped two pieces of elaborate Indian clothing, *a dhoti and a kurta.*

"What are you doing with Indian clothes now? Planning to get married?"

Samlall muttered, "My son, Pradeep, brought them here today. He is getting married this Sunday. He wants me to attend and do the duties as a father."

"So you have to go. You brought him up and sent him to college. Now you have to give him away to a woman with your blessings."

Samlall did not reply. Sarju stared at the top of a coconut tree in the distance.

"I never had that chance, Samlall. I will never have that chance. You are a very lucky man."

Samlall gazed at Sarju, who seemed to be lost in contemplation. "You can have my luck then, Sarju. You can go as his father. It is only a ritual. Not very important."

Sarju met his brother's gaze. "But it is necessary in a Hindu wedding. How can I do that when the father is still around?"

Samlall waved his hands toward the dilapidated hut and the overgrown yard.

"Look around and see where I live. What kind of father are you talking about? Almost as blind as a bat, without proper glasses, and with empty hands."

His voice quavered. "My son, Pradeep, is getting married, and I have nothing to give! All because of that thief, Motielall."

Sarju replaced the clothes in the package and placed them gently on Samlall's lap. "You don't think your son and the whole island know your situation?"

Sarju put his hands around Samlall's shoulders. "But that doesn't matter to him. He wants you to be a part of the ceremony. He wants the blessings and good wishes of his father—not his money."

Samlall inserted his hand into his pocket and pulled out an envelope. He handed it to Sarju.

"He brought an invitation for you too. I told him that you were here." Samlall looked intently at Sarju. "You should go with me then. He would need your blessings as well."

Chapter 19- The Lawyer

It was early in the afternoon when Sarju hopped off the agricultural trailer on the main road of Belle Plaine. He pulled the cap that Hassan had given him very low on his head, and his spring jacket, compliments of Sing Sing, was zipped to the top. He had grown up in these parts and did not want to draw any attention to himself. He knew that there was a stigma applied to prison inmates by all rural people, and he was not keen to face any embarrassment. He did not know how much of the circumstances of his past in America had filtered down to Wakenaam, and he tried his best to avoid exposure. He had instructed Neblet to keep his visit to the island a secret, and he knew he could trust him.

Far ahead, Sarju noticed a man leaning against the fender of a parked car. The man's belly was resting on the hood, and as he turned and twisted impatiently, it looked to Sarju like a balloon filled with liquid. Sarju smiled at the picture, but as he drew nearer, he felt sure that he knew the man. The man changed his position to face Sarju, and with his belly now hanging freely, Sarju recognized his seatmate on the plane home—Esau, Mr. Barrel Stomach!

Sarju stopped beside the car and hailed, "Esau! What are you doing here? I thought you were going to Berbice."

Esau gaped at Sarju for a while, then recognition dawned on him. "Oh, it's you! My friend from the plane!" He reached out to shake Sarju's hand. "It took me a while to make you out with that cap. And besides, I had too many drinks on that plane."

"So, you're visiting the island?"

Esau's expression changed. "This was not in the original plan, but I had to come here because of a conniving lawyer. I paid the man in the States to evict a squatter from my land, and when I called him from Berbice, the mother cunt claimed that I didn't give him any money. I swear I gave the man five hundred dollars as a down payment at my friend's birthday party. I promised to pay him the balance after he throws the squatter off the land."

Esau banged the hood of the car. "If my wife was not there, I would have smashed his fucking face. It would have cost him more than five hundred dollars to restructure his mouth."

"So, how are you going to get the squatter off the land?"

"Only one way, now. Follow my brother's advice. Go directly to the court and start bribing everyone, from the toilet cleaner to the judge. It is time that we cut out the middleman, the damn lawyer."

"Well, that was an important lesson you learned for five hundred dollars."

"You think I lost? No, he paid for the experience. He is always visiting New York to collect money from people and doesn't declare that as income. That is called money laundering. And his family lives there illegally. I am going to report them to immigration. If he can claim that I didn't give him money, then they will have to deal with American immigration.

Sarju peered into the car. It was empty. "So, where is your wife?"

Esau looked across the road at a clothing store. "Oh, she is over there with a friend who lives here. She wanted to visit her, and we decided to kill two birds with one stone. I just forgot to walk with a suitable stone for that fucking snake of a lawyer."

Two women crossed the road and walked to the car. Esau eased himself clumsily through the passenger's side door. The strange woman smiled at Sarju and got into the car, behind the wheel. Esau's wife opened the back door.

Sarju smiled at Esau's wife. "How is the little boy?" he inquired.

The woman looked at him haughtily and mouthed, "Do I know you?"

She plunged into the car and slammed the door.

Sarju was suddenly enraged. He leaned down and shouted through the open window. "Oh, you don't remember that your son kicked me in the balls at the airport?"

The car pulled off. Through the back windshield, Sarju discerned the woman, mocking him with her middle finger.

———————◉———————

SARJU STROLLED DOWN the main road and stopped in front of the house that Samlall had described. He mounted the short flight of stairs and pushed at the wooden door. It opened, making a creaking sound. A pretty black girl sitting at a desk looked up as he entered.

Sarju approached the desk. "I am here to see the lawyer."

She viewed him with interest. "Do you have business with him? Is he expecting you?"

Sarju nodded slowly. "Yes, we have business to complete. I am from New York."

The girl rose slowly to her feet and went to the lawyer's door. She knocked, entered the door, and remained there for a few minutes. She emerged and stood by the door. "The lawyer will see you now."

Sarju nodded his thanks and entered the office. The lawyer was seated at his desk. He looked at Sarju over his glasses. He was the same man that Sarju had seen on the plane. The same man who apparently robbed Barrel Stomach.

"What is your name, sir?"

"Sarju Beepat."

Naitram leaned back on his chair and adjusted his glasses properly on his nose. "I don't think we have represented you before, Mr. Beepat."

Sarju held on to the back of a chair and rocked it towards him. "You have, in a weird kind of way. You represented my brother,

Samlall Beepat, a few years ago. At the same time, you misrepresented my interest."

Sarju let the chair drop. The legs made a sharp sound on the thick wooden floor.

Naitram's countenance hardened. "I beg your pardon."

Sarju growled, "I had half an interest in a property at Zeelandia. My brother took a loan of two thousand dollars from your client and friend, Motielall, and he ended up losing the property to that thief."

Naitram emitted a light sneer. "I don't know anything about that. I can't discuss your brother's affairs with you."

"I am not here to discuss his affairs. I never gave oral or written permission to anyone to dispose of my share of the property," Sarju boomed. "You, sir, submitted false or forged documents to effect the transfer of my rights to that swindler, Motielall."

"I submitted whatever documents your brother tendered," fumed Naitram. "I am not a detective to verify your signature or determine your consent. The land court would decide, and obviously they did. I had nothing to do with that end of the business."

"But now I am giving you the opportunity to work with your client to have the documents rescinded and the deed or title reverted to my name," sputtered Sarju, his eyes glinting in anger.

Naitram scowled and rearranged some papers on the desk. "Mr. Beepat, you have every right to be upset if what you allege is correct. I served as an advocate for both your brother and Motielall. Your brother had no money, so out of kindness, I acted pro bono. He supplied all the documents to effect the transfer of property."

He wagged his finger at Sarju. "And if the documents were forged, then when an investigation is done, your brother can be charged with very serious offenses," he warned.

Sarju glowered at Naitram. "And he is prepared to face the court and serve time if necessary. But that is his problem. All I want is to be compensated."

Naitram recoiled as Sarju leaned over the desk. "The value of the property at the time you were involved in this malpractice was fifty thousand U.S. dollars. The loan you arranged was a mere two thousand. You owe me and my brother the difference."

Naitram's nose flared, and his lips curled with menace. "Is this a joke, Beepat? This island may be very far from America, but I know who you are and how much time you served in Sing Sing."

"So, you know me?" Sarju retorted and removed his cap.

Naitram leaned forward to get a better look at the uncapped Sarju. "You were the guy on the plane? And you said you had no problems?"

"But now you have the problem," Sarju chided.

"You think I am some backwater lawyer, eh? But I have connections all over. The police sent me a list of all the deported prisoners from America. Do you think you can just waltz out of an American prison and enter my country without the police taking notice of you? You are nothing but a jailbird, and you don't scare me," mocked Naitram.

"I am not here to scare you, Mr. Lawyer," hissed Sarju. "I willed everything that I owned to my children in America. Everything, including my share of the property you stole from me. I understand you have the wherewithal to bribe all and sundry here in Guyana, but when the U.S. Embassy intervenes on my behalf, the U.S. government will expose you and all your bribe-taking minions."

Naitram removed his glasses and shook them at Sarju. "There is an old Guyanese saying you may be familiar with, Beepat, *smart fly always gets trapped in cow's ass*. Don't play smart with me, or you will find your sorry ass trapped in another prison. And remember, this lawyer doesn't forget."

"Oh, you don't, eh? Did you forget that you took five hundred dollars from Esau in New York? How many more people did you swindle there? And did you forget that you travel to America while your family lives there illegally?"

Naitram's eyes popped. "I don't take threats from jailbirds, Beepat. Especially weak ones."

Sarju leaned over the desk to be face-to-face with Naitram. He whispered through gritted teeth. "I may appear feeble, Naitram. The man who violated my daughter thought so too, but I took his life. Just think, Mr. Lawyer man, what would I do to people who steal the birthright of my children?"

Sarju placed his cap on his head, kicked a chair against the wall, and stormed out of Naitram's office. Naitram rocked back in his chair and tapped his pencil against his nose.

Chapter 20- The Swindler

It was evening. The Belle Plain main road was painted in patches of darkness and light, as the few street lights did not cover the entire area. Sarju walked along the road, heading towards Motielall's house, flanked by Neblet and Samlall.

"I don't know why you so insistent on going to Motielall's yard," Samlall argued. "You didn't hear when we told you that the man gave me a serious beating when I entered his property?"

"I am going to pick some mangoes, Samlall. The fruits from your grandfather's tree," Sarju replied in a casual tone.

"You would be in serious trouble, Sir Beepat," warned Neblet. "Stealing fruits is called praedial larceny. That means the thiefing of agricultural crops; that could lead you to jail."

"I am not a thief, Neblet. I am only going to harvest the fruits of my grandfather's labor."

"Your grandfather probably planted those mango trees, but now they are standing on another man's land. You have no rights there, Sir Beepat," cautioned Neblet, putting a restraining hand on Sarju.

Sarju shrugged off Neblet's hand. "A man is entitled to reap what he sowed, eh Samlall?"

"But I can't understand why you want mango now! This island full of mangoes, and now you want to walk into a death trap," Samlall responded.

They stopped in front of Motielall's house. The motorboat was gone, but the two jet skis were still there. The yard lights were on, and the area was bathed in pale yellow light.

Sarju pointed to the trees. "Look, the trees are laden. The mangoes are calling."

"Sir Beepat, what is wrong with you? Go home. I will bring you mangoes tomorrow. Last night I picked a big bag from the tree over Old Roger's grave."

Sarju pushed aside Neblet, ducked under Samlall's hand, and crossed Motielall's bridge. He stood before the wrought-iron gate and fence and pulled a shopping bag from his pocket. He whipped the bag like a kite in the evening breeze to expand it. Then he flung the gate wide open, stumbled into the yard, and headed for the mango trees.

Neblet and Samlall moved from the gate; they huddled against the fence, peering through the bars like two agitated dogs.

"Madness run in your family, Samlall. Sir Beepat is more crazy than you. How could an educated man turn into a thief overnight?" whispered Neblett.

"Go behind him, Neblett. If Motielall comes down, he will find himself in serious trouble. Not forgetting a sound thrashing."

Neblet glared at Samlall. "I look like I mad. That is two charges you are talking about. Trespassing and praedial larceny. I don't have money to bribe the police and pay a lawyer. They wouldn't think twice to ship my poor ass to a prison cell."

Samlall peered through the fence. Everything seemed blurry to him. "What is he doing now?"

The dim light from a slow-moving tractor splashed over them. The tractor stopped.

The driver called out, "Samlall, what you doing there? Is that you, Neblet?"

"Is that fool, Yattieram," whispered Neblet.

Samlall waved his hand at the driver. The man cut the engine and joined them by the gate. Yattieram was an old Indian farmer. He peered through the fence. "What's going on there? An alligator in the yard?"

"Nah, a mango picker," whispered Neblet.

"Picking mango in the night? That man thinks this is a foreign country to pick fruits in the dark?"

Sarju was at the bottom of one of the trees. He stopped and picked up several fallen mangoes. He inspected them, tossed the bad ones by the jet skis, and dropped the palatable ones into the bag. He looked up and saw a set of the delicious fruit hanging about ten feet above. He examined the area under the tree and then stooped to pick up a long bamboo pole with a metal hook at one end. He raised the pole and hooked the fruits. The mangoes tumbled around him. One hit him on the head and pressed his cap firmly onto his scalp.

"What is he doing now, Neblett?" Samlall tugged at Neblet's hand.

"He is thiefing mangoes," uttered Yattieram.

Sarju had filled his bag. He took a mango and smelled it thoroughly. He pressed it to his nose and kneaded the fruit with his fingers. He brought the mango to his lips, bit a piece of skin, spat it out, then sucked on the delicious fruit.

"He is eating a mango," spluttered Neblet.

"That man is completely mad! He thinks he is at a restaurant eating dessert. Why he don't get out of there now?" croaked Samlall, squinting through the iron bars.

The front door of the house opened. The flickering light from the TV danced on the open door. Motielall emerged onto the landing and peered over the railing to survey the yard.

"Why is that madman sucking a mango? Motielall is going to catch him," whispered the tractor driver.

Neblett pressed his nose against the fence as Motielall climbed down the stairs.

"Run, Sir Beepat, run!" he shouted.

Sarju heard the shout. He glanced at the open door but walked casually to the front of the yard, where he came face-to-face with the enraged Motielall.

"What you doing in my yard, Beepat?" bellowed Motielall. "You were not only satisfied with snooping around; now you are trespassing on my property!"

Sarju sucked at the mango and observed the irate Motielall. "I came to pick some mangoes," he casually declared.

"You come here to steal mango off my tree? Your grandfather planted those fucking trees?"

Sarju squeezed some more mango juice into his mouth. He waved the bag in the direction of the mango trees. "Yes, those trees were planted by my grandfather. And the mangoes taste the same as when I was a boy in this yard."

"Good. But you are not a boy now, just a fucking thief," Motielall screamed.

A woman appeared at the doorway. His wife. She leaned over the railing and yelled. "You want me to call the police and tell them we have thieves in the yard, Motie?"

"No, no. Get inside. I don't need the police. I know this thief. I will deal with this crazy cunt myself."

The woman disappeared inside.

Sarju looked carefully at the house. Motielall followed his gaze.

"Why are you afraid to call the police, Motie? We can show them the paperwork to identify the real thief when they come."

Motielall flexed his hands menacingly. The gold rings on his fingers glinted in the light.

"What do you want from me, Beepat?" Motielall growled. "I never transacted any business with you. Why are you bothering my lawyer?"

"I just paid him a visit to let him know that my advocate from the U.S. Embassy would be in contact with both of you shortly. I hope all your documents are in order."

"Go to the law court and find out. Every inch of this property is documented there." Motielall's eyes flickered in anger. "Look, man, it looks like you are shopping for a coffin. Don't test my patience in my own yard before somebody got to dig your grave. I never transacted any business with you."

Sarju stared him in the face. "Transaction is a legal term, Motielall. But you don't know about anything *legal*! You owe me money for this property."

Motielall sputtered. "You are crazier than your drunken brother. You want me to smash your fucking teeth into your brain?"

Motielall chucked Sarju in the direction of the gate. Sarju spread his legs out, and dug his feet into the ground, resisting Motielall.

"You seized my property and didn't pay for it. You cheated my brother."

Motielall grabbed Sarju forcefully by the arm and turned his body to face the house. "Look at this house! You think this is yours? I tore down your old shit house and built this. You ever live in a palace like this? If you are looking for a place to squat, go and live with your brother in his shithouse."

Sarju wriggled out of his grasp. "This is legally my property, Motielall."

Motielall stared at Sarju in disbelief. He raised his hands in resignation. "It's a fucking madman I'm dealing with! Okay, if you want this property, go to the real estate office and make an offer. If I agree with your price, I will sell this palace to you."

"I want the money that you owe me, Motielall," Sarju insisted.

"And I want you out of my fucking yard," Motielall yelled, and with both hands, he pushed Sarju's body towards the gate. "I don't do business with American jailbirds. Get off my property, mango thief."

Sarju wobbled with the sudden push. His legs felt like jelly. He held onto Motielall for support, but Motielall punched him in the head several times. Sarju pitched forward, clutching and ripping Motielall's shirt with one hand, while his other hand held on to the bag of mangoes. Sarju panted rapidly as a sharp pain enveloped his chest.

"What happen, now? You can't talk? The American jailbird getting an epileptic fit," grunted Motielall as he tried to extricate himself from Sarju's body which was leaning against him.

Sarju heaved suddenly, and a green liquid gushed from his mouth, to cover Motielall's shirt and pants.

Motielall jumped away from Sarju. "You sick piece of shit," he yelled in disgust. "Don't spray your filthy vomit over me. Get out of my yard. If you ever come back here, I will kill you and nail your guts to that mango tree."

Sarju panted heavily, but his quavering voice reached the street. "You are threatening to kill me in front of witnesses! Look, the whole street heard you threaten to kill me. Look at the witnesses outside your yard."

Sarju appealed to the onlookers, "All of you are witnesses. You all hear Motielall threaten to kill me," he croaked.

Motielall gave Sarju a wide berth. He kept about six feet from him and looked at his fence. The three men were still clutching the bars and peering into the yard like constipated monkeys.

"And if your witnesses don't move from my fence, I will rip the skin off their bones, and you can be their witness too," shrieked Motielall and kicked Sarju in the rump. "Get off my fucking property, you diseased dog."

Sarju stumbled out of the yard with his bag of mangoes. He crossed the bridge and collapsed on the road, clutching his chest.

Motielall kicked the gate shut, spat in the direction of the men hovering over Sarju, and mounted the stairs to his house.

"You feeling okay, Sir Beepat? You getting a heart attack?" Neblet inquired anxiously.

"I am okay, Neblet," moaned Sarju, "just a little pain. Samlall? Here, boy, these are the mangoes of our youth. When last you tasted mangoes like this?"

Samlall leaned over his brother. "You are bleeding, Sarju."

"That is the price we pay for our heritage. We pay in blood for our own mangoes."

"That is your brother, Samlall?

Samlall stared at Yattieram and muttered sadly, "My little brother!"

"Oh, he is the one that left the island a long time ago? He used to be a teacher here. He come back for the wedding?"

"What wedding?" snapped Samlall with annoyance.

"What wedding? Your son's wedding. I got the invitation from the bride's family," persisted Yattieram. "It said the groom's father is Samlall Beepat from Belle Plaine. You is not the father?"

"This is not the place to discuss weddings," reprimanded Neblet. "This is a matter of sickness—bleeding from the forehead and a possible heart attack."

Sarju held out the bag to Samlall. He clutched at his stomach and panted.

Neblet looked into his face. "You are not okay, Sir Beepat. Let me take you to Dr. Morris."

Yatieram took a hard look at Sarju. "Yes, yes. You don't waste time when a heart attack is on the way. Put him in the trailer, and let's go to the hospital."

Sarju shook his head feebly. "No hospital! No hospital! I don't want to go to any hospital."

"No, no," assured Neblet. "He is not at the hospital. Dr. Morris is at home now. He will treat you at his house."

"I hope you learned your lesson now. This is not some foreign land that believe in talks. The next time you come to fight Motielall, you must walk with a garden fork and shovel stick," Yattieram warned and jumped on the tractor.

Neblet and Samlall hoisted Sarju by his arms and legs and slung him into the trailer. Sarju lay on the floor, which smelled of grass and dry coconuts, with his head cradled on his brother's lap.

Yattieram engaged the clutch, and the old tractor clattered away, with the three men in the trailer bouncing up and down like rag dolls.

Chapter 21. The Doctor

The tractor stopped in front of a two-story wooden house. Neblett vaulted over the side of the trailer and rushed into the yard.

"Dr. Morris! Dr. Morris!" he yelled, flapping his hands wildly.

A window on the second floor opened, and a head pushed out slowly, like the head of a turtle.

"Who is that? Neblet?"

"Yes, yes, it is me. I have Sir Beepat here in the trailer. He is very sick."

"Okay. I am coming. Bring him into the yard," drawled the head.

Neblet strung Sarju over his shoulder, and with the support of Samlall and Yatieram, he hauled him to a door on the first floor.

The door creaked open to reveal Dr. Morris, a tall black man with a pointed goatee and a small afro. "Take him to the bed," he ordered.

Neblet, who was familiar with the house, trudged to a small bed in a corner of the room and carefully swiveled to deposit Sarju face-up.

Dr. Morris scrutinized Sarju's face. "What is the matter with him?"

"Motielall beat him up. We all witnessed it," volunteered Samlall.

"He collapsed with a heart attack," added Neblet.

"I would check out his lungs, too. He not breathing too right," proffered Yatieram.

"Why didn't you take him to the hospital?"

"He is more determined than a jackass not to go to the hospital, Dr. Morris," informed Samlall.

"Okay, I will examine him now," decided Dr. Morris, "but all of you will have to wait outside."

The men left the room and sat on the trailer.

Dr. Morris put on a white coat and slipped on a pair of gloves. He stood at the side of the bed and waited for Sarju to open his eyes.

"Okay, Mr. Beepat, just sit up and unbutton your shirt."

Sarju raised himself slowly and painfully to a sitting position and unbuttoned his shirt.

Dr. Morris put on his stethoscope and stared at the mountainous bulge on Sarju's stomach.

"On second thought, I think you should remove your clothes."

"All my clothes?"

"Yes, I need to give you a complete examination."

As Sarju removed his pants, his pill bottle fell out. Dr. Morris leaned over, picked it up, and examined the label and contents.

Dr. Morris gave Sarju a thorough examination, as he promised. He probed and pressed with his tender fingers, and completed by listening to Sarju's heartbeat and breathing with the stethoscope.

He looked at the gash on Sarju's forehead. "How did you get this laceration on your forehead?"

"He hit me very hard."

"His hands were made of steel?" chuckled Morris.

"No, he had giant gold rings on his fingers."

"Well, that explains the cut in your skin. It just needs a bandage."

"How did you get involved with Motielall, Mr. Beepat?"

"He swindled my brother out of our property. I went to his house to confront him."

Dr. Morris shook his head in displeasure. "He is not a man to trifle with, Mr. Beepat. Motielall is involved in a lot of shady business and has connections to cover his crimes. To such people, the lives of their enemies don't mean much."

"What kind of business are the police not investigating?" Sarju inquired.

Dr. Morris paused. He opened a bottle of alcohol and cleaned the cut on Sarju's forehead. "The drug business. He has several fishing boats. I hear that he has communication with

drug runners in Venezuela and Columbia. They fly over the Atlantic and drop their bundles of drugs in the water. Motielall's sailors fish them from the water and transport them to bigger ships in the Atlantic or to Surinam."

"He does all that, and he was never caught?" Sarju was incredulous. "They found no evidence to put him away?"

"They caught him with a bale of marijuana once," Dr. Morris shared, "but it wasn't enough to put him away."

"But why not? A bale of marijuana is very heavy," Sarju declared.

Dr. Morris applied a bandage to Sarju's forehead. "When they presented the evidence in court, it wasn't a bale of marijuana. It was a bale of dry grass."

"I don't believe that the plane dropped a bale of grass. Somebody tampered with the evidence," Sarju suggested, searching Morris's face. "Who switched the marijuana with grass?"

"Who would be in a position to do that?" probed Morris, smiling.

"The police?"

Dr. Morris nodded. "That is why you should stay away from him."

He removed the gloves, tossed them in the trash basket, and washed his hands at a small metal sink.

"You can get dressed now," he instructed and stepped to a cabinet under the stairs that connected the ground floor to the second floor.

He tossed an adult diaper at Sarju, who was struggling to pull up his pants. "Put the other one in the garbage. I will give you a pack to take with you."

"I have diapers at home, Dr. Morris."

"And now you will have a dozen more," declared Dr. Morris and took a chair near the bed while Sarju finished dressing. He held the pill bottle up to the light and examined the label again.

Sarju glanced at Dr. Morris. He looked so refined and polished, very much unlike the rough and weather-beaten Neblet. He seemed like a professor, ready to give an important lecture at a seminar. A lump came to Sarju's throat. This man was once his student, and he had risen so high in the world. He was so proud of him! How proud Dr. Morris's parents would be of their son! Then he suddenly thought of his own son, Mitra, and a heaviness descended on him.

Sarju dressed and sat on the bed.

"Neblet said you came from America. When are you returning?" queried Dr. Morris.

"I will not be returning, doctor," Sarju muttered. "I am here to the end."

"I see," declared Dr. Morris, shaking the bottle of pills. "Do you know why you are taking these tablets, Mr. Beepat?"

"It is for the pain, doctor. Pain is a constant companion now."

"What did your doctor in America tell you about your condition?"

Sarju paused and looked at the wall behind the doctor. "You probably suspect after that examination. I have stomach cancer, Dr. Morris."

"That was not hard to determine. The tumor in your stomach is quite sizeable. I suspect that it has spread to other parts of your body as well," stated Dr. Morris. "We have only the basic facilities on the island. But I can refer you to Georgetown, where we can have a CT scan done to see how far it has progressed."

Sarju smiled sadly. "I already did that, Dr. Morris. A few weeks ago, the doctor pronounced on my lifeline. The sand in the hourglass is running out. I only came here because your friend, Neblett, insisted."

Dr. Morris sighed. "Well, this medicine would not be as effective as before. I can prescribe a stronger dosage. If the pain doesn't recede, you will have to go to the hospital. That is unavoidable."

"Thank you, doctor, but no hospital," Sarju grinned ruefully. "Now, I have to convince Neblet."

"Does he know about the cancer?" queried Dr. Morris, with his hands clasped.

"No one on the island knows but you, doctor," Sarju confided, "and I prefer to keep it that way."

"I understand," replied Dr. Morris. "Well, if not the hospital, you can come here every evening, and I will give you some of the strong stuff—morphine. That is all we have for the pain. There is nothing after that."

"I know. And after that, I will be nothing. Just a memory to some. How much would the treatment cost?"

Dr. Morris smiled. "Nothing! Absolutely nothing! Service to a former teacher, that is all."

Sarju examined Morris's face. "Do you remember me, Dr. Morris?"

Dr. Morris chuckled. "You think Neblet is the only one who remembers you? Whenever I hear the old saying, *Spare the rod and spoil the child*, you always come to mind. You didn't just spare the rod; for the short time you were my teacher, you beat the love of learning into me."

Sarju's eyes brimmed with tears. He muttered, "I am sorry if I was too harsh with the whip."

"But you instilled the love of science in me, Sir Beepat," Dr. Morris admitted. "Neblet remembers his story well. But he wasn't the only one impacted by your lesson on the life cycle of the salmon."

Sarju smiled with tenderness as he looked at his former student. "Imagine that the three of us are connected by the story of the salmon."

"Imagine that, eh?" reflected Dr. Morris. "I am here as a doctor because this island of Wakenaam is where it all began. Where my interest in science started. Because of you."

Sarju looked down at his shoes, stained by the island's mud. "Neblet is still searching for his salmon, but he has overlooked me. I am the salmon that has returned to die."

For a while, Sarju and Dr. Morris were silent. There was nothing more to say. The river breeze entered the room carrying the strains of a folk song that was being sung by Neblett, Samlall, and Yattieram. They cocked their heads to listen:

One day me been to Wakenaam
And me see Sitira on de dam
And me ask Sitira
What she ah do deh
Sitira raise up she petticoat
And wine like a boxing board
Sitira more man deh
Oh, Sitira more man deh

Sarju struggled to get off the bed. Dr. Morris helped him to his feet, put his hand around his shoulder, and led his old teacher to join the singers on the trailer outside.

Chapter 22- The Wedding

Sarju mounted the stairs to the upper level of Hassan's house. He was dressed in a brown cotton shirt and beige pants. His clothes were new, purchased at a clothing store in Belle Plaine. There was a tailor on the premises, and he made the necessary alterations. Sarju had a close fit, unlike the loose clothing that he had been wearing owing to his rapid weight loss.

He stepped into the dining room and joined Arifa and her parents at the table.

Nizam whistled. "Are you sure you are not going to get married today? You look like a groom, man."

"Yes, Mr. Beepat, you look very elegant indeed." Fazeela grinned and handed him a plate with toast and a slice of avocado.

Arifa giggled. "And I have something for you that would make the people at the wedding very jealous."

Sarju grinned, biting on a piece of toast. "Thank you, but it is just common clothing. I couldn't get the elaborate Indian garments."

He finished the toast and avocado and took a sip of water. He placed his hand in his pocket and removed a small pouch of white powder. He put a spoonful of the powder in a glass of water and stirred vigorously.

Arifa observed the spoon spinning in the glass. "Why are you mixing the milk powder with water? Don't you want to put it in your coffee?"

Sarju raised the water to his eyes. "This is not milk powder. It is a kind of medicine that was invented by Dr. Morris."

"Oh, what does the medicine do?" quizzed Arifa.

"Well, it relaxes the muscles in the stomach. It fools the muscle to believe that everything is alright," explained Sarju.

"It still looks like milk powder. How does it taste?"

Sarju took a sip and wrinkled his nose. "Not tasty at all. It tastes like chalk."

"Does it work better than the other method?"

"Other method?" Sarju was puzzled.

"The bucket, silly. Do you still have to use a bucket or a bag?"

"It is better. Dr. Morris prepared a very effective medicine, and I am getting used to it. But I still keep the bag or bucket nearby. Just in case."

Nizam looked at Arifa and smiled. "Dr. Morris is a very good doctor. You will be like him one day."

Fazeela beamed at Sarju. "And Arifa, do you know that Mr. Beepat once taught Dr. Morris?"

Arifa squealed. "He did? You taught a doctor? A real doctor?"

Sarju grinned. "Well, when I taught him, he wasn't a doctor. He was around your age. But very smart. Like you."

A big smile lit up Arifa's face. "Oh, I forgot to thank you for the mangoes. It tasted like someone had drizzled honey on the flesh. Where did you buy them?"

"I didn't buy them. They came from my grandfather's tree."

"*You* have a grandfather? How old is he? As old as this island?"

Sarju and her parents laughed. Arifa looked puzzled.

"The trees were planted by my grandfather a long time ago."

"Oh, I see. So, now you own the mangoes."

"In a kind of way," replied Sarju. "My grandfather's father planted the first tree. When the tree produced mangoes, my grandfather ate the fruits and planted the seeds on his land. Four trees grew. Now, only two remain."

"So you and your father didn't plant any?" Arifa inquired solemnly.

"No. There was no need to, then. We were living on the land. We had lots of mangoes from the four trees." Sarju took a sip of the milky liquid. "The mangoes are very special to me."

"Because they are very sweet?"

"No, because they remind me of the hands of my grandfather and great-grandfather. When I eat a mango from the tree, I think of their hands planting the seeds. The hands that fed me and helped me."

Atifa considered that and nodded her head thoughtfully. "Do you have any land here, Mr. Beepat?"

"No, unfortunately, all is gone."

"But we have land here. You can plant a mango tree here."

Nizam winked at Sarju. "That is true, Mr. Beepat. We have lots of space for your mango tree."

"Yes," Arifa agreed. "You can plant one, and I will remember your hands. Even the hands of your grandfather and great-grandfather."

Sarju gazed into her innocent eyes. "Okay. We will plant it together. And you will remember it as your own, too."

Arifa scraped the eggs off her plate. "Your student, Dr. Morris? He remembers that you helped him."

Sarju choked on the liquid he was sipping. He gulped and contemplated Arifa. "Yes, he remembers that, Arifa."

"Oh, so he has a story with you too! But different from the mango one."

The puttering sound of a tractor came through the open doorway.

"Sir Beepat, Sir Beepat!" someone shouted.

Nizam poked his head through the window. "It's Neblet and Old Yattieram."

Sarju rose from the chair.

Arifa frowned. "Neblet was your student too, Mr. Beepat?"

"Yes, yes," Sarju admitted. "I taught both of them in your primary school."

Arifa pushed her chair back. "Well, you didn't do a good job with Neblet. I can see that he never paid attention to your lessons."

Sarju chuckled. "How can you tell, Arifa?"

"He just roams across the island without a care. And the students caught him picking mangoes from a tree that is over a grave. A *dead man's* grave!"

"Oh, I will tell him to stop," promised Sarju, and turned to the door.

"Don't leave yet. I have something for you."

Arifa ran to the kitchen and returned with a rose on a short stem. She had cut the flower from a tree in the yard.

She stood in front of Sarju. "Let me pin this to your shirt. You will look better than all the other wedding guests."

Sarju held on to the back of a chair for support. He kneeled so that Arifa could get to his shirt pocket. She bit her lips as she worked the pin through the stem of the rose. He examined her small face so close to him, and memories of his daughter as a child flooded his mind. She finished her task and gave him a peck on the cheek. Sarju reached forward, collected her in a great hug, and with eyes brimming with tears, he stumbled down the stairs to the road.

———————⟡———————

NEBLET AND YATTIERAM were well-dressed for the wedding. Yattiram wore an Indian kurta over black pants. His feet were still clad in his farmer's rubber boots. Neblet, on the other hand, was dressed in a blue jacket and blue pants with shiny black shoes.

The trailer attached to the tractor was well-swept and cleaned. There were three plastic chairs tied to the sides. Neblet was seated on one and extended a hand to help Sarju climb in. Sarju took his seat, and Yattieram's old tractor clanked and puttered to Samlall's house.

The tractor stopped on the road in front of Samlall's hut.

Neblet jumped off the trailer. "You wait here, Sir Beepat. I will get him. I will get the father of the groom."

Yattieram looked over to Sarju. "Your brother is a lucky man today. The son is marrying a rich man in Maria's Pleasure, while the father chooses to live like a drunk in that old house."

Neblet returned to the trailer with a sour expression on his face. "The man is drunk, Sir Beepat. He is dead drunk and won't wake up."

"Fucking fool," muttered Sarju, and he hopped off the trailer. He and Neblet hustled down the passageway to the hut. Samlall lay fast asleep on the bench. His mouth was open, and a bee was buzzing around his nose. An empty bottle of rum was at the base of the bench.

Sarju kicked at the bottle, which flew and shattered against the fence.

"You didn't tell him that we would pick him up this morning, Sir Beepat?"

"Isn't he the one who arranged for Yattieram to pick us up? I am his brother, not his keeper! Why do I have to remind him to be sober for his son's wedding?" retorted Sarju angrily.

Samlall snored loudly, and the bee rocked back and forth with the current from his open mouth. Neblet leaned over Samlall to brush the bee away. "We should toss him in the canal to sober him up, but he might just sink and drown."

Sarju looked at his brother with disgust. He glanced at the overgrown bushes in the yard. "I wish an alligator would crawl out and bite him on his ass. We can't do anything else. We have to leave this drunk here."

"But he is the father. He has to go," protested Neblet, waving the bee from his friend's open mouth.

"Go to do what? Create more embarrassment for his son?" remarked Sarju bitterly. "That bee should enter his mouth and live in his intestines. Sting him every time he takes a drink."

Neblet entered the hut and tossed the package with the Indian wedding clothes to Sarju.

"Well, you have to do his job now. Change your clothes now for the ceremony."

Sarju dropped the package on the bench next to Samlall's head. "Leave that here. If he sobers up and comes to his senses today, he will need his clothes. The wedding will still be on. I am sure his son will still welcome him."

———————◉———————

THE TRACTOR PUTTERED its way out of Belle Plaine and parked outside a small Hindu temple that was in the middle of a spacious plot of land. Sarju and his two companions joined a group of men standing outside the temple. The men were observing a team of Indian *tassa* drummers tuning up their drums. A wide wooden bridge led to the temple's entrance, where a welcoming arch was decorated with hanging tassels of marigold flowers.

Neblet crossed the bridge and joined the crowd of people standing by the temple's main door. An old man emerged from the temple and conversed with some people. Sarju recognized him. He was the pandit or Hindu priest. He had been his father's friend and had officiated at many family events.

Neblet and a young man dressed in an Indian wedding outfit left the crowd and walked across the bridge.

Neblet introduced them. "This is your uncle, Pradeep. He came from America for your wedding."

The lithe young man had a neat, small beard, and his face was very familiar.

Pradeep embraced Sarju. "Thank you for coming, uncle!"

"I appreciate your invitation. You look like your grandfather, you know!"

"That is what my mother tells me."

Pradeep surveyed the people gathered on the road. He looked at Neblet, who had gone to observe the *tassa* drummers. "I don't see my father. Didn't he come with you and Neblet?"

Sarju coughed in embarrassment. "He couldn't make it. He was not feeling well."

Pradeep grunted in displeasure. "But why did I expect him to come? He made his choice. Rum wins out over his family again."

Sarju reached out to touch his hand. "He asked me to stand in for him."

A woman in a red sari glided across the bridge to them. Sarju recognized Saroj, Samlall's wife. She had aged gracefully over the years. Her hair was streaked gray, but she still maintained her beauty.

She hugged Sarju. "Sarju! What a surprise! You look ..."

Sarju looked into her eyes and could read her thoughts as she viewed his almost skeletal frame.

She touched his hand affectionately. "We thought you had forgotten the island for good. But I am glad you are here to witness your nephew's wedding."

"Your husband is not here, Ma!"

The smile disappeared from Saroj's face. "I don't know what to say about that man. He changed from being a saint to the disciple of the devil in a rum bottle."

"I will perform the duties as the father if you wish."

"Thank you, Sarju. His wedding will still be special without Samlall. Who did you come with?"

"Oh! Two men from the island."

"I mean your family," she laughed. "Did they come with you?"

"No, I came alone to the island. I left them on another island, New York."

The pandit came up to them. "What is happening now? How long are we going to wait for Samlall? He thinks he could just make a son and forget to attend his wedding ceremony!"

The pandit had not lost any of his brusqueness with age. His unsmiling face was now marked with more frown lines since Sarju last saw him. The hair on the lobes of his ears was longer now but completely gray.

Saroj tried to placate him. "We can start now, Pandit. Samlall is not here, but his brother will stand in as his father."

The ancient priest stared at Sarju. "You, the boy who left for America and didn't return?"

"Yes, Pandit," admitted Sarju sheepishly.

"You know, I did all the religious ceremonies for your parents. Even the last one, where I prayed for their souls to receive *moksha*, or salvation." He glared at Sarju with disdain. "I didn't see you at their funerals."

Sarju stared at the priest and smiled. A thought played in his mind: *Don't worry, your job is not yet done, Pandit. Very soon, you will be performing a ceremony to help another soul attain nirvana.*

The pandit inspected him from top to bottom. Sarju felt like he was having a colonoscopy all over.

"You don't have to do anything special. No speeches, nothing. Just stand by his side when the bride's parents welcome him to the family and stand behind him when I conduct the religious ceremony."

The priest glanced at the *tassa* players and gave a signal. The drummers' hands attacked their instruments; the air was split by the rhythmic riot of the drums, and a crowd of people began to dance, flailing their limbs to the pulsating beat. Saru saw a blue jacket weaving and undulating in the crowd. It was Neblet. His limbs moved with fluidity as he matched the antics and artistry of the other dancers.

With the beat of drums echoing in the background, Sarju, Pradeep, and a gathering of people from the groom's side made their way across the bridge to the entrance of the temple, where they were greeted by the parents of the bride. The pandit recited a few prayers, and he led the way into the temple, which had been principally occupied by the bride's friends and relatives.

The people sat on sheets of white cloth that were spread on the wooden floor of the temple. Sarju and Saroj sat behind Pradeep as the pandit conducted the wedding proceedings in Hindi and English. The smoke from the incense rising lazily into the air and the sweet aroma from the various items the pandit was burning in an iron box or *kund,* reminded Sarju of his own marriage. It was a cold day in New York when he and Meera sat in a basement temple, surrounded by a few relatives and friends, as the pandit droned on and on. Sarju still remembered a part of a prayer from his marriage. It was a prayer to the Hindu God, Krishna: *Oh, Krishna, when you are with me, I am everything; when you are not with me, I am nothing.* He glanced at the profile of Pradeep, shimmering from the light of the leaping flames of the *kund,* and detected a feeling of happiness and contentment as he sat beside his adoring bride.

The ceremony came to an end when the bride and groom stood and circled the holy fire seven times to signify their commitment to each other for seven lifetimes. Sarju thought of his brother Samlall. *What a fool he was to have avoided this occasion.* He shut his eyes and prayed that Pradeep and his bride would be happy forever.

Pradeep and his bride were escorted to two throne-like wicker chairs at the far end of the temple. People lined up to congratulate and offer gifts to the newlyweds. Sarju considered joining the line but decided against it as the line was long; the people there were all relatives or close friends who were excited to be in the company of the newlywed couple.

Sarju left the temple through a side door and came upon a spacious backyard, half of it covered by a shed. Under the shed were several long tables coupled to benches, and enormous iron pots bubbling over wood fires sprayed the air with delicious, spicy aromas.

Some of the wedding guests were already seated at the tables. Neblet and Yattieram beckoned for him to join them.

"That was a long session, Sir Beepat. After listening to the word of God, now is the time to celebrate with the "seven-curry"—the wedding food." Neblet was excited at the prospect of savoring the vegetarian meal served at Indian functions, which consisted of several curries.

One of the young temple assistants distributed a lotus leaf to each diner.

Yattieram noticed Sarju staring at the leaf and laughed. "That leaf is not part of the salad, you know. That is used as a plate."

Sarju smiled. He knew that, but he thought that the tradition of serving food on a lotus leaf had died on the island. He was pleased to note that the past was still wedded to the present.

Another assistant came by with a large stainless steel basin of rice. Sarju raised his hands in alarm when he saw the sizeable mound of rice in the large pot spoon. "Just a little bit of rice, please."

The assistant dumped half of the spoon and moved on.

Sarju saw Neblet form a hole with his finger in the center of his mound of rice. He remembered and did the same. A man with a bucket of *dhal*, the thick, yellow, split pea soup, hovered over and ladled a helping of the liquid into the hole on the mound of rice. Sarju immersed his senses in the yellow dhal, speckled with pepper, cumin, and tiny bits of roasted garlic. Other servers came by, one by one, to spoon out the various vegetarian curries. Sarju accepted the spinach and pumpkin but declined the others. He looked at the mixture in his leaf and realized that it was too much load to put on his stomach.

Neblet noted Sarju's very light leaf. "This is not a two-curry event, Sir Beepat. You are missing five."

With his leaf filled to maximum capacity, Neblet waded into the food expertly using his fingers, as was the tradition. Sarju had not eaten with his fingers for years and was looking at Neblet and Yattieram with envy when an assistant noticed.

"Do you need a spoon, uncle?"

Sarju was relieved by the offer.

Yattieram commented through a spoonful of rice mixed with various vegetables. "He is an American. He forgot all we customs in Wakenaam." He nudged Neblet and laughed. "Don't give him a knife before he cut up that leaf and eat it like lettuce."

The food was delicious. It tasted the way his mother cooked. Memories of his mother stirring a rice or curry pot over the wood stove flickered in his mind.

Sarju closed the leaf, leaving a lot of food inside. He didn't want to throw up in the full view of the guests and create an embarrassing scene at Pradeep's wedding. He walked over to a garbage bin and deposited the leaf, then returned to the table, where he took a glass and poured some water from a carafe there. He reached into his pocket and retrieved Dr. Morris's pouch. He stirred some of the powder into the water.

The young assistant, who had provided the spoon, rushed over. "You don't have to do that, uncle. We have milk in the kitchen!"

Sarju smiled at the kind young man. "Thanks. But this is not milk. It is medicine for my stomach."

The assistant smiled with relief and moved away.

Neblet looked at Yattieram. "Milk is good for ulcerated stomachs, you know."

Yattieram gave him a disapproving look. "I can't use milk. It lacerates my stomach. Anytime I drink milk, I got to run to the shit house."

Neblet's and Yattiram's leaves were empty. They looked around and beckoned the servers for seconds.

Neblet noticed Sarju's expression. "You think this second round is still seven curry or fourteen curry, Sir Beepat?"

The shed was almost filled with wedding guests. He knew that the line to greet the newlyweds would be manageable now. He left his two companions flexing their fingers in the many curried rice and reentered the temple through the side door.

There was no line, but some people were gathered by the two throne-like chairs. He recognized Saroj and the bride's parents, who had welcomed them earlier. A tall, burly, elderly man stood nearby, twirling his thick mustache.

Sarju shook Pardeep's hands. "Congratulations, Pradeep. Consider this your first step to eternal happiness."

Pradeep beamed. "Thank you, uncle. This is my wife. Nanda."

Sarju joked. "You forgot that I was a witness to your wedding?"

Nanda laughed. "Thanks for coming, uncle. Pradeep said it was the first time you saw each other."

Nanda was indeed very beautiful. Pradeep was a lucky man.

"Yes, it is the first time. And the best time was because I saw him get married."

Sarju reached into his pocket and dug out an envelope. He handed it to Pradeep. "A little something for your wedding. I forgot the card. Sorry."

Pradeep accepted the envelope. "Thanks, uncle. The card is not important. You are."

Nanda nodded in agreement. "How long are you here for, uncle?"

"Just a few days more. Then I will leave the island."

Nanda's father, Dilip, stared at Sarju. He scratched his head. "I remember something about you. Didn't you teach in Zeelandia many years ago?"

"Yes. A very long time ago."

"And you married an island girl?"

Sarju replied. "No. I married a girl from Berbice. We got married in New York."

"Oh, well, that was just a rumor then," declared Dilip.

"What rumor?" his wife inquired.

"There was a rumor that he eloped and married the caretaker's daughter. A common woman named Lalita."

Nanda's mother put a hand on her husband's shoulder. "And now you know that it was just another island rumor."

"Why don't you come over to the house? We are having a reception after we leave here," Nanda invited.

The elderly man with the mustache blew his nose loudly, placed a handkerchief over his face, and walked away.

Neblet and Yattieram appeared at the door.

"Yes, uncle. And you can invite your friends. We would love to have you all," added Pradeep.

———◦———

A PROCESSION OF VEHICLES left the temple for Nanda's parents' house in Maria's Pleasure, a few villages away. The few cars and minibuses in the procession were decorated with banners and garlands of artificial flowers. Bringing up the rear was Yattieram's old tractor, with Neblet and Sarju reclining on their plastic chairs.

The two-story house in the village was huge, a giant compared to the ant-sized houses nearby. A marble stairway led to the first floor, and on the second floor, a large glass door opened out into a balcony.

The vehicles parked on the side of the road and the wedding guests were met at the gate by another pandit, a young man, who welcomed the newlyweds with some relevant chants and prayers.

The yard was very spacious, and under a white tarpaulin tent, many round tables with accompanying chairs were placed around the periphery, exposing a wide area in the middle. This area was the dance floor for the more enthusiastic guests.

There was a bar at one end and a long buffet table where attendants in white clothing were laying out an assortment of dishes. The food on the table was not only vegetarian fare, but there was a great variety of meat dishes.

A man with an ice pick stood in a corner of the yard, striking at a massive block of ice. He dug his pick into the ice to break it into slivers and cubes to be used at the bar. Specks of ice flew up and stuck into his beard like snowflakes. It reminded Sarju of snow. Sarju loved the snow. He remembered the last time he walked through the snow in New York City with his two children. Mitra had stuck his tongue out and had walked several blocks, trying to catch the snowflakes. Aarti had teased him that his tongue would freeze and break off his mouth like shattered glass. Like the specks of ice that flew into the air, a cold and dark thought swirled around Sarju's mind. Now that his children were grown, independent, and distant from him, he could now melt quietly into the sunlight of Wakenaam.

Sarju chose a table at the back, far from where the speakers of the music set were being installed. Neblet and Yattieram joined him.

Yattieram leaned forward conspiratorially. "They *speechifying* in the house, Sarju. All the relatives and important guests are toasting the married couple. Why don't you go and say something nice about the boy?"

Neblet snickered. "Say what? Is today he meet the boy! Remember, I had to introduce him? He wouldn't know if the boy was good or bad."

"If they ask me to *speechify*, I would say the boy is a good boy. One time I went to the bank in Georgetown to get a loan, and the people there gave me a royal run around; Pradeep stepped in to help me. He didn't ask me for a bribe like the others, so he is an upstanding boy."

"You should go and make a toast with that speech. That is what the uncle-in-law Buddhu would want to hear," encouraged Neblet.

"I can't do that," admitted Yattieram. "I am not officially an invited guest to the reception. I only get a written invitation for the temple."

"And the only thing I know about Pradeep is what he did for me whenever I find Samlall drunk and lying in the street. When I pick up his father and take him home, he would always give me a few dollars. He is a very good tipper."

Neblet sniffed the air. He looked at an area by the fence. A man was barbecuing chicken, and the aroma of roasting meat permeated the surroundings.

Yattieram rubbed his stomach. "I have no room for food now, but I can certainly take a drink."

Neblet laughed. "You are too old for this business. My stomach can stretch like socks. After the music start, I will find room for that chicken. I will start the party now with a drink."

Yattieram got up. "What you drinking, Sarju? You have to make a toast at your nephew's wedding. That milk powder is no substitute for a drink."

Neblet interjected. "Sir Beepat doesn't drink. He is not like we island people. He is a *sophisty* kind of man."

Sarju chuckled at the description. "Thank you, Neblet. My stomach rejects alcohol now. I will toast with water."

"Well, I will bring you our island special—coconut water," offered Neblet, and he and Yattieram bounded off to the bar.

The music started, and Hindi film songs vibrated the air. Sarju's eyes were captivated by the dust on top of a large speaker. The tiny dusty particles jumped up and down in a current of air. Neblet and Yattieram returned with their drinks and a glass of coconut water for Sarju.

"What you looking at, Sarju? That loudspeaker is not important. Let we drink to the health of the couple," offered Yattieram. "This is whisky. My stomach only rejects milk."

"Yes, let we drink out Buddhu whisky," supported Neblet.

The men downed their glasses while Sarju took a careful sip of the coconut water.

A few men and women were on the dance floor, moving like the dust on top of the speaker. The music attacked Neblet; he began to shake his feet. He put down his glass, hung his jacket over the chair, and joined the shaking frenzy on the dance floor. Yattieram, infected with the merriment, downed his glass and joined Neblet. Yattieram's rubber boots were impeding his movement. He kicked them off violently to free his feet; one flew to the top of the tent and landed behind Sarju's table. Sarju chuckled as he retrieved the boots and stored them under the table for safekeeping.

Pradeep, his wife, and the burly mustached man who had been with them in the temple were weaving between guests, shaking hands, talking, and laughing.

Pradeep spotted him and ambled over to the table with a glass in hand. "Where were you, uncle? We were in the house, meeting friends and relatives from both sides. I wanted you to be there with me."

"I was here observing the set-up. I will meet the others in due course."

Pradeep sat with a glass in hand. He looked at Sarju's glass. "Coconut water?"

Sarju smiled at his nephew. "As good as any liquid to toast your happiness."

He raised his glass, and Pradeep took a drink with him.

Pradeep observed Sarju. "Thank you again for being part of the ceremony, uncle."

"I am truly sorry your father couldn't make it. But I am sure he is sending good vibrations and wishes to you."

Pradeep sighed and ran his hands through his hair. "His best wishes are curses with his absence today. But what difference does it make? Many years ago, he abandoned my mother and me for alcohol."

"I don't know what happened to Samlall, Pradeep. I was out of the picture for too long."

"It doesn't matter now, uncle. He was not here for the final act. The time for him has passed." Pradeep looked outside the yard at the approaching darkness. "This day is almost over."

Sarju touched his nephew's hand. "No, son. Not over. Another aspect of your life has begun. Neither sun nor rain can erase the fact that he is your father and would want the best for you."

Pradeep looked sadly at his uncle. "That is the most painful part. I wanted the best for him; that is why I needed him here today."

Pradeep turned around and saw his wife beckoning. As he got up, the burly, mustached man ambled over to the table and nodded to Pradeep.

Pradeep introduced the man to Sarju. "Here is a chance to meet an important person in the family. This is Nanda's uncle, Buddhu. Her father's elder brother and head of the family."

Sarju stretched out his hand; the man ignored him and pulled up a chair as Pradeep made his way to his wife.

Buddhu emptied his glass and looked around. He beckoned to a man, probably a helper at the bar. "Bring me a large whisky. No ice. What are you drinking?"

Sarju shook his head and displayed his half-filled glass.

"So, you are the American, Sarju Beeepat, eh?"

Sarju nodded his head.

The man swiveled his head, his eyes taking in the operations under the tent and the house at the side. "Your nephew is a lucky man. He has married into a royal family."

"Royal?" Sarju inquired curiously.

"Yes, look around you. This is how we live. Compare this to how your brother lives!"

The helper returned with the drink. He handed it to Buddhu and quickly slid away.

Sarju observed Buddhu with distaste. "He didn't live like that all the time, you know! Somebody robbed him of his property."

"So he says. So he says. But, fortunately, I didn't object to the marriage. Samlall worked as a clerk in my rice mills for many years. He was a good and reliable man until he embraced the evil of drinking. I had to fire him. But I don't believe children should pay for the sins of their fathers."

Buddhu sipped on his drink and smirked. "Unless they commit murder and are convicted felons."

Sarju's eyes narrowed in anger. "What are you saying, Buddhu?"

"I am saying that if it were your son, I would have chased him off the island. No relative of mine would get the chance to ruin my reputation by marrying the seed of a convicted murderer. Yes, Sarju Beepat. I heard you lived in Sing Sing, but on this island, we sing another song."

"Do you know how I ended up in Sing Sing?" Sarju demanded.

"It doesn't matter what you did. All that matters is what the police, jury, and judge said. They found you guilty and put you away because you were a menace to society."

"So there is no justification for a crime?"

"In my experience, no. I have donated to prisons and have spoken to many prisoners. All said they were innocent. If that is the case, then we should jail the judges and the juries and let the criminals loose."

"I never said I was innocent. I accepted what I did."

"Yes, but you were convicted. People are accused of murder and are put before the court. They have no records unless they are convicted. People judge criminals by their conviction, not by their reputation."

Buddhu took another drink and turned to face the dancers. He pointed to a tall man with a yellow shirt, twirling his hands in the air and gyrating his hips to a racy Hindi song.

"That man was accused of murdering his brother and his nephew four years ago. The police held him because there was a witness. A fisherman saw when he shot his relatives. The witness provided a sworn, cast iron statement to the prosecution."

Sarju sneered. "So, where is your justice system now? The murderer is free to dance at your niece's wedding. He is a respected guest of yours."

Buddhu gazed at Sarju. "But the system worked. The man faced his day in court, and the defense lawyer asked for the witness to testify in court."

"So, why is he free?" demanded Sarju.

Buddhu emptied his glass and beckoned to the bar helper.

"They couldn't produce the witness," he declared firmly. "The fisherman was lost at sea. The ship's captain, Crankshaft Willie, reported that he fell overboard during a storm. No witness, no conviction."

Sarju stared incredulously at Buddhu. "Crankshaft Willie? The murderer who is in the Venezuelan jail."

"Yes. For Pradeep's sake, I am glad you did not make his acquaintance," Buddhu continued. "The dancer is free of murder, while *you* were convicted of murder. I only learned of your crime a few days ago. It was too late to raise any objection. And Pradeep has proven to be a fine young man, despite the condition of his father."

Sarju's eyes narrowed. "And the man who is responsible for his condition is probably a business acquaintance of yours."

Buddu looked around for his drink. "Don't involve me in any other business, Beepat. My business has always been rice. I buy the farmer's rice and feed it to my mills. I only sell rice."

"And you are okay if your business acquaintances rob, steal, and murder to get their way?"

"I told you that I deal only with rice. There is a business fraternity on the island. There is also the law, but that is not my business either. And the reputation of my family should not be clouded by your actions. Understood?"

The helper returned with a glass of whisky. Buddhu seized the glass. "I suspect you are trying to keep *your past* a secret, too! That is okay by me. My lips are sealed. But when are you leaving this island?"

Sarju put down his glass and got up. "Soon. But not soon enough. I won't cloud your home with my presence any longer."

Sarju weaved his way among the dancers under the tent and out into the yard. Saroj and Pradeep were standing by the gate, bidding goodbye to a few wedding guests.

"Are you leaving so early, uncle?" Pradeep queried.

"Yes, yes. It was a long day."

Saroj smiled. "We are so happy that you came. Will you be seeing Samlall tonight?"

"Yes, I may drop in to see him before I go home to Zeelandia."

"You mind taking a bag of food for him? At least he can have a taste of his son's wedding."

"I will take it for you. No problem."

Saroj walked back to the house. Sarju glanced back at the tent. Buddhu was at the table conversing with Yattieram, who was yanking on his boots.

"I notice you had a long conversation with Buddhu. Did you know him while you lived here?" probed Pradeep.

"I didn't know him personally. I knew that his parents owned the rice mill. That is about all."

"It seems that you hardly know anyone here, uncle."

"Even though the island is small, I never moved around much. Most of my friends from high school left the island. I was one of the few who returned but finally left."

Sarju looked at the house. "You have married into royalty, Pradeep."

Pradeep snorted. "That is what he told you? Well, I don't want anything that isn't mine."

"How did you meet your wife, Pradeep? On this island?"

"We attended the same elementary school here, but we didn't know each other then. She left to attend high school in the city. After I completed high school on the island, I went to the university, where we met and got to know each other. We both graduated and ended up working at the same bank. The rest, you know."

"Did Buddhu know that Samlall was your father?"

Pradeep paused and gazed at the tent. Buddhu was still sitting with Yattieram. "He knew eventually. But I don't think it mattered to him."

"But he fired your father," asserted Sarju.

"Yes, but after several warnings. My father messed up several of the man's accounts and made him lose money. He had to let him go. Buddhu protects his family by preserving their assets."

Saroj walked up to them and handed Sarju a large shopping bag. "Here you are, Sarju. I have packed for both you and Samlall."

Sarju hefted the bag several times. "So much food? Do you think we have another wedding at Samlall's place?"

"It is not a lot. Just a variety. You and Samlall will finish it in no time."

"Well, thank you, Saroj. I had better go before Samlall's food gets cold."

Pradeep looked back at the tent. "How are you getting home, uncle? You shouldn't trust a drunken man behind the wheel of a tractor."

Sarju chuckled. "Don't worry. I am not going with him. I will walk out to the main road. A minibus is bound to pass for Belle Plaine."

The front door opened, and a man and a woman stepped out.

Saroj looked at the door. "You don't have to walk. These people are driving to Belle Plaine. They will give you a lift."

Chapter 23- Revelations

Sarju crept gingerly down the dark path to Samlall's hut with the bag of food in his hand. The door of the hut was open, and the lone light bulb attached to the ceiling cast an elliptical patch of light over the bench.

Samlall was lying with his eyes closed. The package with the wedding clothes had slipped off the bench and was resting against an empty rum bottle lodged against the rail at the bottom. The stiff river breeze had bent it against the bottle, and the package looked like a little child trying to evade the restraint of a parent.

Sarju rested the food bag on the bench and observed his brother. He shook him vigorously by the arms.

Samlall opened his eyes, glared at Sarju, and then sat up with his elbows on his thighs and his palms over his eyes.

"What? Not awake yet? The entire day in a drunken state?"

Samlall removed his hands from his eyes and glared at his brother. "Who said I am drunk? I was just sending good vibrations to my son."

Sarju sat beside him and pushed the bag across. "And your wife felt your vibrations and sent some wedding food for you. Your son would have appreciated it more if you were there gyrating at his wedding."

A little smile crossed Samlall's face. "That is why I sent you. You were always the better dancer."

"Your son was very disappointed," Sarju pointed out softly.

Samlall barked, "You think I wanted him to be unhappy? Look around you, man. This is where I live. Do you see a palace here?"

Samlall reached down and retrieved the package of clothing. He placed it against the bag of food. "I couldn't keep my job! I couldn't keep a wife and family. I couldn't hold on to my house, and you want me to be a proud father?"

"Then ask yourself what created all this?" Sarju persisted.

Samlall snorted. "And you think the answer is alcohol? The *American* knows the answer to every problem!"

"Didn't you promise him you would attend his wedding and perform the duty of a father? But, of course, you were too drunk to open your eyes this morning."

Samlall gave his brother a scornful look. "And what would have been my wedding gift? I live like a beggar. It was easier to pretend to be drunk."

Sarju leaned down, grabbed the empty rum bottle from under the bench, and waved it in Samlall's face. "Pretend? What is this? Medicine?"

Samlall swatted the bottle away. It pitched behind the bench and rolled into the thick grass. "You should thank me. I gave you the chance to be a father."

Sarju shook his head in disappointment. "That was your duty. It was your son. Take some responsibility for your actions, man." He sighed. "You are not a child, Samlall. Your brain is still functioning. You should have done the right thing today of all the days."

Samlall shouted, "And for once, I did the right thing, and you blame me!"

"*You* did the right thing."

"You think it was easy, Mr. American? I did the right thing. I sent you. You are his father."

Sarju's eyes popped. His mouth opened several times, but no sounds came. Finally, he shouted, "What? What the hell are you saying? What other drug have you been using?"

Samlall grabbed Sarju's hand and stared into his eyes. "It is true. You are his father."

Sarju wrenched himself from his brother's grip and got to his feet. "This is crazy talk. It is useless talking to a drunk like you."

Sarju began to walk out of the yard. Samlall lunged and held on to him.

"That is what you did," Samlall whimpered. "You got her pregnant, and I got the baby."

Sarju tried to shake him off, but Samlall shifted his weight, and both men fell to the ground.

"You are a crazy man," Sarju shouted as he struggled to his feet and headed for the road. "You need help."

Samlall scrambled to his feet and called after his brother. "Don't go, Sarju. Don't go! We can't keep secrets forever. You are Pradeep's father. Lalita is the mother. He is your son."

Sarju stopped and faced his brother. "Lalita? Cyril's daughter."

Samlall nodded his head and returned to the bench. "Yes. She admitted that you were the father."

Sarju shuffled back to the bench. He sat beside his brother and stared at his folded palms.

"How can this be? We had something going on," he confessed, "but I used protection with her. I always did."

Samlall sighed and contemplated his brother. "Yes, cheap Chinese condoms that couldn't protect you from your destiny."

Sarju shook his head and appealed to Samlall. "Are you sure, Samlall? I don't believe this. You have to be joking. After thirty years, you tell me this! But what about you and your wife? Am I crazy? Lalita is not your wife."

"And my wife did not give birth to him," Samlall announced sadly.

Sarju put a hand on his head and massaged his temple. "I am confused," he muttered. "I don't know what to think."

"Apparently, before you left for America, pieces of you seeped out of your cheap Chinese condom."

"So, how did you get the child?"

Samlall hesitated a while. He delved into his mind to uncover a painful experience. "My wife was pregnant about the same time. She lost the baby. We lost our son, and she was depressed for a long time."

Sarju patted his brother on the knee. "I am sorry, Samlall."

"One day we woke up and found a baby in a box outside our door. He appeared like the baby Moses from the Bible."

"Lalita dropped the baby on your doorstep?"

Samlall sighed. He slapped a mosquito on his arm. "We didn't see her. We didn't know who dropped the baby. And Lalita had left the island shortly after you left for America. We kept the baby. My wife bonded, and over the years she forgot that we found the child."

Samlall looked into Sarju's eyes and grabbed his arm forcefully. "In her heart and soul, she believes that the baby came from her womb. She must not be reminded otherwise."

"So, how are you so certain that I am the father?" inquired Sarju desperately.

Samlall looked at his brother with sympathy. Mosquitoes were swirling around Sarju's face, but he was oblivious to them.

"Keeping secrets is very painful, Sarju. Years ago, about the same time you were sent to jail, someone brought a secret message to me from Lalita. My wife didn't know about the message. Lalita wanted to see me urgently. She was in the public hospital in Georgetown."

"No doubt, having another baby," retorted Sarju with bitterness.

"No," replied Samlall softly. "She was dying of cancer."

"Cancer?"

Samlall scrutinized Sarju's face. "Yes, cancer! She wanted to let me know who the mother of the child was. And who was the father."

"But why did she want to disclose that after all those years?" demanded Sarju.

"The secret, Sarju! She wanted to set her soul free. But it imprisoned me."

"But why would the secret harm you?" murmured Sarju.

Samlall searched Sarju's face. "How would you react if you suddenly learned that the child that you loved so dearly was fathered by an American prisoner and a loose woman? How could I disclose that to my wife? And to my son?"

Sarju looked at his brother with new-found respect. "And that caused you to take to drink."

Samlall looked at the ground in shame. "Yes, take to drink and finally lose the love and respect of my son. Your son."

Sarju held his brother by the arm. "You didn't lose his love."

"That may be so, Sarju," Samlall retorted with a pained expression on his face, "but I have to live with that secret. You don't know what it is to live with that. Sometimes I think Lalita should have died without telling me anything. She should have taken that secret with her to the grave. Some secrets belong there, Sarju."

Sarju leaned his head against the headrest of the bench. He closed his eyes and shook his head in confusion. "I don't know. I don't know what to do or think now."

"Don't think. Just suffer like me," Samlall whispered with a grim look of resignation. "Now, you must share this burden of the secret with me. I can't let my wife know. She must spend her final days as the mother of Pradeep, our beloved son."

The brothers sat side by side, engrossed in their own thoughts, and wept quietly.

Sarju stared at the dark passageway that led to the road. "There are secrets from America to this island, too," he whispered.

Samlall nodded in understanding. "I had to keep the secret of your imprisonment here, too. Not many people know about what happened to you and your daughter in America."

"But there is another secret," insisted Sarju.

"No more, no more secrets," Samlall objected. "We have said enough for one night. No more."

Sarju grasped Samlall's wrist. "But you should know this," he mumbled. "Like Lalita, I have cancer too."

"You, too?" Samlall was aghast.

"Yes, my brother. I returned to Wakenaam to die on the island where I was born."

With tears in his eyes, Samlall edged over and embraced Sarju. "My little brother! You, too, will be taken from me. What did you do to deserve so much suffering?"

Sarju shut his eyes and sat back, his hands hanging feebly at his sides.

Samlall wriggled his way back to his end of the bench. He stared at his folded hands. "How much time do you have, Sarju?"

Sarju stirred. "Anytime now. A few days, a few weeks, a few hours. But definitely, I am leaving my Wakenaam."

Sarju rose from the bench. He looked at his watch.

"Where are you going, Sarju?"

"Home. To rest a few hours. To be prepared for the long sleep."

Samlall grunted. He opened the bag and took out several bowls of food, which he arranged on the bench.

"Did you eat, Sarju?"

"I am not hungry. I have a stomach problem, you know."

"Eating will not kill you. That is not your enemy. Tonight, we will have a special meal to celebrate our son's wedding."

Samlall left the bench and entered the hut. He returned to the bench with two plates and a bottle of rum.

Sarju glared at him with contempt. "Rum again? From the beginning of the day to the end? And on this day too, Samlal? After all that was said, Rum?"

Samlall set the plates down on the bench. He opened the bottle. "The secret burdened my soul. You don't know how much it affected me, Sarju. Rum was the only medicine available to drown it out. But no more. The secret is out. My soul is now free."

Samlall tilted the bottle and poured the rum ceremoniously in front of the bench. The mosquitoes swirled around to escape the pungent vapor. "I don't need this anymore, Sarju. I don't need a jailer anymore."

Sarju looked at the liquid slowly seeping into the ground. "You think it is so easy to get over being an alcoholic? There will be withdrawal pains if you stop suddenly."

Samlall filled a plate and handed it to Sarju. "My pain is insignificant compared to yours, Sarju. That bottle is history."

———— ◉ ————

SARJU STOOD AT THE side of the road for a long time, waiting for transport. He considered trekking the few miles to Zeelandia when, on the opposite side of the road, a minibus crawled to a stop like a beetle.

The driver leaned over and shouted, "Where you going, uncle?"

"Zeelandia," Sarju remarked.

"Well, you coming over to the bus, or you want me to send a plane for you?"

Sarju crossed the road and opened the passenger-side door. The bus was empty except for the driver, who was a little boy no more than sixteen years old.

"Do you have a license?" inquired Sarju with his hand on the door.

"Did I ask you to show me your money?" The boy retorted rudely. "If you don't want to travel with me, you can walk or make your bed on the side of the road."

Sarju boarded the bus. As it took off down the road, Sarju noticed a few specks of facial hair around the boy's mouth.

"Which part of Zeelandia you going?"

"Three houses before the road ends," Sarju answered. "You are not afraid of the police?"

The boy gave a short laugh. "Police on the road on a Sunday night? The police party all day on Sunday, and now at night they are taking a rest. Only murder and mayhem could make them leave the station."

"And what about your father?" Sarju persisted. "He knows that you are driving his bus?"

The boy snickered. "My father is just like the police. He drank all Sunday, and now he is sleeping. He won't wake up until tomorrow. Now, I take the chance to drive around the island to make some spending money."

The bus braked before a pothole. Sarju's chest thudded into the dashboard.

"That is why they have seat belts on vehicles, you know," the driver laughed. "Don't worry. You are safe with me. I was driving since I was ten."

Saju grimaced and put on the seat belt.

"Where you living, uncle?"

"Didn't you hear when I said Zeelandia?" Sarju snapped.

"I mean the country you come from. You don't sound like a Wakenaam man."

"America," muttered Sarju, looking at the passing houses.

"I hear people in America work hard every day and don't have time to enjoy their lives," shared the boy, glancing at Sarju.

"They have to pay their bills, you know. Everything over there has a price."

The boy nodded his head in agreement. "They say that they work like donkeys in America; then they come back to the island to relax."

"Yes, they deserve a vacation after all that non-stop work."

"Yes, they enjoy their vacation here," observed the boy, "but like donkeys, they return to America. I don't see the sense in that. Stay where you can enjoy life. When are you going back, uncle?"

Sarju looked sharply at the driver. "I am not returning."

The boy glanced at Sarju with a smile forming around his lips. "Oh! So, you are not a donkey! You are the business kind of American! What kind of business you involved in?"

"Land business, if it is any of your business," retorted Sarju.

"Oh, so you buying up all the land! You are getting into agriculture or manufacture?"

"No. I am just selling some land."

The minibus rolled into a pool of water, and the vehicle swayed like a ship. Sarju unbuckled the seat belt.

"I will come off here," he instructed as he saw the little street that led to the school.

"You said by the road end. We not there yet," observed the boy, but stopped the bus.

"This is okay. I will walk home from here." Sarju murmured and handed the boy money for the fare.

Sarju opened the door and stood on the school street.

"You know, there are no houses there!" The boy declared. "That street leads to the school."

"I know it leads to the school," remarked Sarju coldly.

The boy poked his head through the window of the bus. "I hope you are not drunk. It is not safe to go near that school at night."

"What does being drunk have to do with school?" barked Sarju.

"That school is haunted," the boy confided. "The headmaster is buried on the school grounds. People say that they buried him with his whip, and he comes out at night to whip anybody who enters the ground."

Sarju laughed. "Thanks for the warning, but I don't think he would whip me."

The boy looked hurt. "A lot of drunk men won't agree with you," he continued. "Some of them fall asleep on the bridge, and they wake up to lashes all over their bodies. I am just trying to help you."

"Oh! So that is what happened to that minibus driver here last night!" Sarju whispered in a conspiratorial tone.

The smug look disappeared from the boy's face. "What happened to him?"

"He was slowed by a pothole when a ghost entered the bus and began to whip him all over his body. He had to leave his bus and run for his life."

The boy's eyes bulged. He wound up all the windows and sped away, lurching from pothole to pothole in his haste.

———◉———

SARJU'S FACE CREASED with a mischievous smile as he made his way down the short street to the entrance of the school. The quarter moon was out and spread its weak glow on the street. He trudged to the bridge and leaned on the railing. The wooden gate to the school was locked. The caretaker's house that was once close to the schoolyard was gone, probably demolished to expand the playground. On the other side of the school building, the lone mango tree looked like a dark blob under the moonlight, and the dark shadow on the ground around the trunk shrouded the tomb of Mr. Rogers. Sarju raised his sight to the attic-like room above the second floor, and his eyes settled on the two windows flanking the boarded-up one in the middle. The memory of the broken window flashed through his mind as he remembered Lalita.

She had come to live with her parents about two months before Sarju left the country for America. One morning, while he was teaching his class, he chanced to glance through the window that overlooked the caretaker's house. He noticed a strange woman on the stairs, beating out a carpet. The dust swirled around her like a fine mist, and when it settled, he detected a delectably plump young woman with ample bust and thighs. An animal arousal stirred in him, and he stood by the window for a long time, observing her while the class was at work. Finally, the intensity of his gaze caused her to look in his direction, and she threw him an inviting smile. He remained by the window for the rest of the day, and from time to time she would find some pretext to go to the stairs and cast a furtive look in his direction.

One afternoon, after school was dismissed, as he rode his bike home, he encountered her on the road. She was heading for Belle Plaine, about two miles away, to do some shopping. He was elated that she chose to walk rather than wait on any kind of motor transportation, so he pushed his bicycle alongside her, and they engaged in a long and amorous chat. She confided that her husband had left her alone in Georgetown while he went to the interior to prospect for gold. When he didn't return after three months, she made her way to her parents' home—the caretaker's cottage. Laita loved her husband and was confident that after he had had enough of *whoring and wilding* in the gold fields, he would retrieve her from Cyril's house. But Sarju detected that, while she was not interested in any kind of romantic relationship, she was not averse to satisfying her physical needs.

School supplies were stored in a little attic room that could only be accessed by a steep staircase from Sarju's classroom on the second floor. Being the only male in the school, apart from Headmaster Rogers, Sarju was tasked with taking notebooks, chalk, textbooks, stationery, and other items up to the room and removing supplies as required for the functioning of the school. The moving of these items was often done after the students were dismissed. Mr. Rogers had entrusted Sarju with a spare key to the room.

Supplies had arrived from the city, and with the school empty of students and teachers, Sarju started unpacking and carrying the items to the attic room when Lalita entered the second floor with a broom in her hand. Her mother, who used to sweep the second floor, was ill, so Lalita was helping. When Sarju saw her, he immediately experienced a great rush of desire; he closed the door behind her, quickly took her hand, and she willingly followed him up the staircase. Rapidly, he flung some boxes off a narrow table that was close to the windows and converted it into a makeshift bed. On that narrow table, Lalita was a ravenous lover and teacher and found a willing student in Sarju. Their lovemaking was rapid and exhilarating as they kept their ears out for any stirrings from Cyril, who was in charge of sweeping the first floor.

They met a few times a week after Mr. Rogers had left the building. Sarju found every excuse to be in the building after school was dismissed. Apart from attending to supplies, he would stay back late, ostensibly to grade students' work, create lesson plans, or make teaching aids. To ensure that it was safe to rendezvous, Sarju would tape a sheet of paper on the window to signal to Lalita when Mr. Rogers had left.

They had spent a month or so in lustful bliss when Sarju received a letter of acceptance from a university in America along with an official application form for a student visa. One of the conditions for the visa was proof of financial support in America. Sarju had no money or relatives in America. One of his teachers from the training college that he attended had changed professions and was an important functionary with the Ministry of Foreign Affairs. Many times, in the newspapers, Sarju had seen photographs of the man in the company of important U.S. Embassy officials. Sarju took a few days off from work and traveled to Georgetown.

He met his former teacher, Mr. Johnson, at the ministry and explained his situation. Mr. Johnson made a call to someone at the embassy, gave Sarju a letter, and instructed him to head to the embassy with his passport the next day. Early the next morning,

Sarju arrived at the embassy, and without any hassle or an interview, he was granted his student visa.

He remembered vividly the last afternoon he made love to her. Mr. Rogers had left after dismissal, and Sarju waited anxiously by the door. Lalita arrived and without any hesitation, she eagerly followed him up the steep staircase. Even before arriving at their narrow bed, the two starved bodies were intertwined in ecstasy. The days without him had turned her into a feral cat, and in the throes of orgasm, she kicked out violently, and her foot smashed the window pane. After she left, Sarju cleared the room of pieces of broken glass.

Early the next morning, Mr. Rogers climbed the staircase and returned to the second floor almost immediately. He glared at Sarju, his face livid with rage, but didn't say anything.

After the class went home for lunch, Mr. Rogers reappeared and beckoned to Sarju to follow him up the staircase.

"Do you know how this window got broken, Beepat?" Mr. Rogers bellowed, probing at the broken window with a yardstick.

"No, Mr. Rogers. It looks like a student pelted a ball at the glass," Sarju gulped.

"If the ball came from outside, the glass has to be inside here. Find me the glass, Beepat."

Sarju turned his head to inspect the floor.

"You take me for an ass, Beepat?" Mr. Rogers yelled, poking Sarju in the chest with the stick. "Tell me, what is that?" He pointed with his stick at something on the floor.

Sarju leaned down and retrieved a condom wrapper. He put it quickly in his pocket.

"What is that, Beepat?" He growled. "Did the ministry use its precious funds to supply you with condoms?"

Sarju was silent. He hung his head in embarrassment.

"This is a school, Beepat. You are a trained teacher. We are here to instruct the students in reading, writing, and arithmetic, not in sex education. You hear me, Beepat? This is a school." Mr. Rogers yelled.

"Yes, Mr. Rogers," squeaked Sarju, "this is a school."

Mr. Rogers gritted his teeth. "I am glad you are aware of that, Beepat. This is a school, not a whorehouse. You hear me, Beepat?"

"A school, not a whorehouse, Mr. Rogers," repeated Sarju.

Mr. Rogers curled his lips in distaste. "I heard rumors that you were seeing that woman, but I never believed that you would be so foolish and reckless to use my school as your bedroom."

"I am sorry, Mr. Rogers."

"Sorry? You are putting my job on the line, and you are sorry?"

"I wasn't thinking, Mr. Rogers," muttered Sarju.

"You were thinking alright, Beepat," sneered Mr. Rogers. "But you weren't thinking with the right head. All of you young men have your brains in your shorts."

He poked Sarju in the crotch with the stick. Sarju stepped aside quickly.

"If the ministry hears that you turned the government property into your private house of pleasure, you will not be the only one kicking bricks on the street," Mr. Rogers declared and slapped the stick down on the tabletop.

Sarju winced as the stick broke against the table.

"You used this table as your bed, Beepat?"

Sarju nodded his head sheepishly.

Mr. Rogers pursed his lips in disgust and kicked the table aside.

"Give me the damn key to this room," he commanded.

Sarju removed a key from a key chain and handed it over.

"You will not come up here unless I am here at the school. And you will leave the school at dismissal every day. Am I clear, Beepat?"

"Very clear, Mr. Rogers," squeaked Sarju.

"You are a big man; she is an older, more experienced woman, and I can't stop you from being with her. But not in my school. Not in this compound. Take her outside the village. Take her to your house. I don't want a scandal here. I am not going to lose my job for you."

Sarju remembered that it was a Friday, the last day he spent at the school. He went to Georgetown on Saturday and booked his ticket for America. Two days later, he was gone from Guyana. Gone without informing Lalita or Mr. Rogers.

The dark clouds were rolling in from the Atlantic. The moonlight was fading, shrouding the school in darkness. Sarju faced the street and wobbled in the direction of Hassan's house. Lalita was gone, buried somewhere in an unmarked grave in Georgetown. Mr. Rogers was resting under the mango tree, his ghost skipping between the shadows with a whip in hand. Sarju was the only one left but within reach of the licking shadows.

Chapter 24- Instructions

Sarju reclined on the bed and watched mesmerized as the liquid in the intravenous bag emptied into his wrist, drip by drip. His pain had increased, and Dr. Morris prescribed and administered that final treatment.

Dr. Morris, in his white coat, inspected the now almost empty bag. He turned off the machine, removed the drip tube, and placed a bandage on Sarju's wrist.

Sarju raised himself to a sitting position while the doctor took a seat in the swivel chair close to the bed. Dr. Morris stretched his long frame out on the chair and placed his palms together, tapping his fingers softly.

"How do you feel, Mr. Beepat? That was your first drink of morphine."

A frown appeared on Sarju's face. "Okay, I guess. I am feeling..."

Dr. Morris looked at Sarju with a grim expression. "You don't have to hide your feelings, man. I am your doctor."

Sarju pressed the fingers of his right hand on the bandage on his left wrist. He felt a sharp pain where the needle had pierced his flesh.

"I feel like shit, doctor. Or, if I were to be more honest, *I wish I felt like shit*. My pain is worse than shit." Sarju gestured to the empty IV bag. "This morphine you gave me. Isn't that addictive?"

"To some people, yes. But addiction is not a concern in your case, Mr. Beepat.

"So, we are very near the end, eh, Doc? The pain terminates with me!"

Dr. Morris swiveled slowly. "Your time is running out, Mr. Beepat. If there was anything that I could have done, rest assured, I would have done that already."

Sarju smiled. "I know. You are a doctor of medicine, not a doctor of miracles. A doctor told me that once."

Dr. Morris stroked his beard with his long and stately fingers. "Neblet told me that you are living with some friends. Don't you have family here with you, Mr. Beepat?"

Sarju gazed at the empty morphine bag. "I have a family in America. I was married but now divorced."

He leaned down, opened a bag at his feet, and handed an envelope to Dr. Morris. "I have two adult children."

Dr. Morris opened the envelope and stared at the photograph. "A very pretty girl. She is a nurse?"

"My daughter, Aarti," beamed Sarju. "It is my hope and prayer that she turns out to be as caring and compassionate as you, doctor."

Dr. Morris returned the envelope to Sarju. "I have no doubt about that. What better inspiration can there be with you as a father!" He grinned at Sarju. "I am sure she is infected with the spirit of this island."

"My children have never been here."

Morris peered into Sarju's face. "You don't expect them here? Shouldn't they be here with you?"

Sarju slowly replaced the photograph in his bag. "The memories of their father have faded. But there is something that you should know about me, Dr. Morris. Before you hear from anyone else."

Dr. Morris stopped swiveling. "What is there that I haven't already heard from your pet student, Neblet?"

Sarju pinned Morris with a piercing stare. "My daughter was raped. She was only fifteen."

Morris gasped, "Oh! I am sorry to hear that."

"And I shot and killed the man who raped her. I am a murderer, Dr. Morris."

Dr. Morris looked somberly at Sarju. "You took the law into your own hands?"

"Then the law took me into their hands. I spent sixteen years in prison. I was only released because of this disease."

"You had a terrible experience as a father, Mr. Beepat. Are you still close to your daughter?"

"I have always been close. My daughter would never leave my soul, Dr. Morris. I would do anything on earth for her. Even spend a hundred years in any prison."

Dr. Morris stared at Sarju, a frail and broken specimen hunched on the bed. "I am sure she loves you very much, Mr. Beepat."

Sarju coughed to clear his throat. "She blames me for the rape, doctor. She blames me, and she is right. I didn't protect her as a father. I took the easy route to avenge her, and that made me an outcast in her life. Now the world has discarded me as a monster and condemned me as a murderer."

Dr. Morris rubbed his eyes. He leaned back in the chair. "You know, Mr. Beepat, we live in a world with different contradictions. Soldiers kill in wars to protect their country, and they are called heroes, not murderers. Policemen kill to protect innocent citizens and are hailed as heroes. Animals kill to protect their young. Sometimes even doctors kill when trying to save lives."

"I am not a hero, Dr. Morris. I am just an animal that failed to protect his young, and my animal story is near the end."

"I am so very sorry about what happened to you. I can't judge you. I have no children, but I can understand why you reacted that way. I assure you, if there was any way to help you, I would have left no stone unturned to do so."

"I know, Dr. Morris," Sarju muttered. "You did your best, and I am very grateful. I wish I had more time to get to know you better. This country is very lucky to have a doctor like you."

Dr. Morris smiled. "And I am grateful to all the people who helped me along the way." He peered at Sarju over his glasses. "Do you have your affairs in order?"

Sarju glanced at Dr. Morris's computer desk. "There is just one thing left to be done. Can I use your computer to type and print a letter? There is something that I believe you can do for me."

"Anything within my power, consider it done."

Dr. Morris walked over to the computer desk. He pulled the chair for Sarju. "This computer is only accustomed to medical issues. It has never experienced a last will and testament."

Sarju adjusted himself on the desk chair. "Not a will, but a set of instructions."

Dr. Morris left Sarju and went upstairs. He returned later and handed Sarju a glass of coconut water.

Sarju had finished typing and printing. He took the glass and handed the paper to Dr. Morris.

Dr. Morris stood by the computer desk and read the paper carefully. Sarju sipped the coconut water and swiveled on the chair with his eyes on Dr. Morris.

"This letter is granting me permission to inform the U.S. Embassy and members of the Guyana government that you were swindled out of your property by Motielall and Naitram!"

"I believe that is common knowledge to all the people on the island."

Dr. Morris tapped a finger against the paper. "Why don't you make a formal complaint in the court system? I know a lot of people there. They can be of assistance if what you allege is true."

Sarju sneered. "You really believe your people would take the word of a murderer over the word of a powerful attorney and his business confederate?"

Dr. Morris pursed his lips. "What about the word of a doctor who would support the murderer?"

"And how long would your contacts in the court system take to rectify the matter?" inquired Sarju skeptically.

"About five to ten years to have satisfaction in your favor," responded Dr. Morris. "But this is how the court system works. Justice in this country takes time. You have to exercise patience."

Sarju sipped and considered Dr. Morris. "Do you think I have time for the process to work? It just allows unscrupulous people to prey on the weak and deprive them of their property."

Dr. Morris returned to the paper. "And who is Pradeep, the person who would benefit from any proceeds if you succeed?"

"Pradeep is my, my brother's son."

"And your children? There is no mention of them."

"They are well provided for. And they are not of the island."

"And why do you think this plan of yours is going to work, Mr. Beepat?" pressed Morris.

"Because time is compressed. I must do what I can to hasten the process," explained Sarju.

Dr. Morris looked at Sarju thoughtfully. "I hope you are not planning what I am thinking."

Sarju stretched out his hand for the paper. "I don't know what you are thinking, but what I am planning requires my signature, doctor."

Chapter 25- Last Gasp

It was late at night in Wakenaam. The foot and vehicular traffic were almost at a standstill in that agrarian community. A slow-moving motorcycle interrupted the sedate evening with its barking exhaust; the glare from the headlight illuminated three characters trudging their way along the Belle Plaine road.

Samlall held Sarju by the arm to support him as he walked with unsteady steps.

"You should be home resting, Sarju. You are not well; now isn't the time to have any dealings with Motielall."

"He is right, Sir Beepat," supported Neblet. "You didn't go to Dr. Morris for your injection yesterday, and you purposefully missed today. You should be in bed."

"Dr. Morris is a busy man. He has more deserving patients to attend to, Neblet," Sarju wheezed. "I know that you steal mangoes from the schoolyard. You ever thought of stealing mangoes from Motielall?"

Neblet guffawed. "I prefer to steal mangoes from a dead man, but never from a gunman."

Samlall stopped and gave Sarju some time to rest. "That house is not ours anymore, Sarju. It is no use going to confront that man."

"You are right, Samlall," Sarju declared firmly. "We don't own a nail on his new house, but he doesn't own my land. I never sold him a leaf from the mango tree."

Sarju took a few deep breaths and continued walking.

"The last time you entered the man's yard, he assaulted and threatened to kill you, Sir Beepat," Neblet insisted. "What you think will happen this time?"

Sarju chuckled. "This time, the business transaction will be over. Finally, over."

"Old people always say that you must never do business at night, Sir Beepat."

"But the old people were wrong. Samlall lost everything during the day, so now we have to try at night." Sarju inserted a hand in his pocket and removed a shopping bag. He flapped the bag open. "We will have mangoes tonight, Neblet. I got up this morning with a sudden yearning for my own mangoes."

They stopped in front of Motielall's house. The latch was off, and the gate was a few inches open. Through the front windows of the house, they saw the flickering lights from the TV.

"For the last time, Sarju, this is madness," Samlall protested. "Let me take you home. This is trouble you looking for. You can't enter the man's yard. The law is on his side."

"And we can't enter the yard to help you," declared Neblet. "The police ordered me and Samlall to keep off his property, or they would send we to prison."

"You don't have to come with me. All I want you to do is witness the transaction."

Sarju shrugged off Samlall's hand and shuffled slowly to the gate. He kicked it open, and it shrieked on its hinges. He stumbled to the mango trees by the fence. The jet skis were gone, and the area by the trees was bathed in the yard light. He looked up at the tree and noticed bunches of mangoes bursting with ripeness. The long pole with the hook at one end was still by the fence. He tottered as he raised the pole and hooked a bunch of mangoes. The fallen mangoes thudded against the fence and rolled on the ground. Sarju leaned over and selected one. He bit the end of the mango and sucked noisily on the golden yellow juice.

The front door suddenly opened. Motielall appeared on the landing of the front steps. "Who is that?" he thundered. "Who is hiding by my fence?"

Sarju crept from the shadows under the tree and stood in the light. He held out his hand with the mango. "The lawful owner of the land, Sarju Beepat," he proclaimed loudly. "I am just here to pick my mangoes and share them with the neighbors."

Motielall bounded down the stairs and advanced to Sarju. "What the fuck are you doing here? Didn't I tell you not to enter my fucking property? Why you come here again, Beepat? You want to make me jail bait tonight?"

"This is still my land," bellowed Sarju. "I don't need your permission to enter my property. You never finished paying for it. It is money or life today. Pay me my money or lose your life over my land tonight."

Motielall's wife appeared on the steps, peering over the banister. "Don't argue with that madman, Motie," she shrieked, "just call the damn police and let them take him to the lock-ups."

The commotion had attracted a few spectators by the front gate. From the adjoining house, a man and a woman leaned through the window to get a better view of the yard.

Motielall sputtered, "Don't test my patience, man. Get off my property or you won't live to see America again."

The curious spectators gathered courage and pressed forward against the gate to get a better view of the confrontation.

Sarju appealed to the people at the gate and the neighbors by the window. "This man owes me money for the land he is standing on. He owes me money for the land he built his house on."

Motielall fumed, "You want your land? I will kill you and bury you right here if you don't leave."

Sarju swiveled around so that he could see the faces of the neighbors at the window. "Did you hear him? This thief is threatening to kill me because I am demanding the forty-eight thousand U.S. dollars that he owes me and my brother."

Motielall spat in Sarju's direction.

"We have witnesses now, Mr. Businessman Motielall. Tell them when you are going to pay me the money that you scammed my brother," Sarju shouted. "Tell them when you are going to pay your debts."

"That is a lot of money," hissed Motielall. "Where am I going to get all that cash? By prostituting your wife and daughter?"

"Don't confuse my family with yours, Motielall," growled Sarju. "Prostitution and cocaine are your family business."

Sarju glanced at the crowd by the gate. "Pay me what you owe me now," he shouted. "Pay me for my land now, and you may live to sell your drugs tomorrow."

Motielall grabbed Sarju by the hand and twisted it behind his back. "How are you going to fetch all that money? On your head?"

Sarju waved the shopping bag in his other hand. He groaned in pain. "Fill this bag, and we can call it quits, or I will have to bury you under my mango tree."

Motielall released Sarju, grabbed the bag, and turned it over his head. He began to pummel Sarju all over his body. Sarju swung his arms blindly and landed a few ineffective blows.

"You are trespassing on my land, and your American law gives me the right to kill you."

"You are a coward. You are not a man," shrilled Sarju, tearing the bag off his head. "You have lost your balls to cocaine. Kill me if you are a fucking man."

"You invaded my yard and are questioning my manhood?" screamed Motielall.

"Drag him out of the yard, Motie," supported Motielall's wife. "He is too presumptuous to enter our property and throw insults so that the low-class neighbors can hear and repeat."

Sarju threw a dirty look in the direction of the woman. "But that is what your wife says when she goes to bed with other men. You are a wimp, not a man."

Motielall lunged at Sarju and grabbed him in a chokehold. "Fucking American jailbait. You will die here today. I will kill you on your own land."

Sarju twisted his body, raised his legs in the air, and both men fell to the ground. Motie snatched the bag and attempted to strangle Sarju with it. He jumped to his feet and kicked Sarju repeatedly in the stomach and the head. Sarju whimpered as blood and vomit escaped his mouth.

"Leave that man alone," Neblet roared from the gate. "He is a sick man; leave him alone."

Motielall's wife rushed down the stairs and separated her husband from Sarju. She grabbed him by the arms and pushed him up the stairs into the house. "He got what he deserved. Let his friends take him out of the yard."

Samlall and Neblet sprinted to Sarju's side.

"He is bleeding badly, Neblet," croaked Samlall. "That man damaged my brother."

Samlall removed his shirt and tried to stem the flow of blood from his brother's mouth.

Neblet looked at the front door of the house. Motielall's wife was blocking the door, preventing Motielall from leaving.

"Let's get him out of the yard before that madman returns with a gun and kill the two of us."

Two of the spectators by the gate rushed in and helped Neblet and Samlall transport Sarju out of the yard. They laid him down by the side of the road.

Neblet leaned over and listened to Sarju's heart. "His heart is barely beating. He has to go to the hospital immediately. We have to get an ambulance."

"Which ambulance? The ambulance crashed into a tractor last week. We have to use private transportation," advised one of the men who helped ferry Sarju out of the yard.

"Look, a minibus is coming this way," pointed out the other man, whose face was covered with a thick fuzzy beard.

The men formed a wall before the minibus. The bus stopped, and the two male passengers stared at the men with annoyance. The driver, the same young man who had driven Sarju to the school street on the night of the wedding, demanded. "What happen? Why you stop the bus?"

The man with the beard opened the door and peered at the passengers. "We have to take a man to the hospital. You have to get out."

The young driver objected. "But they didn't reach their destination. I have to drop them off first before I take on another passenger."

Beard Man was determined. "They can walk to their home. You have a new destination. This man is injured and has to go to the hospital now."

The young man relented. He came out of the minibus and walked over to where Samlall was wiping the blood from Sarju's mouth.

Samlall and Neblet attempted to lift Sarju into the minibus.

"Wait, wait," cautioned the driver. He opened the trunk and removed an old blanket, which he threw over the seats. "Put him down now. The nurses at the hospital only clean the patients. They don't clean minibuses."

The men assisted Samlall and Neblet in loading Sarju into the bus. Samlall sat in the back, cradling Sarju's head in his lap and wiping his mouth with the shirt. Neblet jumped into the front seat beside the driver. The bus made a U-turn and headed for the hospital.

The young driver glanced over to look at Sarju. "I know that man. He is an American."

"How do you know him?" queried Neblet.

"Last Sunday, I dropped him off by the school in Zeelandia. I warned him about the ghost in the schoolyard."

"Which ghost?" scoffed Neblet.

"You know! The one who lives under the mango tree and whips people who hang around the school," continued the driver and looked over at Sarju. "Who beat the American?"

Neblet sighed. "A different jumbie beat him under his own mango tree."

"Like he stopped breathing, Neblet. Like Sarju stopped breathing," shrieked Samlall.

The minibus accelerated and screeched to a halt outside the hospital door. Neblet jumped out and sprinted through the doorway. He returned with two porters pushing a gurney. The porters loaded Sarju and wheeled him into the hospital, with Neblet and Samlall following.

The young driver, unsure of what to do, leaned on the hood of the bus and waited. Samlall and Neblet emerged a few minutes later, accompanied by a security guard. Samlall walked to a bench across from the entrance and sat head down, looking at the bloodied shirt in his hands.

"We have to get Dr. Morris," Neblet shouted to Samlall, who did not respond.

Neblet jumped into the bus. "Let's go and get the doctor."

"Isn't the doctor here at the hospital?" the driver queried.

"*Their* doctor is on lunch break. We have to get we personal doctor. Drive, man, drive!"

The minibus took off and returned a few minutes later. Dr. Morris, in shorts and T-shirt, leaped from the vehicle and bolted through the open door of the hospital, with Neblet behind. The security guard at the door waved off Neblet with his truncheon and ordered him to stand away from the door.

Unasked, the young driver leaned against his bus and waited. He could not understand why he lingered to hear news of the man he had transported to the hospital. The daring and bravado on his face disappeared, replaced by a feeling of empathy and concern for the men he had recently met. The young driver observed Neblet as he paced up and down in front of the hospital's entrance. Samlall, in a trance-like state, stared at the shirt in his hands. Then Dr. Morris emerged and stood in the doorway. He ambled over to Neblet and placed a comforting hand on him. Neblet's shoulders drooped as they made their way across the concrete apron of the hospital to his friend. Samlall raised his eyes to the dark sky as he felt the hands of his friends on his shoulders.

A wave of sadness and loss overcame the young man as he witnessed the three grown men huddled together in tears.

Chapter 26 – Restitution

Dr. Morris mounted the stairs to the front door of the stately wooden colonial building. The office on the first floor was closed and bathed in darkness. An ancient metal knocker was mounted on the door that led to the upper floor. He knocked twice and waited. After a few minutes, he heard thudding footsteps. Naitram opened the door and peered at him.

"Good evening, doctor. It is very late for a business visit, but no doubt, you will educate me over a drink or two."

Naitram moved aside for Dr. Morris to enter and climb the stairs to the upper flat. Dr. Morris was acquainted with the building; he had been invited to several social gatherings there before.

They made their way into the living room of the house. Naitram walked over to a table and picked up a glass that was already fortified with a drink.

"What is your late-night drink, Dr. Morris? You aren't on duty, now."

Dr. Morris raised his palm to signal his refusal.

Naitram tipped his glass and coiled himself on a recliner. On the wall behind him was a huge photograph of him and his wife posing before the Statue of Liberty in New York.

"Have a seat, man. What brings you here so late at night? You didn't mention your business when you called. I hope it is not about my medical records, because, as you see, I am fine."

Dr. Morris lowered himself onto a sofa. "This call is not about your medical records, Mr. Naitram. It is about an illegal operation."

Naitram looked quizzically at the doctor. He took a drink and smacked his lips. "Whatever quagmire you have found yourself in, doctor, I am pretty sure I can use my legal skills to extricate you."

Dr. Morris leaned forward and looked Naitram in the eyes. "And you will have to use a lot of your skills, Mr. Naitram, because *you are* in a quagmire."

Naitram choked on his drink. He wiped his mouth on his sleeve. "I am not following you, doctor."

"Do you recall a man named Sarju Beepat?"

Naitram took a tiny sip of his drink. "I can vaguely recall that name. Is he a patient of yours?"

Dr. Morris leaned back on the sofa with his eyes locked on the lawyer. "*Was*, Mr. Naitram! He was a patient, but more importantly, a friend, until he was pummeled to death by your friend and client, Motielall, a short while ago."

Naitram spilled his drink as he raised his glass to his mouth. He glared at the doctor. "That is news to me. But why are you here? If a murder has been committed, that is a matter for the police. Not me!"

"I am quite aware of that, Mr. Naitram," Morris announced coldly. "And I am certain that you know that your client, Motielall, is presently enticing the police not to take an interest in the matter."

Naitram glared at the doctor and shook his head in irritation. He went to a small bar at one end of the living room and mixed a drink.

The lawyer returned to the recliner and swilled his drink. "That is neither here nor there, Dr. Morris. Motielall, or any other citizen, enjoys the right to associate. Likewise, in my profession, I am bound to represent anyone who seeks my services. And as you very well know, I have no control over the police."

Dr. Morris shook his head aggressively. "But you can control your dog, Motielall."

Naitram looked at Morris with distaste. He took a drink and grimaced.

"I took the liberty of taking written statements from people who witnessed the vicious attack on my friend."

Naitram took a drink and frowned. "Is taking witness statements for an alleged crime part of your duties as a doctor?"

Dr. Morris rose. He looked pointedly at Naitram. "No, but it was the duty of a friend to do so." He slapped the back of the sofa. "I will now cut to the chase," he declared sternly. "I have documents to show that you and Motielall conspired to deprive my friend of his property."

Naitram leaned forward on the recliner and gave the doctor a scorching look. "You are being very careless with your remarks, doctor. Remember, my profession seeks the truth, and I am the master of arriving there. That man you proudly hailed as a friend, do you know what dastardly deed he committed in America?"

"I know what he did, Naitram. He protected the honor of his daughter and paid the price." Morris gestured with his chin to the photograph behind Naitram. "Would you do the same for your wife? For your daughter?"

Naitram swiveled to view the photograph, and his drink spilled on his pants.

"A common criminal who took the law into his own hands."

"Oh, he was forced to do that because you lawyers take the truth, turn and twist it to expose holes, then insert your legal technicalities."

"And how is your legal philosophy connected to me?" Naitram sneered.

"That is why I called you tonight. You are quite aware of how you personally manipulated and forged instruments to take the land of the simple and trusting brother of Sarju Beepat."

Naitram rose to his feet and waved a finger at Dr. Morris. His voice trembled in anger. "Repeat that in public, and I will sue you for slander and take the shirt off your back and everything that you own."

"Everything will be revealed to the public if forty-eight thousand U.S. dollars are not delivered to me within five days," responded Morris with quiet determination.

"Are you aware that you are engaging in extortion, Dr. Morris?" fumed Naitram.

Dr. Morris looked at the lawyer with disdain. "Is that what lawyers say when they cheat people of money and property?"

"You are an intelligent man, doctor. I would hate to see you defending yourself against slander."

"But I won't be defending myself," insisted Morris. "I am putting you on notice that I will appear as a willing witness to see that justice is done to my friend. And, by the way, there are people in New York who would also testify that you robbed them of their money."

Naitram looked at Morris in amazement. "Dr. Morris, we are part of the professional fraternity on this island. How can you take the sides of those degenerates against your own?"

"Are they degenerates because you took their money and did not give them representation? Or are they degenerates because they plan to complain to the tax bodies in America that you took money and did not declare it as income? What about Samlall Beepat? Did you represent him in the eyes of the law?"

Naitram laughed scornfully. "I think you are taking some of your patients' medications, doctor. Motielall is the man you want. He is the man in control of the property formerly owned by the Beepat brothers."

"I am quite aware of that. Sadly, it was on the same property that Motielall delivered the fatal blows that killed Sarju Beepat."

Naitram took a drink and scowled at Morris.

Morris continued in a low, conspiratorial tone. "Now, my instructions are to deliver and send certain documents that clearly implicate you to the American Embassy, the president, newspapers, and other agencies in and out of the country if the estate of the Beepats' is not made whole."

"And you expect an accomplished lawyer like me to fall for your demands?" Naitram challenged.

"Yes, because if you do not do what is right, on a single click of a mouse, a damaging email will be sent out. I expect you to heel your dog, Motielall, if you care for your reputation and assets. If the money is not delivered to me within five days, start seeking more accomplished lawyers to defend you against money laundering, forgery, and other legal malpractices."

Naitram snarled at Dr. Morris. "You think it is so easy to make accusations against a leading member of the bar and an upstanding member of this community?"

"Oh, and as your doctor, I would not advise temporary insanity as your defense. Good night, Mr. Naitram; you have five days. I will see my way out, thank you."

Dr. Morris nodded his head to the lawyer, and as he was making his way down the stairs, he heard a tinkling sound as a glass was thrown against the wall.

———————◉———————

IT WAS MIDMORNING, and there was a strong breeze whipping over the river bank when Naitram drove up and parked beside the sea wall. He emerged from the car with a water bottle in hand, did a few warm-up exercises, and began to jog along the track beside the river bank.

It was not very hot, but he was thirsty from drinking the night before. He stopped beside a tree to take a few gulps of water when he saw a Motielall in the distance walking towards him. Naitram leaned against the tree and waited.

Motielall approached, lit a cigarette, and blew the smoke towards Naitram.

"So, why did you ask me to meet you here? What is wrong with your office?"

Naitram wiped the sweat from his face and took a drink of water. "Why did you go to the police station about that man, Sarju Beepat?"

Motielall looked at the lawyer with suspicion. "Because the police are cheaper than lawyers. When I am in legal trouble, then I see you. But why did you want to see me this morning?"

"Because you have put me in a predicament. You killed that man in front of witnesses."

"Who told you that, counselor?" Motielall protested and drew on his cigarette. "The man killed himself. He was a walking dead. I heard he had cancer! My blows didn't cause his death."

Naitram sighed in exasperation. "But he died in your yard, and your blows, according to witnesses, hastened his death. That is homicide and is a matter for the law."

"So, aren't you the lawyer?" Motielall sniggered. "You don't have to worry about witnesses. A few dollars would make them blind. A few witnesses are like pesky mosquitoes. I swat and kill them with dollar bills."

"They have written statements. And pesky mosquitoes can spread diseases," Naitram objected. "This is precisely what I am trying to avoid. This has gone too far, Motielall! You should have paid that man for his property, and we wouldn't be in this mess."

"I paid you," Motielall exploded. His lips curled in anger. "You knew the plan was not to pay him. He got the loan. I got his land."

Naitram surveyed the area for eavesdroppers.

"Well, now you have to pay him," he replied forcefully. "If you don't pay him the balance, then the U.S. Embassy, the president, and God knows who else would be invited to your party."

Motielall sucked on his cigarette and blew the smoke in the lawyer's direction.

"The U.S. Embassy can kiss my wrinkled black ass. They revoked my visa because they suspect that I engage in underhand activities. I am not interested in what they think."

"Well, I am," objected Naitram. "My visa is valid, and I use it regularly. I don't want to be caught in your net."

Motielall flicked his cigarette over the sea wall. "Why are you so agitated about one property? You knew what I was doing. You advised me that everything was above board."

"I knew you brought me documents that you declared were genuine. As a lawyer, I looked at the documents and accepted your word."

Motielall sighed and glowered at the lawyer with distaste. "I see. You are using your lawyer's tricks on me. You knew very well that I had to forge documents to show that Sarju Beepat gifted his portion of the property to his brother."

Naitram raised his hands in denial. "Again, I have no knowledge of what you did. But why didn't you pay all the money?"

"You are hiding behind your crooked law book training again," fumed Naitram. "The drunk was content with two thousand U.S. dollars until the damn U.S. government released his cancer-ridden brother."

"Now, you made his cancer our problem."

"Don't worry, counselor, it is not a problem. The man will be cremated, and the problem will go up in smoke. You'll see."

"You think so, eh? How many properties have you acquired using forged documents?"

"As if you don't know? How are the other properties related to this matter, counselor?"

"Because if you don't pay off, the authorities are going to dig into all your interests and examine all the documents with a fine-tooth comb."

"So, what? You are my lawyer. You are paid to legalize documents."

Naitram shook his head in defiance. "Not this time. This time, they will have enough evidence to examine me. You will have to engage another lawyer. I have to look after myself, and I may have to take another lawyer as well."

"What are you saying? We can't win? That is why you asked me to meet you here. You didn't want me to come to your home! You want nothing to do with me."

"Motielall, business is not only about acquiring things," Naitram retorted, "it is also about holding on to things you have acquired illegally. If you don't pay off Beepat, you stand a chance to lose all your properties. The only thing you may be left with is a jail cell. And I don't want to join you there."

"So you are advising me to pay the forty-eight thousand U.S. dollars to settle all claims?"

Naitram shook his head and took a swig from the water bottle. "Sixty thousand dollars."

"What shit is this?" bellowed Motielall. "Somebody wants to rob me. I only owe them forty-eight thousand dollars! That twelve thousand U.S. dollars is for you?"

"Just like how you have to pay off the police, I have to pay people to make this go away."

"You know how many politicians I could buy with those twelve thousand dollars?" hissed Motielall, his eyes narrowing as he looked at the lawyer. "Look, man, one thing I can't stand is when people take me for a fool and want to rob me blind. It is then that I take action to eliminate the pests that bother me."

"I know how you feel," agreed Naitram. "I am also involved. I need this to go away quickly. I need to retire with my reputation intact before I migrate to America. Look, I will put out five thousand dollars, but do the right thing and save yourself. You are just an island man. All the officials in Georgetown will conspire to bring you down at the whiff of a scandal."

Motielall coughed and spat a gob of mucus over the wall. "When do they want the money?"

"They wanted this business to be over in two days, but I explained that it was unreasonable. I persuaded them to give you five days to arrange the money."

"And this would be the end of everything?" barked Motielall. "No other half-dead cancer man will appear to give me trouble?"

"No more trouble unless you create it," cautioned Naitram. "Deliver fifty-five thousand dollars to my office, and all the paperwork will be done to put all this behind us. But this time, I will prepare all the documents—legally."

Chapter 27 – Final Rites

The funeral chapel was packed. Although Sarju had kept a very low profile, the island people, as was their custom, would attend the wakes and funerals of any islander, and Sarju's family was well known on the island. Buddhu, the patriarch of Pradeep's wife's family, was seated in the front row with members of his family. He had arranged for the musicians from the nearby Hindu temple to deliver religious songs that would usher Sarju's soul to a better place.

People filed by the coffin and offered silent prayers to the departed soul. The funeral director, a tall, thin man dressed in an oversized black suit with the appearance of Count Dracula, buzzed around carrying plastic chairs from a shed at the back of the funeral home to the chapel to seat the new arrivals. Samlall and Neblet stood by the head side of the coffin, eyes closed and hands clasped, saying their respective prayers.

Samlall concluded, lit an incense stick, and stuck it in an incense holder beside the coffin. Neblet's eyes followed the curling trail of scented smoke as it lifted toward the ceiling.

"I hope Sir Beepat is in a better place now, Samlall."

"Any place where there is no pain is better for him. He is at peace now," responded Samlall.

Neblet noticed the new pair of glasses on Samlall's face. "How come you have new glasses? Sir Beepat left that for you in his will?"

Samlall sighed in annoyance. "My son, Pradeep, gave them to me. He took my prescription to Georgetown after the wedding and promised to post the glasses to me. Now, this happened, so he brought them himself."

"All I can say is keep out of Motielall's way," warned Neblet, "because when he sees your new glasses, he will make sure that you won't see anything after."

Hassan, who had arrived the night before from New York, was standing in a corner, conversing with Dr. Morris. Samlall and Neblet moved from the coffin to join the two.

Hassan turned to the two, who stood awkwardly by Dr. Morris. "How come the two of you didn't enter the yard and stop Motielall from beating him?"

Samlall looked down at his folded hands. "He told us not to enter the yard. He said he had a plan, and we should only intervene when he called for help."

"He knew Motielall had our names at the police station, so he didn't want us in the yard. He wanted to transact his business in private; that is why we were outside—waiting for him to call," Neblet confessed.

Hassan shook his head in disappointment. "And did he call?"

"He never called," Neblet declared with regret. "We were waiting for him to call. I even had a stick ready to beat Motielall, even though he always carried a gun with him."

Dr. Morris grunted. "And do you know why he didn't call for help?"

Samlall glanced over at the coffin. "He wanted to be in that box."

"You are right," agreed Dr. Morris, and he too looked at the coffin. "He wanted Motielall to be responsible for the fatal blow."

Hassan nodded and looked at the three men. "I am glad that in his final moments, he was surrounded by people who cared for him."

"And he would be very happy that you left everything and came all the way from America just to say farewell," Samlall uttered, his voice choked with emotion.

"Yes," responded Hassan, "he was my brother. I had to be here for him. He once said that we began and will end on this island."

"He loved this island," Dr. Morris intoned, "and we all do."

Hassan looked at the people streaming past the coffin to pay their respects. He muttered. "I wish that the people that he loved so dearly were here in his final moments."

The lawyer, Naitram, glided into the funeral home with a briefcase in hand and joined the line of people waiting to view the body in the coffin.

"Why he come here with briefcase? Like he come to read the will." Neblet remarked.

Samlall stared at Naitram's back. "Well, I know he is not here to seize the coffin because Dr. Morris made all the funeral arrangements."

Naitram took a cursory glance at the deceased and beckoned to Dr. Morris, who joined him by the door.

"I hope everything is okay, Mr. Naitram,"

"You said the business had to be concluded by the fifth day," rejoined Naitram, slapping his briefcase. "I have everything here. Business is business. My client just needs the signatures of you and Samlall to put an end to this tragic episode."

"Your client doesn't need the thumbprint of the deceased as well?" Dr. Morris chided. "Do you normally conduct your business in these surroundings?"

Naitram looked at the doctor in amusement. "I have done a few at my client's behest. But if you prefer, you can visit my office anytime today to take possession of what is yours."

"That is reasonable," agreed Dr. Morris as he observed Dracula passing by with a chair balanced on his head. "Well, since you came to do business here, I won't disappoint you. Settle the bill for the funeral expenses with the director and deduct it from the principal we agreed on."

The old pandit, who presided over Pradeep's wedding, arrived late with an oversized bag in his hand, and he and Pradeep huddled in an animated conversation by the coffin. Pradeep signaled to Samlall to join them.

"Dad, the pandit wants to know what kind of religious ceremony you want to be performed."

"I know your parents were Hindus, but your brother spent years in another country. Is he still a Hindu? I have to ask because a lot of we people go overseas and find Jesus as if he was ever lost," remarked the pandit.

"I never asked him about his belief," declared Samlall. "But I know he was married according to Hindu rites, and his children have Hindu names."

"Okay," decided the pandit, "so we will do the religious ceremony. Where is his son? He has to partake in the rituals."

"Well," murmured Samlall, "his son is not here. We will have to skip the rituals."

The pandit appeared stunned. He looked at the coffin. "What kind of man was he? Why is the son not here at the funeral?"

"It is a long story, Pandit," piped Samlall, "but do we have to use all the rituals? Can't we just say some short prayers? Wouldn't that satisfy God?"

"What do you know about what *Bhagwan* wants?" rebuked the pandit caustically. "It is written in the scriptures that the eldest son must partake in religious rituals to intercede on the soul's behalf. I don't know if that is true. You don't know if that is true. We don't know because we are not dead yet. But what if we are wrong? Do you want the soul to experience any kind of hardship because we didn't want to dedicate a few minutes to meditate and pray?" fumed the pandit. The hair on his ears wriggled in exasperation.

"Can anyone else perform the duties, Pandit?" queried Pradeep.

"If there is no son, another relative can substitute," conceded the pandit.

"Then I will participate in the rituals for my uncle."

"You will do it, Pradeep?" gasped Samlall.

"Well, now that we have settled that part, come and help me set up the prayer items, Pradeep. And while I am setting up, if anyone wants to say anything about Sarju, let them come now."

The pandit spread a sheet on the floor and laid out an assortment of religious items for the farewell ceremony.

Samlall looked at his son, and his eyes welled up behind his new glasses. He hesitated, took a few steps forward, and then captured his son in a tight embrace. "You are a good son, Pradeep. I am sorry I wasn't at your wedding. Your uncle would be so proud of you."

Samlall beckoned Hassan over. "While the pandit is preparing, someone has to do the eulogy. I believe you should do it."

"Why me? You are the brother," objected Hassan.

"But you knew him better, Hassan. You were with him in his youth and in his exile in America. Please, Hassan, his soul would rest easy with your words."

Count Dracula, anticipating Hassan, moved a small podium from a corner and positioned it in front of the mourners.

Hassan went to the podium. He viewed the audience. He knew many of the faces, in particular the old heads of the island, and unlike Sarju, he was a regular visitor.

"My friends, today is the last time my friend's mortal body will be on this planet. This afternoon, after cremation, it will be returned to all its original elements, and the only thing that will remain with us is memory."

There was no microphone, and the people leaned forward and paid rapt attention. Hassan glanced at the pandit, who was still busy setting up for his prayer service.

"The pandit will no doubt tell you about the journey and rebirth of the soul according to Hindu belief. The actions or karma of this life will determine your rebirth or your attainment of godly bliss. I knew my friend, Sarju, and from his actions, I am sure that he will take rebirth in a better situation.

Sarju and I grew up together on this island. We were very close. His brother, Samlall, recently reminded me how closer Sarju was to me than to him. That was so only because Samlall was older than Sarju, about nine years, and older brothers tend to keep a distance from their very younger siblings. But Sarju loved his brother, Samlall, and when he returned, their bond became closer and stronger.

Many people leave this island and return. Sarju left, but the island did not leave him. I was close to him for over thirty years in America. I attended his wedding, the birth of his children, and other major events of his life. His love for his family was as pure as the nectar from the mango blossoms of his father's trees. It was this love, this devotion to family, that led to the loss of his freedom. In the darkest of moments, the memory of this island kept him alive. The birds singing their morning songs; the river lapping on the shore kept flowing through his mind. So, my brother Sarju never left this island.

Like all of us, he had his weaknesses and made his mistakes, but he had a special gift that touched the people that he met. My niece's daughter, a little girl, told me of her love for him. How he patiently taught her and how she loves math because of him. Sarju was a teacher for a few years on this island, and I know he left this world a very satisfied man. His actions made this world a better place. Among us today, we have two of his first students. Neblet, the jolly wanderer of our island, never forgot him. He also inspired a young boy to love science, and this boy finally became a doctor and devoted his life to the people on this land. I know Sarju's heart was filled with joy by the presence of his noble student, Dr. Morris.

His final moments were passed in the presence of his beloved brother and his two former students. He was born in a yard in Belle Plaine and ended his life there, beside his treasured mango trees. To those who knew him and loved him, his memory will remain a part of us until we part company with this island."

Hassan concluded as the melodic chanting of the Hindu priest commenced. The priest sat on the floor with Pradeep and conducted his service to free Sarju's soul from earthly bondage. When he was finished and the congregation joined him in the final prayer, the funeral director closed the coffin, and the four pallbearers, Neblet, Samlall, Dr. Morris, and Hassan, lifted the coffin on their shoulders and slowly walked out to the hearse.

———◉———

THERE WAS A SMALL CONVOY of vehicles behind the hearse as it wended its way out of the yard of the funeral home. The hearse crawled out of the yard and came to a stop on the main road. The driver made several attempts to restart the vehicle, but with no success. He left the car, opened the hood, and stood looking perplexed at the exposed engine.

The funeral director briskly strode up to the hearse, his oversized black jacket flapping like the wings of a vulture. A few men left their vehicles and followed him.

"What is the problem, George? Why did you stop?"

"The engine shut down, Mr. Lucas. It is not turning over. It sounds like the electrical coil again," mumbled the driver.

"Well, you have to fix it. You are blocking traffic," rebuked Dracula.

"I am not a mechanic. I don't know how to fix a coil," rejoined the driver.

"So, how are we going to get the body to the cremation site?" barked the director.

"You want us to push the hearse?" George suggested.

Yattieram, who was watching the proceedings, laughed. "Let we push this old hearse off the road so that the people can pass."

Yattieram, George, and the young minibus driver who had driven Sarju to the hospital helped push the hearse to the side of the road.

Hassan came up to the crowd of men around the hearse. "So, what now? How are we going to get there?"

The funeral director scratched his head. "I have to get a mechanic. The other hearse is down."

"It looks like your vehicles need to be cremated too," Hassan scolded.

The director scowled. He opened the door of the hearse to expose the coffin.

"If you remove the seats from my minibus, I can carry the coffin," the young driver offered.

"That would take too long," snorted Yattieram. "Put the coffin in my trailer. That trailer took him around when he was merry; it will take him now to his final place."

Samlall placed a hand on Yattieram's shoulder and looked at Hassan. "Yes, I think Sarju would prefer that."

Hassan nodded in agreement. "Yes! Sarju would like that. Let his dead body experience the island for the last time in the open air, not confined in a hearse."

Neblet poked his head through the open door of the hearse. "This simple man loved his island. We must show him that the island loves him too."

The pallbearers lifted the coffin from the hearse and loaded it on the trailer. They mounted and held on to the sides as Yattieram's tractor puttered its way to the riverside.

Yattieram stopped the tractor outside Motelall's house for a few minutes. There was a padlock on the gate, and all the windows of the house were shut.

Yattieram banged the side of the tractor. "This is where everything happened, Sarju. This is where your life began and ended."

The cremation site was on the bank of the Essequibo River. The old man in charge of the operation had made the funeral pyre by layering logs of wood and filling the spaces with very combustible coconut shells. The coffin was placed on top, and after the priest recited his final prayers and chants, Pradeep used a flaming torch to set the pyre on fire. The wood and coconut shells quickly sizzled and combusted; in a few minutes, a roaring flame, fanned by the river breeze, hovered intensely over the pyre and erased the body of Sarju Beepat.

———— ◉ ————

IT WAS LATE IN THE afternoon when Samlall and Neblet rode up to the cremation site. The sun was slowly dipping into the river, and the cremation fire was long over. On the ground was a layer of gray ash. Samlall dropped his bicycle and kneeled beside the ash. He used a scraper to gently remove the top layer and filled three containers. He put two containers in a backpack and walked to the river with the third.

Neblet leaned on his bicycle and watched Samlall wade knee-deep into the dark water of the Essequibo River with the container of ashes in his hands. Samlall faced the dying sun, mouthed a few words in prayer, and then poured the ashes gently into the river. The wind whipped the water, and a wave curled over, its ends like silver fingers, snatched the ashes of the late Sarju Beepat.

Samlall returned to the shore, picked up the bicycle with a shovel tied to the crossbar and handle, and pedaled off with Neblet following.

"Where you going now, Samlall?"

"Going to get some mangoes from Motielall."

Neblet rode beside him. "You gone crazy, Samlall? You want to lose your glasses again? You might even end up as ashes, like Sir Beepat."

Samlall sucked his teeth. "You didn't notice the house this morning, Neblet. There was a lock on the gate. The man didn't want to stay for the funeral. His police contacts probably advised him to leave the island for a few days."

————————◉————————

THE HOUSE WAS DARK, and the lock was still on the gate. Samlall and Neblet dropped their bicycles by the parapet. Samlall removed the shovel that was tied to his bike.

"What you doing with a shovel? You plan to do agriculture in the man yard?"

"I will fertilize the yard while you pick some mangoes."

Neblet peered over the fence. "Let me go first. Just in case Motielall is hiding in the yard, I can escape faster than you."

"Alright," whispered Samlall, "but take this shovel with you."

"What will I do with that shovel? The man has a gun. You think that shovel would block the bullets from blasting my ass?"

Neblet jumped the fence and reconnoitered the yard. He returned to the fence and helped Samlall over. They crept silently under the mango tree. Samlall used the shovel to dig a hole in the earth of his childhood home. He opened his bag, took out a container, and carefully poured the ashes into the hole. Neblet kneeled beside him, and the two men, in their own way, silently said a prayer for the departed soul.

Chapter 28- Legacy

Pradeep entered the yard and peered under the house. The door and windows to the small, self-contained apartment were locked.

From the top of the stairs, Fazeela called out. "If you are looking for Uncle Hassan, he is not awake yet. He came in late last night."

"I was not looking for him. I came to see you and Nizam."

"Well, come up, Pradeep. Join us for coffee."

Pradeep climbed the stairs to the dining room. Nizam pulled a chair for him.

Pradeep took a seat, and his eyes roved over the room. "I am just here to thank you for all you did for my uncle."

"You should thank his friend, Hassan, not us. He was Hassan's guest."

"But it must be said," insisted Pradeep. "He told my father how you and your daughter cared for him."

Fazeela brought Pradeep a cup of coffee. "That is the same chair your uncle used when he was here." She nudged Nizam. "Look at him! He looks so much like his uncle."

"Well, Mr. Beepat was the uncle. They share the same genes."

"We are really sorry about Mr. Beepat," Fazeela lamented. "We had no idea he was that sick. He hardly ate the cooked food here, but he helped our daughter with her homework."

"We have to thank your uncle for helping her with her maths," declared Nizam. "He made her into an expert in maths, and she is helping her friends now."

Pradeep grinned. "I wish I had him to help me when I was growing up. I was very poor in maths. But where is she?"

"She is spending a few days with her cousins," sniffed Fazeela. "She loved your uncle. She is still grieving for him."

Pradeep reached across and patted her hand. "I envy her. I only met him once. I didn't spend enough time with him to love him."

Nizam sighed. "Life is like that! You don't get to know people until it's too late. But he was a good man."

"So I heard. My father told me that Arifa wants to become a doctor."

Fazeela smiled. "She is obsessed with that profession. She was always advising your uncle what to eat and how to eat to avoid throwing up his food."

Pradeep took an envelope from his pocket and handed it to Fazeela.

"My uncle would want her to have this. A token of his gratitude."

Fazeela looked into the envelope and quickly handed it to Nizam, who examined its contents with a perturbed expression.

"We can't take this," Nizam objected. "This is a lot of money. Your uncle doesn't owe us anything. His friend Hassan took care of all the expenses."

Pradeep looked at the couple. "My father mentioned that he learned something from your daughter—*paying forward*."

"Oh, that!" responded Nizam. "She said it means helping a complete stranger, so when you need help, another stranger will help you. She learned that from her teacher, and she believes in it."

Pradeep chuckled. "So, they had a lot in common. This money is from her *stranger*. This is to help her go to college so that she can help more people like him."

NEBLET STOOD ON THE riverbank, holding a long fishing rod over the water and humming a folk song. A bird cage hung on a pole next to him. Samlall approached from behind and strummed his fingers on the wires of the cage. The screeching sound caused Neblet to turn around, and the song fell from his lips.

"Hey, boy! Where you going all dressed up in your Sunday best? You going to a church wedding?"

Samllall grinned. "No, man. I am heading for Georgetown."

"Then you going on an interview for a big job. The prime minister got fired? His job vacant?"

Samlall eyed the fishing line swaying over the water. "I am going to live with my son. We are going to form a family again. Pradeep is planning to build a house in Georgetown, and I will find a job there to help with the expenses."

Neblet wedged the end of the pole between two rocks. "That is good news, man! Now that you are a changed man with new clothes and glasses, we must take a drink."

Neblett rummaged in a backpack and produced a bottle of rum.

Samlall waved his hands. "No more of that, man. I made a promise over the dead body of my brother that I would not touch that stuff again. I have no secrets to hide anymore."

Neblet tilted his head and smiled in admiration. "Well, I have no brother, and I never made that promise to Sir Beepat." Neblet chugged a drink and wiped his lips. "I wish you luck in the city." He sniffed the air. "But what is smelling so?"

Samlall laughed. "That is my after-shave lotion. I must smell good when I go to the city."

"Nah, that is fruit I smelling."

"Oh!" declared Samlall and opened his bag. "I have mangoes here. From my grandfather's tree. You want some?"

"Nah! But when you run out of mangoes, let me know. I will steal them from Motielall."

"You don't have to do that. I am saving the seeds to plant in my son's yard. I have to tell him about the history of the mangoes."

"Yes. He must know that is how Sir Beepat met his end."

Samlall took an envelope from his bag and slapped it against his wrist. "He liked you, Neblet. You were his friend. He left a little something for you."

Neblet took the envelope and raised it to the sun. "A little something?" he gasped. "This is a big little something, man!"

Neblet clasped the envelope to his chest and looked up into the sky. "Thank you, Sir Beepat."

"I hope you catch a lot of fish today, Neblet. But I have to leave now to catch a ferry."

A lump came to Neblet's throat. He croaked. "You intend to return to the island, Samlall?"

Samlall nodded slowly and considered his friend. "One day, Neblet. One day I will return."

Neblet gazed at the river. "We will all return, Samlall. Just like the salmon, Sir Beepat returned."

He turned around and removed the cage from the pole. He whistled at the bird and then presented the cage to Samlall. "As you are leaving, take a piece of the island with you. This will remind you of your friend, Neblet."

Samlall took the cage and hugged Neblet. He walked off with the strain of the folk song that he and Neblet had sung on numerous occasions trailing after him like a distant memory.

<hr />

GIOVANNI'S DRIVEWAY was lined with vehicles. Hassan parked on the road in front of the house and trudged up to the front door. He raised his hands to knock on the door when it suddenly opened to reveal Meera. She was in a simple black dress.

Meera looked at Hassan through red-rimmed eyes. She embraced him, and he felt her wet cheeks on his.

"Thanks for coming here, Hassan. The children are waiting for you."

Meera led him into the house. There was a baby carriage in the living room, but there was no baby in sight. In the dining room, Aarti and Mitra were seated at the table and looked up somberly as he entered. Giovanni stood behind a chair with a bottle of beer in his hand.

Giovanni grinned at Hassan. "What are you having, Hassan?" He showed Hassan the bottle. "Need something stronger than this?"

Hassan shook his head.

Meera tugged at his sleeve. "Have a seat, Hassan. The children want to know about the funeral in Guyana."

Hassan sat down at the table and examined the solemn faces of Mitra and Aarti.

"Very simple," he remarked coldly. "There was a cremation. Sarju went up in smoke. No one will ever see his miserable face on this earth again."

Meera let out a sudden cry. Mitra leaned across to hold his mother's hand.

"No one told us that he was—gone," she wept. "You didn't tell us anything. How did you expect us to know about his death?"

Aarti rose and stood behind her mother. She wrapped her hands around her.

Giovanni put down his bottle and glared at Hassan. "At least you could have told us you were going to Guyana. Someone could have gone with you."

Hassan drummed his fingers on the table and faced Giovanni. "How would that have made a difference? Did anyone care? Was anyone interested in why he went to Guyana?"

"That was part of the deal he made with the government to get parole," snapped Mitra. "He told me that when I visited him."

"Is that all he told you when you paid him that visit?" Hassan chided. Mitra averted Hassan's gaze. "Did he tell you that he was dying of cancer? And that was why he was returning to Guyana."

Aarti sobbed quietly and placed her face on her mother's head.

Meera raised her hand to pat her daughter. She whimpered, "But he didn't say anything about being sick, Hassan. He told me that he was suffering from indigestion."

"Yes, indigestion to people who didn't care to know about the details of his life," asserted Hassan brusquely. "But stomach cancer to people who cared for him in his final days."

Giovanni swept up his bottle and took a swig. "So, why are you so angry with them, Hassan? If the man chose to die without anyone knowing, what do you expect them to do?"

"Nothing! Absolutely nothing," retorted Hassan quietly. "The man was a prisoner of both the state and his family. A simple and loving person who became a convicted murderer because he sought his own justice for the violation of his daughter."

Aarti left her mother and returned to her seat at the table. She buried her head in her hands.

"No one told him to take justice into his own hands," snorted Giovanni. "Vigilante justice never solved a problem. And he knew that."

Aarti lifted her head quickly. Her eyes flashed with anger at Giovanni. "Shut up! Shut up! He was my father! He was my father!"

Aarti sobbed; her body shook, and her hands trembled as they rested on the table. "All this happened because of me, and I never saw him before he died. I never visited him in prison. I never saw him when he came out of prison, and he died without seeing his granddaughter."

Meera reached across and hugged her daughter. Mitra stared at them with tears welling in his eyes.

"You didn't care to see him, but he cared to see you," Hassan berated, "and you didn't even recognize him."

Aarti reached for a napkin on the table and wiped her nose. "Where did he see me?"

Hassan stared at Aarti's cheeks, red and puffy from the tears. "He went to the park close to your house. He saw you with the baby," he announced sadly, "and he recognized your husband."

Aarti's red-rimmed eyes opened wide. "Oh, God! I am sorry! Oh, Daddy, I am so sorry."

Aarti rested her head on the table. Her shoulders shook as she sobbed. "You never had a chance to know my husband. He became a fine husband and father and never hated you."

Mitra rested his hand on his sister's shoulders. His voice shook. "Where did he die, Uncle Hassan? In a hospital? Who was looking after him?"

Hassan swallowed. "Strangers who cared. Strangers who saw the devotion and goodness in your father."

He looked at Aarti, shuddering with her head in her hands. Hassan's voice oozed with reproach. "A little girl who did not turn away from him in disgust while he was heaving his guts out. A little girl who comforted him in his pain. He died surrounded by loving strangers while his own flesh and blood abandoned him like a diseased dog."

"Oh, God! What did we do?" shrieked Meera. "What did we do to your father?"

"Daddy, daddy, oh, daddy. I wish I could see you one last time to tell you how sorry I am. To tell you that I love you," mumbled Aarti through her tears.

"You really should have told us something, Uncle Hassan! I could have gone with you," asserted Mitra.

Hassan glared at Mitra. "Alive and in the flesh, you ignored him when you had the chance. Did you visit or ask about him after you interrogated him, Mitra? Now in death, you mourn for what is lost."

Giovanni sat down heavily and rapped the table with his bottle. "The children are not cold-hearted, Hassan. They would have gone to say goodbye to their father. Meera would have accompanied them. Even I would have gone to pay my respect."

Hassan stood up and glared at Giovanni. Aarti and Meera ceased sobbing and looked at Hassan.

"So, you all want to say goodbye?" Hassan turned his head to inspect all of their faces. "Well, it is never too late. Just give me a minute."

Hassan left the room. Their eyes followed his back as he exited the front door. He returned a few minutes later and plunked a coffee can on the table in front of them.

"What is this?" Aarti blurted and sat up straight to look at Hassan.

"You can say goodbye to your father now," whispered Hassan. "I brought his ashes all the way from the island of Wakenaam."

They all recoiled in shock and horror. Meera placed her hands over her mouth. Giovanni pushed his chair back quickly, scraping the floor. Slowly, Aarti reached out and gingerly touched the top of the can. Mitra looked at his sister and did the same. Meera glanced at her children and slowly extended her hand to cover theirs. Hands that once loved Sarju Beepat in life hovered over a can that represented his demise.

*****************THE END****************

About the Author

Somnauth Narine is a Guyanese-born writer who holds a bachelor's degree in mechanical engineering and a master's degree in education. He has published an anthology of short stories—*The Call of the Ocean and Other Stories,* a children's book—*Anansi and the Alligator's Diamond*, screenplays, and two novels. Four of his screenplays have been converted into independent movies: *Brown Sugar Too Bitter for Me (Parts 1 and 2), Forgotten Promise,* and *Protection Game.* His first novel, *Rage from the Backwater,* has been awarded the *Guyana Prize for Literature 2023—Second Prize for Best Book of Fiction.*

He is a retired New York City Public School teacher and lives in Brooklyn, New York.

Printed in the USA
CPSIA information can be obtained
at www.ICGtesting.com
LVHW040804141024
793415LV00009B/35

9 798227 780287